Homage

Homage

Julian Rathbone

First published in Great Britain in 2001 by
ALLISON & BUSBY Limited
Suite 111, Bon Marche Centre
241-251 Ferndale Road
Brixton, London SW9 8BJ
http://www.allisonandbusby.ltd.uk

A catalogue record for this book is available from the British Library

ISBN 0 7490 0530 0

Printed and bound in Spain by
Liberdúplex, s. l. Barcelona

JULIAN RATHBONE's first book was published in 1967 and has been followed by a further thirty novels and one work of non-fiction. He has been translated into fifteen languages. Twice nominated for the Booker Prize, he has been awarded the Deutsches Krimi Preis and the prestigious Macallan Short Story Award, presented by the Crime Writer's Association.

A contributor to various newspapers, magazines and periodicals, he is also a succesful television and film scriptwriter whose work has been broadcast in over forty countries. After long spells in Turkey, France and Spain he is currently living in Hampshire.

Chapter 1

We stood side by side, my hands clasping the cast iron rail, his left hand loosely lying in the crook of my right elbow. Together we looked down into one of two small coves on a headland sixty feet or so above shingle and sandy beaches and watched the rollers heave themselves out of the deepest purest blue I had ever seen, before rumbling over brown rocks and breaking into sierras of white, whiter than any snow. They scurried up the sand which turned the water emerald, and finally, like children using a playground slide, they hurried gleefully round to the back again for another go. On their way they pulled the kelpy hair of mermaids, just for fun.

'I have never seen light like this,' I said.

'Light anywhere else is merely virtual. This is the real thing.'

On the surface his voice rasped a little. But underneath there was always a bass note, not unlike the one you can hear on a beach where the surf thunders in for forty miles in either direction.

'Why?'

'The ocean of course. You are looking at more unbroken water here than almost anywhere else in the world. It is a huge mirror. It reflects the light and the sky back into the light and the sky, and back it bounces again. Ad infinitum. Anyway, until sunset.'

He laughed and we turned, leant against the rail. His hand slipped out of my elbow, and twiddled the sparse but glossy black hairs in the scrap of goatee he'd grown.

There were public gardens facing us now, lawns, cedars of some sort, some of their ancient limbs supported on crutches, and buildings climbing a hill. Apart from one big ugly block they were modest, rarely more than four stories high, in tree-lined avenues. Modest in size, but Jefferson told me when he first moved into La Jolla, The Jewel, not modest in price. Raymond Chandler lived here. Gregory Peck. You had to be a dentist or a gem dealer at least. Or, like him, a more than averagely successful private eye.

I made as if to cross the road to the park. He put his big brown hand on my forearm, then let it drop.

'You go,' he said. 'If you don't mind, I'll stay here a bit longer.'

Apologetically almost, he touched the bullet hole in his right temple with the pale nail of his dark index finger. I crossed the road, sat on a wooden seat, lit a cigarillo. By the time I looked up he had gone.

Grief and shock do strange things to your mind. Or do they? Perhaps they just make you more receptive to what's going on around you all the time. Hi, Mum. Looking for Dad? He just went round that corner. Anyway, I thought, I'll have a drag, pull myself together, then go back to his flat, apartment, and start tidying things up. Phone the police, that sort of thing.

I don't smoke. A tin of ten cigarillos a year maybe, kept in reserve for moments when I know I must take it slowly, think it through, get over the shock. I'm a gumshoe, too, and such moments do occur. Occupational hazard. So I hoisted a mouthful into my lungs, let the dizziness shift to a mild euphoria, then the smoke bit and I coughed. A shadow fell across me. Wrapped itself over me. The sun, while not actually hurrying yet, had got low enough to sit behind her head.

'Do you mind?' she said. 'Children use this park.'

I looked around.

'Dogs too,' I said.

'They could inhale your fumes.'

Not only the largest expanse of water in the world was behind her but the largest lump of unpolluted air, some of it coming in over the rail in a soft intermittent breeze.

And she was fat. No. Obese. Beyond obese. It's the American disease. I'd seen pictures, read articles. There had been a couple in the domestic flight departure lounge at LAX, after I'd been through Immigration. But this one was really going for it. The hems of her outsize shorts dug into blotchy pink dimpled thighs. The thongs of her flip-flops cut canyons across the tops of her feet. Her toes were like the nipples on a not quite fully inflated joke balloon. I hardly dared to raise my eyes, but when I did I was shocked at the hate in hers, deep amber, beneath brows plucked to a curve like a sailmaker's or surgeon's needle. Her black hair was scraped back and tied with a silk red scarf. Hate? Perhaps she had once been a heavy smoker, gave up, and now blamed her obesity on oral deprivation.

'You're standing in my sun,' I said.

'It's against the law.'

'Good.'

'I mean, smoking in a public open space.'

'Shit,' I said, stood on the butt, got up and began to move away.

'Hey,' she called. She was looking at the butt like it was dog-poo I should have scooped. But that was going too far. I walked off, back up the hill.

*

Jefferson had lived in a near cube of a building, just four floors, four apartments, his on the second floor, which we Limeys call the first. The hill was steep. Below the building there was a run-in just wide enough to take a car to parking spaces at the back; above it a six inch gap separated it from its higher neighbour. The pavements were wide, the paving edged in granite, and planted with mature jacarandas, still in bloom in July, with little circular seats set round their bases. A couple of corners away was the main drag with speciality restaurants, boutiques, giftshops and even a supermarket or two. I'd sussed out that much from the taxi that brought me from Lindbergh Field International. Back in Bournemouth, England, where I come from, a courier service had brought me a set of Jefferson's keys which I'd used to get in an hour earlier and which got me in again now.

Passing through a small vestibule the first room you came to was the study. Bookcases, a desk, an office chair, computer and so forth, nice American Native or African rug (all right, can you tell the difference?), a Chinese-type lacquered and painted cabinet on four thin, elegant legs, the top a good height to make an occasional table, and an off-white, leather-covered low settee.

An hour earlier, when I arrived, Jefferson had been sitting on the floor, with his head lolling against the edge of the seat of the settee. Some blood had pumped out of the entry wound in his exposed temple, but not more than four or five heartbeats' worth and most of it had run down the side of his face, down his neck, and on to his dark navy jacket. There was an exit wound on the other side that had left a splash of blood and bone on the back of the settee and an FMJ 9 mm or maybe .44 inch slug embedded in the leather. I guessed he had been sitting in the settee when shot, had perhaps turned his head away from a full frontal at the last second, and had then slumped or slid to the floor. Lacking forensic equipment there was no point in trying to guess how long he had been dead. Given the ambient temperature which was near human blood temperature since the windows were closed and the air conditioning off, not less than half an hour, not more than eighteen seemed a safe estimate.

There had been a fly too. Washing its eyes and face the way they

11

do, on the edge of a spot of blood that had arrived on the Chinese table. I'd killed it with the copy of the *L A Times* I'd picked up at LAX (JFK Junior still missing, Search for Piper goes on). It was still there, where I had left it. The fly I mean.

And now I was back again and Jefferson had gone. And all the blood, apart from that drop on the table top, had been wiped up, and the slug prised out of its nest in the settee. There was a hole in the leather with a three-way split I could push my little finger in and feel the horsehair beyond. The air was filled with the scent of a lemon-flavoured antiseptic, anti-bacterial cleaner and spray. I found the empty container in a kitchen garbage pail, but not the cloths that had been used.

I looked at my watch. They'd worked fast. I had been gone for thirty-five minutes.

Chapter 2

The phone rang. It was on the desk. I used the handkerchief I keep in my breast pocket for the occasions when I might mess up or confuse a SOC, picked up the handset. Click. Dialling tone. I put it back, waited. They knew I was there. They'd try again in a moment or two. They did. She.

'Wilbur Jefferson?' Husky, female, grown-up female but not old like granny-old, as American as applepie. Educated southern I thought, but I'm no expert.

'No.'

'Is Jefferson there?'

'No.' And then I thought: how the hell do I know? They could have put his body on the bed in the bedroom. Or in the bath. But the way they'd cleaned up, I didn't think so. Not unless I'd interrupted them. That thought brought up the hair on the back of my neck. But she, whoever, was shuntering on quite briskly.

'I've been waiting in his reception room for twenty minutes. His actual office appears to be locked, with no one behind the door. I'm not made happy by appointments not kept.'

Ma'am! I thought, and snapped out an air salute.

'You are Mr Jefferson's English associate?'

Tricky word, but then I remembered the emails that had brought me to southern California, the courier-ed Amex cheques, the air ticket, and the keys. I hardly hesitated.

'Yes.'

'I'll wait. Half an hour.'

She'd given no name. She expected me to know it. There was a Packard Bell personal organiser on the desk as well as the computer. The computer would have to wait, but maybe her name, her appointment was in the organiser, even a clue as to why she was a client. I scooped it up. Half an hour? Tall order to get from La Jolla to downtown San Diego in that time unless you knew the best route. I didn't, but I found a cabbie who did, with a fat five-year-old Merc. Early evening so all the traffic was coming out of town. Usual catechism. I'd had it once already coming up from the airport.

'First visit? How long you staying? Limey are you? We get Aussies but not many Limeys. Business? Buying or selling? Ain't it just always one or the other...?'

13

Meanwhile I fiddled with the Packard Bell and ran straight into password trouble as soon as I hit the 'schedule' button. I closed it down and slipped it into my jacket pocket and looked out the window. Wonderful. Totally wonderful. Freeway. Clear sky just purpling up but the tinted windows may have had something to do with it. Flat land below La Jolla and landlocked water as we came rushing down the long curve, marshy some of it looked and the long line of Pacific Beach between us and the Ocean; then the sweep of the bay, almost black now with an aircraft carrier the size of a small city inching towards the open sea. Finally downtown, wonderful skyscrapers of glass and steel, blue, bronze, gold, flashing back the sun which still had an hour to go, and the Stars and Stripes here, and here and there again, sometimes as big as a tennis court, and with just enough breeze to lift them from the flagpoles. And trees and shrubs and flowers, oleanders, jacarandas, giant begonias, strelizias, plumbago in flower-beds and baskets...

'Not a tree do you see,' carolled the cabbie, who was Hispanic from his accent but with quite a lot of Afro from his colour, 'but it was planted and watered by man's almighty hand. A hundred years ago, this was desert, man. Pure desert. Just sagebrush and a little cactus. Ain't those skyscrapers just beautiful? The newest, see, because only in the last fifteen years have they been able to build real high on sand prone to earthquake. So they are the newest dee-sign. And look there. The Coronado Bridge. Ain't she a joy...?'

On the far side of the skyscrapers a long rollercoaster of narrow white concrete snaked an 'S' out across the bay.

'... high enough to get the biggest tallest ship in the world out of harbour and two and a half miles long.'

A proud man, proud of his city. He dropped me in a street that just about lay on the boundary between downtown and the old gas lamp district, an ordinary sort of street with office blocks that weren't that high, predating, I supposed, the new technology.

There was a white BMW roadster, buttoned up, parked on the kerb. I wondered, and it turned out I was right. I used another key from the bunch the courier had delivered to get through the big glass doors, took the lift to the third floor, counted off the door numbers to thirty-eight, knocked and went in. The lady sitting in the black leather armless chair, with a cup of coffee at her side on a black glass-topped table, did not get up. Not because she was dead or anything but because that was what she was — a lady. She sat up straight

14

though and offered me her fingers.

'China Heart,' she said. 'Heart with an 'e'. You must be Mr Shuvlin?'

'Chris Shovelin. It's a round 'o', not a flat 'u'.'

I held the fingers for a second then let her have them back.

A whisper, gravelly though with that hint of a bull fiddle in back of it somewhere, murmured in my ear: 'Steady as you go, Kit, this one bites.'

Did I need him to tell me? She had red to chestnut hair streaked with gold, bobbed but with a peekaboo lock on the forehead which made it a pricey cut, a good forehead, high and narrow, shaped eyebrows, eyes hazel to green, lashes that were probably paler than they had been painted, a nose that looked sculpted and may well have been. Her mouth was small, her chin just a hint too prominent for perfect beauty, strong enough to say don't mess with me. Her thin, slightly scrawny neck put ten years on her which made the sum add up to late forties, and so did the very slight sag on her upper arms. She was wearing a flame-coloured knitted silk tank top, low-slung white shorts with tiny brass studs, gold sandals. Her navel had a pearl in it; gold bangles flashed on her thin wrists.

'Do you have a key to his office?' she asked.

I fumbled the bunch out from my jacket pocket, selected what looked to be the right one, a brass mortice. She came up behind me and I caught the perfume for the first time — a good one, but undercut with something real, musky, like a hot pavement hit by charged rain. I swear heat came off her too, like from a pavement.

'You don't think he's in there. Dead or something?'

'No. No, I don't.'

Something in my voice.

'You seem very certain about that.'

I pushed the door open. There was nothing there at all, or almost nothing. An empty desk, two chairs in front, one behind, an empty cabinet with a roll-down door, the sort you keep box files in, a filing cabinet I didn't really need to look in to check the drawers had been emptied too. They'd left a pretty potted orchid with eight blooms on it on the windowsill, and a big framed photograph of racing yachts, America's Cup class, under full sail in the bay. You could see the Coronado Bridge behind them. Then I saw it. As carelessly, as naturally as I could, I went and sat in the chair behind the desk and put my forearm over it.

'Why?' She was still in the doorway looking in.

'Why what?'

'Why were you so certain he couldn't be here?'

'Mrs Heart. You rang his apartment and you got me. I'd arrived there about an hour earlier. He was there then. Shot. Dead.'

I don't know what sort of reaction I was expecting, but I got none, except that for a moment or so a sort of stillness seeped through her. Then she gave her head a tiny shake.

'You rang the police?'

'No.'

'Why not?'

'I was... in shock. I locked the door, walked down to the sea front, had a smoke, went back. When I came back I found the body had been moved, it had gone and any signs of a shooting or a death pretty well cleaned up. I suppose a really thorough forensic examination might find suggestions of what had happened, but even they would be open to other, more innocent interpretations. I was wondering what to do when you rang.'

She moved to the window, looked out. The setting sun was on her face and she screwed up her eyes a little against it, though, again, the windows were tinted. It gave her skin a rosy, peachy perfection. I took the opportunity I had been waiting for. The desk top was a pure white, high quality formica-type veneer. A number had been minutely pencilled on it, in a grey patch where others had been written in and later rubbed out. The figures were tiny, neat, Jefferson's. He'd written them down while on the phone to someone. Or perhaps after dialling star-six-nine, the US equivalent of 1471. A shamus needs skills and a good one acquires them. One I acquired early was the ability to memorise a quite long sequence of numbers on one reading.

China turned back from the window.

'Mr Shovelin, I guess we have a lot to talk about.'

I looked up at her.

'Certainly,' I said, 'I need to talk to someone.'

And as nonchalantly as I could I moistened my finger and rubbed out the number.

But not there, not in Jefferson's office. At her suggestion I locked up. We walked a couple of blocks, maybe three, turned a corner. The air was still now, warm and balmy. Globed lights which may or may not have still had gas mantles in them glowed against a sky suddenly velvet in the east and above. There were big square cobbles and frontages made out of painted wood. It all looked as real as a Hollywood set which is what reality is for a lot of people. The restaurant was intimate though large, with fringed lamps low over each table or booth. Red Chinese dragons roamed across a ceiling the colour of bitter chocolate and glittered here and there with gold leaf. It was a classy joint. The oriental maitre d' led us to a booth near the back, shielded by bamboo screens, and offered madame a menu Moses might have brought down from Mount Sinai. She waved it away, murmured something about just coming in for a private chat but we might toy with a cracker or take a look at the Dim Sum trolley. A pot of jasmine tea would be nice. She called him Mr Chang and he called her Mrs Heart.

She looked at me, fingers linked beneath her chin, elbows on either side of the place setting Chang presently gathered away.

I doubt she was impressed by what she saw. Fifty years old, black hair thinning, domed forehead, heavy eyebrows which, like my eyes, droop outwards, gladstone bags below those eyes, big beak of a nose, full mouth, a large mole on one cheek, lots of lines and saggy skin. Middle-of-the-range, off-the-peg, light-weight woollen suit, neutral grey not too dark, double-breasted, widely spaced pin stripes. Brown shirt, no tie. Five foot eleven in my socks, a hundred and forty pounds on a good day.

'Well,' she said. 'You look reliable.'

I smiled.

'Except when you smile. Then you look shifty. Wilbur said you were reliable.'

'You were expecting me?'

'Of course. Wilbur said he needed help he could trust, someone who was not known in the area in which he was working. We approved his suggestion.'

This was too much. I leant back into leather, left my hands on the edge of the table.

'Mrs Heart. Four days ago I received an email from Jefferson —'

'Why do you always call him Jefferson?'

'He hated the name Wilbur.'

'Oh. Go on.'

'— asking me to come out here, now, like right away, and work on a case with him. In my reply I expressed a certain... hesitancy, which

I think he misinterpreted. The next day four thousand dollars worth of Amex travellers, a BA ticket Heathrow to LAX, cheques and a bunch of keys arrived by courier. Almost simultaneously a more urgently phrased email and an explanation of the keys. He might not be able to be in a position to meet me, I was to go to his apartment, make myself at home until he communicated with me.'

'You Brits. You, I don't know, you put long sentences together so wonderfully.'

'I'm sorry if I'm boring you. The point I am trying to make is that that's all I know. Once I realised it was urgent I got a move on. In fact I tore up the BA ticket and flew Virgin instead. The hour I gained got me an almost immediate connection on to San Diego. Consequently I know nothing at all of what any of this is about. Only that Jefferson is dead.'

Her eyes, darker in that light, went serious and she reached across to put her right hand over my left.

'I'm sorry,' she murmured. 'You were close, weren't you?'

'Off and on. We didn't see a lot of each other in recent years.'

A bowl of small steamed and filled dumplings arrived on a bed of crisp shredded seaweed, pre-wrapped chopsticks, and four dips in blue and white ramekins, the glaze on them artfully cracked.

'The Schechuan hot sauce is especially good.'

I'm not too brilliant with chopsticks, but she made the procedure look like the operation of an elegantly designed piece of machinery. She was right about the sauce. It was good, the small clam inside my first dumpling pleasantly chewy. Suddenly I felt hungry as well as almost out of my head with tiredness.

She dabbed her lips, did I mention a brownish-red lip gloss? sipped from the handleless cup.

'Right. I have a half-brother four years younger than me, Jerry. Jerry Lennox. He has gone missing. Disappeared. We hired Mr Jefferson to find him.'

'We?'

'My father and I. General Lennox.'

'How long had he been on the case?'

Still with an elbow on the table she jabbed her chopsticks across at me. The points met, just about on a level with my eyes and not much more than a foot away. I resisted the need to pull back.

'If. If...,' she repeated, 'Jefferson really is dead, then that is a question a police detective could properly ask. I don't see it is any business of yours, unless...'

Down went the sticks, like a wader's beak, came up with another dumpling which swooped towards the dips and hovered.

'Unless...'

'Unless we ask you to continue where Jefferson left off. And you accept the offer.'

This time it was the plum sauce.

'Why should I do that?'

She chewed, grimaced.

'Pork. Chang knows I don't like pork.' She swallowed, making an effort of it, then the sticks threatened again. Like bandarillas. 'One. It's your job. Two. It's what you came out to help Jefferson with. Three. If you succeed you'll also almost certainly find out why he was killed and who did it —'

'If I'm not killed in the process.'

'Four. You get a retainer of ten thousand. A grand a day and all expenses. And another twenty large ones if you find my brother alive, and ten if he's dead.'

'And five, I go to jail without passing go as soon as the police realise I didn't report a death.'

'Yes. Well. That brings me to the most important condition. My father is a very prominent citizen in southern California. Although he is no longer ambitious to hold office himself, he is seventy-two, he is very closely allied to colleagues and friends who are already in positions of power or aspire to be. I am not going into any detail about this but the point is that no breath of scandal should attach itself to our family as a result of anything Jerry may have done, or may have arisen because of his disappearance. Are you with me?'

'I think so. I don't go to the police. The police don't find out Jefferson is dead. Is that it?'

'That's it. What do you think?'

I took a swig of the tea. Smokey, yes. But sharp too and very refreshing. She topped up my tiny cup from the dinky little green and white tea pot. This time a white jasmine star floated on the surface.

'The deal, Mrs Heart. The retainer, the grand a day and so on. Is that genuine? Or is it just a polite way of paying me to be quiet?'

This time her head went back into the shadows where her eyes still glittered, and her teeth shone pearly white.

'Apart from the normal social graces, Mr Shovelin, the Lennoxes don't give a shit for politeness. The offer's genuine, and we expect you to work your butt off to make a success of it. Will you take it?'

'Mrs Heart...,' I looked at my watch, a quarter after four o'clock in the morning, UK time. No wonder I was fucking tired. 'I've had a helluva a day, and night, two days. I've had a fucking awful shock. I'll tell you in the morning.'

'All right.' She dabbed her lips, balled her napkin. 'Papa will want to meet you. Right now he's in L. A. But he'll be at Homage by mid-morning.'

'Homage?'

'Ancestral home. Out in the desert. Where will you sleep tonight?'

'Shit. I don't know. La Jolla I suppose. At Jefferson's.'

'I'll run you back there.'

*

She didn't pay Chang, she didn't even sign a bill. The BMW roadster was hers. She took ten minutes less than the La Jolla cabbie had taken. She followed me up to Jefferson's apartment and walked straight in ahead of me as soon as I got his door open. She went through each room, giving each a brisk but thorough look over. I followed her cocoa butter legs and those twinkling orbs above them like a besotted but very tired bloodhound until she came back to the study where Jefferson had died.

She turned on me. She was holding a small white kid purse now which she'd taken from the glove box under the steering wheel. The way she handled it showed it was heavier than it should have been. Probably held a gun, but not as big as a 9mm Browning or Colt .44.

'You going to phone the police? You going to tell them you found a body in here four hours ago and you didn't report it but you repor-ting it now? They'll lock you up for wasting their time if you do. I'll ring you in the morning, and you'll say yes, and I'll tell you how to get out to Homage. Right?'

'I expect so. But not too early.'

She went. The BMW coughed and purred and brrrm-brrrmed up the street. I looked at the settee. It wasn't the same settee. This one was a three seater and had no hole in it. There was no dead fly on the Chinese table top and no dried drop of blood. But on top of my case in the corner my folded copy of the L A Times still had a smudge of reddish brown and one fly wing dried into it. OK. She was right. Not enough for the police. But enough for me, enough to keep me from thinking I was insane.

I dialled the number I still remembered. It began 00 and went on 52-67- and six more digits. Six buzzes then an answering machine kicked in.

'*Ha llamado a la Farmacia San Cristóbal. No le podemos atender en este momento. La farmacia se vulve a abrir a las diez de la mañana. En caso de urgencia llame al...*'

I hung up, and thought, shit, I should have activated the caller withheld his number routine but then it would have taken Lord knows how long to find out how it went on this side of the world.

There were telephone directories on the shelves across the end of the desk. 00, international. 52, Mexico. 67, one of three possible prefixes for a Tijuana number. Tijuana. Aunt Jane. Perhaps the most famous border town in the world.

Chapter 3

I couldn't sleep in Jefferson's bed, a queen-size with a shot silk buttercup yellow pleated bedspread, fitted corners. In fact I felt like an alien almost anywhere in his apartment. It was spotless, tidy. First the living room, more easy leather chairs, lilies in a copper jug dropping pollen which he would have dusted up, a signed Jasper Johns litho of the Flag over the faux fireplace; then the kitchen which was clean enough for brain surgery and bright enough too with track lighting and stainless steel. You expect bathrooms to be clean but there wasn't even a pubic hair in the shower-stall, let alone a stain in the toilet bowl, even up under the seat. There was a table by the bed. *The Cat Inside* by William S Burroughs for bedside reading and an unopened pack of three in the thin drawer. We live in hope, it seemed to say.

I slouched back to the study. I was really very, very tired by now. Head ached in a systolic rhythm, punching home on the heart beat. Blood roared in my ears also cresting on the pulse. I was very thirsty but beyond hunger. Maybe a total of nearly twenty hours of airline and airport food accounted for both with Mr Chang's dumplings to finish off. Too much salt and flavour enhancer.

I drank the last two tins of Diet Coke from Jefferson's fridge, then some fizzy health stuff full of magic ingredients like ginseng, evening primrose, aloe vera, that sort of thing. It wasn't nice. I knew there were things I ought to do, things I should look for, look into, but I knew I had to sleep first. All I did do was secure the front door. After all, intruders had got in at least three times in the last twenty-four hours. I had a look at the locking systems. As well as a conventional chain there was also a dead-lock with no outside key hole but with its grooved key in place on the inside. Apart from making me feel a whole lot safer, it suggested something else. If Jefferson used it habitually, then he had opened the door to whoever had killed him.

Funnily enough the settee felt all right. It wasn't his, that's why. I took the alarm from my bag, adjusted it to West Coast time, it was still not yet ten o'clock, set it for seven.

Who knows what dreams may come? More to the point: how much do you remember the following morning? Oh, he prowled through them, no doubt of it. Sometimes the way I remembered him from his last visit to Bournemouth, yes Bournemouth, two years earlier: compact, fit, just a touch thicker in the waist than he used to be, short tight curls grizzled a little, skin somehow greyer beneath the dark copper. Laugh lines for crows' feet. And sometimes he came back from an earlier time — lean and muscular, skin with a natural gleam, tight plain t-shirt, baggy jeans, tennis shoes, the way he was when I pulled him, blood pouring from his scalp, out of the path of a water-cannon in Boul' St. Mich' and got him into Raspail, where I had a room, before the next baton charge came. May '68. Anyway the alarm put a stop to all that, the alarm and the Pacific light pouring in through the window I had not bothered to drape.

*

It was a fresh bright morning. Twenty minutes later I stood on the stoop and at the bottom of the street could see the blue-black ocean, flecked with white and near the horizon the aircraft carrier again. I'm going to swim in that surf, I promised myself. Swim in the Pacific before the day's out. The breeze blew away the dreams. The swags of jacaranda blossom above my hand tossed about like pom-poms shaken by cheerleaders and shed a leguminous flower-head or two in my direction.

I climbed the hill, dodging a swiftly sliding sheet of water from where the kitchen boy of a bistro was sluicing down the frontage, turned the corner and caught the full blast of waffle, maple syrup and coffee from a café a few yards further on. A waitress who was all California and therefore down here on a visit from Mt. Olympus was straightening cane chairs under the awning. I paused. She gave me a smile that would have stopped a tank. She pulled out a chair for me and put her head on one side inviting me to all the delights of paradise.

I looked at my watch. I looked up the road at the line of cabs.

'Do you serve takeaway?'

'Take out? To go? Ask at the counter.'

She pouted as if her day was ruined already.

I carried my doughnut and lidded plastic beaker of coffee up to the cab line and got into the front passenger seat of the first cab in the line. Another Merc. What happened to the American car industry?

'Where to?'

'Tijuana.'

He leant across me, opened the door.

'Go fuck yourself, motherfucker.'

23

I got out, got into the second cab. Pepe. The same cabbie who had taken me to Jefferson's office the evening before.

'Where to?'

'The border.'

'San Ysidro?'

'If that's the border.'

'That's the border.'

*

He took us up onto the freeway for ten minutes or so, driving carefully so I wouldn't spill my breakfast. It was the best doughnut I had ever had, and the best coffee from a plastic beaker. Eventually he slewed off to the left following what seemed like a motorway box round the north side of the city leaving Lindbergh Field International, downtown with its glitzy skyscrapers, and the Coronado Bridge on our right.

'Quicker if we take the 805,' he grunted.

'Why didn't the guy at the front of the line want to take me to Tijuana?' I asked.

'No one takes an automobile across the border. The best you can expect is to lose the wheels. But more likely they mug you and take the lot.'

'So how do I get across?'

'I drop you at the bus station and you get the shuttle bus.'

'Why didn't the other guy tell me that?'

'He's a stupid fuck.'

*

The suburbs, clapboard houses, chalet-style or bungalows became almost scruffy, the yards no longer filled with oleander and strelizia, the palm trees unkempt and brown. Then there were four miles or so of industrial agriculture, stripped maize, yellowish brown and rattling in the wind, wind-pumps, giant water-sprays with huge booms inching across salad or strawberry beds, long grey huts with silos and hoppers at the ends, windowless but filling the air from the black turd-like ventilators on their roofs with the stink of chicken- or pig-shit momentarily masking the smell of chemical fertiliser. A line of poplars rose above fences, slipways, a freeway spaghetti junction, a conglomeration of low, ochre and red buildings. The signposts Pepe followed read San Ysidro, leaving those for the frontier to our left. I guessed he knew what he was doing. Beyond the poplars an almost exact replica of the Berlin Wall masked the lower slopes of a long low hill stacked with housing which even at this distance you could see was little more than a shanty town.

Pepe took us into a large dirt-surfaced, chain link fenced parking lot and indicated three buses lined up in front of a kiosk.

'Get your ticket there, get on the first bus. They go every twenty minutes. I could wait for you but it'll cost. As it is you owe me fifty. There's a cab rank over there.'

Since he made it very clear from his expression that a tip of five was totally inadequate, it actually cost me sixty.

*

The main drag in Tijuana, Avenida Revolución, is a wide street of mostly two story buildings stretching for a mile or so down a gentle slope. Almost every joint on either side and that includes side-streets and covered arcades going back a hundred yards or so, target over-the-border tourists, mostly on day trips. Which is not to say by any means that they are tourist traps. From cat-houses easier to find, less uninhibited about what they're selling and cheaper than San Diego's, to fake Tommy Hilfiger T-shirts there are bargains. Especially if you're prepared to bargain. I have a technique.

'How much for these shades?'

'Sixty dollars.'

Walk away.

'They're Ray Ban. It says so.'

Keep walking.

'Hombre, how much will you pay?'

'Ten dollars.'

'Twenty.'

'Fifteen.'

'OK.'

Wearing my new shades I glanced up and down the sidewalk. How to find the Farmacia San Cristóbal?

The problem was every tenth shop was a chemist. Large, neat, spotless. White-overalled shop assistants watched over stacks and stacks of proprietory medicines in gleaming white packs with embossed labels, sealed openings and tops, with placards announcing names and prices, and, in case you hadn't guessed, 'No scrip necessary!'. Borderline hard drugs like methadone and codeine; viagra, cortisone, fifty-seven varieties of antibiotic, beta blockers; and the latest cocktails of HIV controllers were all stacked up with offers, buy thirty, get ten free, a free packet of multivitamins with every pack of Viagra, and so on. I remembered Harry Lime and watered-down penicillin but these places wouldn't stay open if they sold placebos or duds. San Cristóbal, I argued, must be here: with its answerphone message, cool and professional, it wasn't going to be a backstreet apothecary selling snake venom and mescalin.

And sure enough I found it, on the corner of one of the arcades. Closed but about to open. I took a saunter down the passage: big spaces, many of the stall-holders unlocking their lock-ups setting up their stalls. One specialised in dreadful plastic kitsch; another toys, ten thousand Micky Mice. Watches, sunglasses, pottery crudely painted with busty flamenco dancers. Guaranteed silver jewellery, filigree and rings. Pointless knick-knacks, joke or macho keyrings, cigarette lighters with nudes on the barrels, bottle-openers ditto, packs of cards, roulette wheels and those pocket torches that throw a red dot of light a couple of hundred yards or more so kids can think they're laser-equipped snipers. I bought one for my twelve-year-old son. Didn't tell you I had a family, did I? Well, I don't really but there's a family live a mile away from me in Blighty where the kids still call me Daddy, though their mum kicked me out five years ago. Make a mental note. I've bought Richard something he'll like, now I mustn't forget little Rosa.

So back to the Farmacia San Cristóbal. A strip neon sign of the old guy carrying the Infant on his shoulders, and the green cross below it. Big shop. I went right in, well beyond the door, before putting my elbows on top of a glass-topped counter in front of the prettiest girl there. Deep red hair, lipstick the colour of bull's blood, and makeup that had taken an hour and which she reckoned she needed since she had some eczema scars. Overall with cleavage and a tiny emerald encrusted cross just below her clavicles. Eyes sharp and mean enough to open oysters at ten paces, but large dark and liquid all the same.

'I've been sent,' I said, 'to see the boss.'

The cleavage rose and fell, just perceptibly, three times. Her fingers rested on the far edge of the counter, the palms below it. One index finger, the lacquer matched the lipstick, tapped. I could just hear the click of the nail on the glass.

'Who,' she murmured, 'sent you to see the boss?'

English but accented.

I had given that some thought before I went in. Wilbur Jefferson? Mrs. Heart? General Lennox? I settled for Jerry Lennox.

'Jerry Lennox,' I said.

'And your name is...?'

'Christopher Shovelin.'

'Christopher. Like Cristóbal. One moment please.'

She turned a key in her computerised till, extracted it, it was attached to her belt, and sashayed off, still behind the counter, to a polished, panelled door, beneath a sunburst clock, at the back. Just after ten, maybe I was the first customer of the day, except that I wasn't a customer. I jigged around from foot to foot for five minutes, jingled the small change in my trouser pocket, pulled some of it out, turned it over in my palm with my left index finger. I love the quarters. In God we trust. Liberty. The fine relief. The feeling of depth behind the eagle on the other side. Here she comes.

'Señor Guzman does not come into the shop until he has had breakfast in La Cantina on the other side of the road. Maybe he'll see you there.'

'How will I know him?'

'You won't.'

'How will he know me?'

'He will.'

I waited on the corner for the lights but still got caught by a cab taking a right. Yes, a Merc, but ten years older and ten feet longer than the ones from La Jolla and painted red and black. I got the full hispanic open palm above the forehead chopping gesture that signals you are a hijo de puta, but escaped without injury. From the middle I walked in the shadow of a very old man in a Calvin Klein T-shirt and very old, very distressed Nike trainers. He used a stick, had a back hunched by age and arthritis, pendulant ear lobes and a charmed life. I still had a side street to get across but it was narrower and all I scored was a bull-roarer from a bus. The final obstacle was a shoeshine stall, the full monty, fifteen brass-topped bottles in racks, sixteen brushes, and a Fagin-sized bundle of rags — the material of a small, energetic, muscular Indian who had no intention of letting me get past once he had spotted my tan Oxfords.

He sat me on his leather upholstered throne, pulled my right foot onto a thin, worn brass rail, slipped oval guards into the sides of the shoe so no polish would get on my sock, spat on his hands, took a swig from a tequila bottle and got on with it.

I guess reflexology has its roots in the ministrations of shoeshine boys. You come out of it not only with shoes that look as if they have been french polished but in a relaxed and all together happier frame of mind which is not entirely dispelled by the shoeshiner's insistence that one five spot is an insult that can only be removed by a second. Which is unfair when you think about how much a reflexology session can cost.

La Cantina was *tipico* and had had the sense to do little more than exaggerate or point up what it already had so now it was *tipico plus*. Almost everything was wood — the floor, the ceiling, the walls, the tables, the bentwood chairs, the long bar down the inside wall, the six foot long blades of the ceiling fan. The jukebox was not wood, looked old but was probably repro. There were bullfight posters, also old. El Cordobes for Christ's sake. And high up in a corner, near the ceiling a framed and faded newspaper photograph of a square-headed guy, crew-cut, granny specs, military type top — none other than Leo Trotsky himself. The whole place smelled of black tobacco, garlic, re-fried beans, overcooked tomato and coffee.

There was one barman, six customers and a waiter. I ordered a cortado, an espresso with a splash of hot milk, and then went to the *caballeros* for a slash. It was small but as clean as cracked lino, and cracked porcelain would allow. As I zipped up and turned away from the urinal two men came in. The first, a big man with mediterranean features and colouring smashed my face with his open palm so my head cracked against the wall behind me, and the second, who had the bony nose, high cheekbones and parchment skin of an Indian, like the shoeshiner, round-house kicked me in the stomach. Fortunately I'd pocketed my new shades out on the sidewalk.

That was enough kung fu fighting for me and I sat down.

They pulled me up and heaved me back into the main room and dropped me in front of a very old man in a Calvin Klein T-shirt, very old, very distressed Nike trainers. He had a stick, a back hunched by age and arthritis, pendulant ear lobes. He was dipping a large boat-shaped madalena into a large *café con leche* and sucking the gruel he'd made of it between two canines with a big gap between them.

Occasionally a lump of sludge would drop back into the bowl. It took me the same time to get my breath back as it did for him to finish the cake. He pulled a tissue from the dispenser at his elbow and wiped lips as pendulant as his ear lobes.

'The fuck you know about Jerry Lennox?' he asked. His voice was wheezy, his accent thick but penetrable.

'Not a lot.'

He shook a black cigarette out of a paper packet, offered me one which I refused, fired his up with a Zippo. Petrol fumes and thick smoke.

'He's the son of a general,' I went on, 'he's gone missing...'

'The fuck are you.'

'I'm a private inquiry agent. English...'

'The fuck you doing here.'

'I have... I had a friend called Wilbur Jefferson. He's a private eye based in San Diego. He was investigating the disappearance of Mr. Lennox on behalf of the family. He asked me to come over and help him... This gets complicated.'

'I'm not stoopid.'

'I'm sure you're not. Incidentally, you haven't introduced yourself. Are you the Guzman the girl in the chemist told me would meet me here?'

'Chemist?'

'Farmacia.'

'They're not the same.'

'No.'

'I could get angry you think I'm a chemist.'

'I'm sure you're not.'

'OK. The farmacia's mine. How come you're here asking for me?'

He took a last drag on the cigarette so his head almost disappeared in a cloud of smoke then dropped the butt in his bowl where it hissed. From beneath droopy eyelids something glittered in his rheumy dark eyes. He waited.

'Jefferson left me the telephone number of the farmacia.'

'I think I ask Ramon to take you back to the toilet and pull your head off.'

The Mediterranean guy was still by the toilet door, poking his nails. The Indian with the kick was chatting to the barman.

'I'm sure that won't be necessary. There's a problem?'

'Sure there's a fucking problem. You told Victoria Jerry Lennox sent you.'

I sighed.

'This may seem a bit silly to you,' I said, 'but I thought the name Jerry Lennox might, um, interest you, arouse your interest, more than Wilbur Jefferson.'

'They go together. *Maricónes*. One the same as the other'. He linked his gnarled and knobby index fingers in front of his pigeon chest and pulled. Then he coughed, spat an ounce of phlegm onto the wooden floor. 'Wilbur could have come. Why send you?'

'Wilbur's dead. Shot. I found him in his flat, apartment. But then the body disappeared.'

'The fuck it did.'

The old wreck of a man had gone still. Silence spread from him until it hit the wall of sunlight and sound that came in from the street through the long unglazed windows: the shouts of the shoeshiner trying to drum up business, the traffic, crash of gears, hiss of brakes as the lights changed, the shrill blast of a traffic cop's whistle.

'How long you knew Jefferson for?'

'Thirty years and a bit. We met in '68. In Paris.'

'No kidding.'

'No kidding.'

'Show me your passport.'

I handed it to him. He riffled through it.

'Not a AFT agent then.'

'AFT?'

'Alcohol, firearms, tobacco. Gringo law enforcement agency.'

'No.'

He began to stand up but before he made it the young waiter, no more than a lad really, was at his elbow helping him, handing him his stick. He looked at me across the table. His lips shook, he cleared his throat but didn't spit this time.

'Shovelin,' he croaked and handed back my passport, 'go back to San Diego. Go back to England. With Jefferson dead what can you do? But if you do get to Jerry, tell him to cool it right now. Lay off till he hears from me. He'll understand. Sorry we roughed you up.'

'Hang on. Can you not give me even a hint as to what this is all about?'

He shook his head. Not hugely. Not a negative either. Just the incredulity of someone who has been asked a damn fool question.

I watched him go, out into the sunlight. I paid for the coffee I hadn't drunk and caught the bus back to San Ysidro.

I have almost no Spanish. I didn't then know what *maricón* means. If I'd bothered to look it up I'd have saved myself a lot of trouble and maybe a life or two. It's slang for homosexual.

Chapter 4

Out on the beltway, perhaps just as the cab was passing the signs for the zoo, the pain from the lump the size of an egg just below my bald patch, where mediterranean man had smashed it into the loo wall, let its fingers slip and became a not so dull ache. Back in Jefferson's apartment, it clawed its way back up to pain as I listened to China Heart on Jefferson's answerphone.

'Shovelin. If you're there pick up the goddamn phone. No? All right, play it your way. But here's what you do. You got Jefferson's keys. There's a small parking lot back of his building. The metallic green Pontiac Grand Am is his. Take the freeway, interstate five, into town. Don't take any of the exits until you get to state highway ninety-four east. Take that, it's signposted Yuma in Arizona but you don't have to go that far. Thirty miles out you go through a small township called Heavengate, one word. Three and a half miles on, on your right, you'll come to a gateway with an iron sign above it, says Homage. There's a guard who'll check out your ID so make sure you have some. There's a wind-pump on a low rise half a mile inside the spread, you can see it from the road. Follow the dirt-track past it until you come to Homage itself. You'll know when you get there. Now hear me Shuvlin, Shovelin. Be there by one or you lose a day's pay. Oh yeah. And watch out for the traffic cops. Without proper documentation you'll end up in jail.'

I looked at my watch. Half after seven. I looked at Jefferson's wall-clock. Half after eleven. Could be possible. If I didn't get lost. Then I thought: fuck it, I'm not in this for the money, I'll take my time.

It was as well I did. I found the wheels, no problem. The key was central locking, but when I got in there was no steering wheel. Well, it was on the wrong side. Next, it was an automatic and the only automatic I'd ever driven before was my sister's Nissan Micra, after she had a stroke, so that took a bit of sorting.

Then of course they drive on the wrong side of the road. That seemed OK. All the cab rides I'd had I was already used to it. I thought. But it slipped my mind at the third junction, the one that took me on to the slipway for the freeway. Fortunately, although it was two-way, there wasn't a central reservation, and no Highway Patrol either.

The Pontiac was OK. Medium-sized family car, all the options, a touch dull maybe. Seemed an unlikely choice for a successful private eye but it had the merit of not drawing attention to itself. It was John Doe's car. A tolerably affluent John Doe. I guessed with a car like that Jefferson could hang on a subject's tail for half a day without being noticed whereas a Porsche or even a Celica would have been picked up on.

I'd already covered the first part of the route that morning on my way to San Ysidro, it wasn't until the intersection south of Balboa Park that I began to cover new ground. Clear of the city the land ceased to be agri-industrial. At that time of year, and maybe any time of year, it looked like desert: flat or gently rolling grit with scattered dried up thorn-bushes and cactus eight feet tall, the sort with arms, not drowning but waving, what I took to be some sort of black vulture on every tenth telegraph pole or soaring between on wings with tips tilted up. Lilac coloured mountains on the horizons. The only thing it lacked was tumbleweed. It got hot. I opened the window and it got hotter. I pulled in, found the manual in the passenger's glove locker, got the air-conditioner running.

Every now and then, over to the right, when a crease in the hills left by a prehistoric creek revealed it, I got glimpses of the Wall, the wall I had seen at San Ysidro. Double fencing, watchtowers, sometimes the concrete with the angled and rounded coping on top.

Heavengate was a score of clapboard houses in a ribbon edged with acacias already in heavy black pod, a filling station, a 7-11 or maybe a Spar, and something official with its Stars and Stripes stretched from its flagpole by the hot breeze. I felt a sudden surge of... what? Hard to put a name to it. Nostalgia? From *The Postman Always Rings Twice* (both versions) to *Paris, Texas*, I've spent a lot of my life in places like Heavengate without ever crossing the Atlantic. There's always at least one of them in the multiplexes I go to two or three times a week.

Sure enough, another three miles on, another blast from the movies. Set back from the road, so the track to it made a crossroads with the one opposite, a brick archway covered with flaking white stucco stood on its own in the desert. A fence, six feet high, chain link with a curly-whirl of razor on top, metal posts, stretched down the road as far as the eye could see. On a hill that made a visual ridge behind it a wind-pump failed to turn because the girders were twisted near the top and the fishtail bent. I slowed, took the right, and stopped ten yards short of the arch. And yes, curly lettering in wrought iron spelt out 'Homage' across it. A Cherokee Jeep, nearly new, swayed a little as a big man with a big paunch dropped his feet down onto the dirt. He was wearing a tan, military-style uniform with squashy peaked cap above tinted glasses and he was carrying a short barrelled, pump-action shotgun. His belt was stuffed with shells.

I dropped the window as he came up. The hot wind fought the air-conditioning to get in and won.

'You Shuvlin? Kit Shuvlin?'

Seemed silly to be pedantic about it so I let it go.

'Get out the vehicle please, show me some ID.'

Oh shit, I thought, my mind still in the movies, this is where he kicks my legs apart and slams me against the bodywork. But he was happy to give my passport a quick glance and me a quick frisk. Nevertheless I felt uncomfortable with that, sort of embarrassed, I suppose it's the Brit in me, and, as his hand slid up the inside of my trouser leg, I glanced past him at the octagonal STOP sign, white on red, a telegraph pole, the mountains, noticeably nearer now. And, of course, the crushed Pepsi tin at my feet.

He flipped through my passport, handed it back, then unhooked a mobile, or more probably an RT, from his belt.

'Gate one to control. Shuvlin's here. He's clean, though I ain't checked out the car... Sure thing. I'll do that.' He turned to me. 'Got to give the vehicle a once-over.'

He took the keys from me so he could open the lockers and the trunk. Nothing there that interested him. He kept the shotgun in one hand all the time so he was pretty awkward about it. Bending into the corners his big behind stuck out. His neck was as red as you'd expect a redneck's to be. If I'd had a mind to it I could have hit him with a brick or a tyre-iron, except I didn't have a brick or a tyre-iron. Eventually he straightened and gave me back the keys.

'On your way, *hombre!*'

I kid you not. That's what he said.

I drove up the rise, past the wind-pump, over the other side. A plain, a range, a spread, almost flat, stretched in front of me bordered on the far side, a good ten miles away maybe more, by what, from where I was, looked like a thin black thread but I guessed was the border fence. There was a lot to look at between and I pulled in and got out.

Way over to the left, towards the mountains, a rocky escarpment was scarred with a mini-canyon and an almost dried up river which threaded out of it through a debris of scree and boulders into the plain. Then it ox-bowed and meandered generally south. River? Should that be barranca, levée, creek or crick? Here and there in the bends there were stands of poplars, already beginning to yellow up in places, and, stretching out irregularly from it for a mile or so, a swathe of dried up meadow, yellow and ochre, through which drifted, very slowly, maybe a hundred head of small black cattle.

In contrast along the slopes above this plain there were more neglected and non-functioning wind-pumps, and even more surprising a cluster of about twenty rusting, motionless oil donkeys with oil rig girder towers above some of them, rusting vehicles stripped of anything useful like wheels, tumbled sheds of corrugated iron and other machinery I couldn't identify. It all told a tale. I reckoned the oil had run out and the aquifer had dropped below the level mere wind power could pump it up from.

Yet, in front of me, still a couple of miles away at the end of the now ruler straight track, was the most surprising feature of all, an oasis. Most of it was screened by trees — palms, broad cedars, pencil cypresses, but not so I couldn't see the dome and part of the façade of what looked at this distance to be a white colonnaded mansion with emerald lawns in front, gardens around and a complex of outbuildings, white and red-tiled to the side.

And even as I watched a white twin-engined Lear jet completed its approach, kicked dust, dropped its tail and taxied out of sight behind the trees.

Five minutes later I pulled up on a wide semi-circle of quartzy gravel that glittered in front of the steps, also set in concentric semicircles, beneath a doric colonnade. To my right what I took to be a Civil War cannon, mounted on a plinth, faced out over lawns where wind-blown spray from sprinklers made rainbows in front of the rich dark green of a Lebanon cedar. There were two flagpoles. The Stars and Stripes on one and on the other, not the Confederate flag I half expected, but the bear of the Republic of California.

A black footman? Butler? in a monkey jacket with a high collar and brass buttons, white kid gloves, black pants, opened the car door before I could. He put a hand under my elbow which annoyed me. I'm only a little over fifty and not a fucking geriatric yet.

'Are you real?' I asked. 'Or do you black up like Al Jolson every morning.'

He grinned.

'Suck my dick, whitey,' he murmured, 'and find out.'

He pushed back the big brass-handled front door. Thing was, we both knew I came from the same side of the green baize as he did, so one day maybe we could be friends. 'I'll tell Mrs Heart you *fin-al-ee* arrived. Keys please.'

'Fuck off.'

'Keys. So Sir's limo can be valet-parked, all right?'

He took them, brushed past some potted palms, yuccas whatever and was gone. Through a green baize door.

I was in a big circular hall that was quite a room. The ceiling, three floors up, was the dome I had seen from the hill. A third of the cylinder it made was glass walled, hung with lots of muslin billowing in front of louvred casements, right from the dome down to the floor where curved doors that kept to the shape of the whole opened out onto terraced gardens. On either side two staircases corkscrewed in spirals to the landings which gave access to the wings. On the ground level the floor was inlaid polychrome marble in trompe l'oeil patterns but the central feature was a tall palm, lean and straight which stopped only six feet below the apex of the dome. Swags of waxy white flowers hung from its crown. Round its base more plants had been artfully arranged in their pots — ceramic, polished copper or brass. There were ferns, yuccas in bloom, and orchids. The temperature was in the mid-eighties which was probably cooler than outside, but the humidity was high. A couple of small birds with plumage like bright enamel darted about and a hummingbird sipped at a syrup dispenser.

I heard footsteps. I moved beyond the palm and discovered that the south facing aspect continued the theme with galleries designed like orangeries though with tropical and equatorial fruits rather than citrus. And along one of these came Mrs Heart herself. China Heart.

Today she was wearing a simple pale blue cotton dress, which looked cool and wasn't really simple at all. The material was textured by the uneven thickness of the threads, the cut was a miracle, making it move where you felt it ought to, but fitting like it was part of her where you wanted it to. I wouldn't mind betting that the label was so exclusive neither you nor I would have heard of it. There were no bra or knicker lines I could see. She was wearing fuck-me high heels of the sort that turn sane men into foot fetishists and a fetishist would have died for. They were the same blue as the dress, but silk covered not cotton.

'You're late.'

'It's only just one o'clock.'

'So it's afternoon. You lost a day's pay. A grand. And I mean it — so's you'll know you don't fuck with us. Now you'd better meet Papa.'

'Who only just arrived?'

'The fuck you know about it?'

Two fucks in five seconds. Very demotic for a class act.

'I just saw his plane land. Ten minutes. A quarter of an hour ago.'

The bevelled curved glass doors took us between ornamental terracotta urns on to a semicircular parterre, part arboured with roses which hung above an irregularly shaped swimming pool. Dazzlingly white statues of exaggeratedly pubescent nymphs hung out on its promontories no doubt hoping for similarly sexy youths to show. After all, all they had was General Lennox, one of the ugliest old men I have ever seen.

'Papa. This is Christopher Shovelin. The private detective from England I told you about. Friend of Wilbur Jefferson.'

'Shovelin. Keep it brief. This time of day I have a swim.'

The voice, which sounded like a spade scraping horse-shit up from concrete paving, came from a face that looked like Mount Rushmore before they carved human likenesses on it. It was deep, rumbling, throaty and chesty at the same time. The voice that is. The face was a pale ochreish grey, fissured with deep lines almost all of which ran vertically. The eyes were hooded behind eyelids that slipped down and outwards, the nose was a hook whose cave-like nostrils supported tufts of yellowish-white nasal hair, the mouth a shark's. His hands, which rested on his bony knees, resembled a bird's claws — an eagle's perhaps, or a vulture's — and were as blotched with liver spots as any I have ever seen.

He was sitting in a sparkling electric wheelchair, beneath a parasol set in a round table. There was a jug on the table with a crown of mint. A mint julep? I wouldn't know a julep from a Pimms, not even if it sat up and bit me.

'China, get him a chair. Pour him a drink.'

'If it's alcoholic...'

'Of course its's alcholic...'

'I'm afraid I can't drink it.'

'Can't? Or won't?'

'Can't.'

37

China unfolded a metal framed chair with wooden slats. I sat on it. She took a semicircular stone seat in the shade of an arbour about five paces behind. A breeze stirred the surface of the water and the white light lines refigured themselves on the blue tiles below.

'Why you dry, boy?'

'A distended liver caused the varices in my oesophagus to burst. I vomited and later shitted blood. I was lucky to survive.'

Very slowly his claw-hand reached forward, closed round the glass he was drinking from. He drank long and slowly and then yes, literally smacked his lips before replacing it.

'When was that, boy?'

'Three years ago.'

'You must have been a regular boozer.'

'That and I was born with weak veins. They go varicose too readily.'

He grunted, wiped moisture from his glass on his shorts. For someone who had just flown in from Los Angeles his clothes were casual, though he could have had time to change them. He was naked apart from shorts and sandals, and as far as decency was concerned he might as well have not bothered with the shorts. They were loose, baggy, but... short. His thin bony knees were spread, and one testicle, like a small walnut, had escaped from their netted lining. His legs were knotted with veins, almost as bad as mine, his toes misshapen, the nails arched down over them like claws. I could go on. Let's just say he made me feel that sixty or sixty-five would be enough. See what I think when I get there.

He fiddled with a cloth bag, tied with a draw-string, on the table next to the jug. Stencilled on it was a picture or badge I couldn't quite make out and the words Wells Fargo.

'What do you say, boy? Who shot your pardner? You ought to know. Damn it, you're a frigging detective aren't you?'

A sound like the rhythmic sighing of a high wind in mountain pines — the general was laughing.

'All rightee, son. I've talked this over with China. She thinks you'll do. Take over where Wilbur Jefferson was cut off. Find my son Jerry. I guess that way you'll find who killed your friend too. You get a retainer of five big ones. A grand a day and all expenses...'

'That's not what Mrs Heart offered.

'It isn't?' He looked across me at her, in the shade behind me. I resisted the temptation to let my eyes follow his.

'The deal was a retainer of ten thousand, twenty more if I found Mr Lennox alive, and ten if he's dead. A grand a day plus expenses.'

White teeth, his own — I imagine he had paid for them — the canine pointed, chewed the corner of his drooping mouth.

'Is that right, honey?'

This time I couldn't resist looking round. A resigned smile... but for me or her father was hard to tell.

'That's right, Pa.'

'The retainer ten grand not five.'

'Yes.'

'And it's in this bag?'

'In the bag, Pa.'

'OK, boy. You got it. She'll give you a hand, fill you in and so on, be a bell away for as long as you need her...'

'No, Pa. That's not what I said. I can give him a week. Then I'm flying to Sydney.'

'Hell, China, I don't expect him to take more'n a week. Not at the rates you've offered. Mr. Shovelin? What do you say?'

At least he had my name right. Southern manners. I shrugged.

'OK,' I murmured. At about four times anything I'd ever been paid in the UK sure it was OK, but I wasn't about to stand on my chair and cheer.

He pushed the bag across to me. I loosened the drawstring and pulled out the first wad of fifties, still fastened by a brown paper wrapper with the Wells Fargo logo on it. Yes, was a stagecoach. Twenty sheets, present and correct. I started on the second. It was while I was counting that the Lear took off again. First the rising roar of the engines then they settled, diminuendo, then back it came on a steadier more even note. The plane flashed over us, sending a shadow skimming across the pool, still low enough for the airstream to ruffle the surface. The pilot made the wings wiggle in salute, then it was gone, over the cedars and poplars.

'Well good hunting to him,' the General cried and took another swig before turning back to me. 'Hell boy, we're not fairground swindlers. If China says it's all there, it's all there.'

I went on counting. All ten bundles. Round about the fifth, he batted at a passing insect with his claw.

'I like your style, son.' And I heard again that rhythmic sound like wind gusting through a pine forest. At last I stuffed it all back, pulled the toggle down on the drawstring.

'Thanks,' I said. I turned to the General. Shake on the deal? But no — the look he gave me said it all: the Lennoxes do not shake hands with trade.

She was standing now, standing behind me. I stood too.

'I'll show you the rooms Jerry used when he was here and fill in some background,' she murmured. Then the voice rasped and the hooded eyes glittered up at us from the deep shadow under the parasol.

'You may find there evidence that my son occasionally broke federal and state laws. You will not use this knowledge to do him any harm or to serve your own ends. Do you understand?'

'I understand.'

'If you break this promise I'll get you locked up in jail. Most of the inmates in such places are negroes with an ill-founded but ineradicable sense of grievance against their masters. They gang-rape, anally that is, any white unlucky enough to fall into their clutches. Most of them have AIDS.'

I stood. China did too. Had my chief concern not been the identification of Jefferson's killer I think I might at that point have chucked in my hand. It was not the silly threat that bothered me. It was just the absolute nastiness of this very nasty old man.

I followed her round the waggly periphery of the pool, feeling somewhat absurd as we did so. The Wells Fargo bag was too big to go in any of my pockets and I let it swing as I walked. Oleanders, strelizia and giant orange lilies brushed our thighs. The air was heavy with frangipane. As we left the pool I noticed a long-legged fly standing in the six tiny black circles its feet created above all the light and colour beneath. The frozen girls at puberty looked down at it.

Chapter 5

A door in a whitewashed wall took us down a couple of brick steps and into a different world. First, it was like an oven. Inside my shirt sweat broke and trickled down my back. Homage was well inland, well away from the cooling effect of the ocean, and at a latitude further south than Marrakesh. Where we were now was enclosed, with no water, no breeze. It looked like, and probably was, the kitchen garden of the original settlement, a Spanish farm house or *finca*. It was laid out like a single story Andalucian farmstead with rooms on three sides of a rectangle connected only by an exposed verandah. There were a couple of big trees, and the outlines of square beds in which kitchen herbs still struggled for survival. There was also a domed stone oven and a well. But the whole enclosure was dominated by a huge tank, no not a water tank, a tank with tracked wheels and a gun half a mile long. Nearly. I have no idea what sort it was. But it looked new, new and evil.

Also parked there, inside the high double gates, were a jeep attached to what I would call a field gun, possibly Second World War vintage, and an armoured car. All were in immaculate condition, metal shone where it was meant to shine, oil and grease glistened in appropriate places, there was not a speck of dirt or even dust on them. In short, they looked ready for use.

We walked down one of the verandahs, our feet echoing on the boardwalks. The windows of the rooms we passed were barred but unglazed and I could see that each room was an armoury dedicated to a different sort of weapon. There were carbines and automatic rifles racked in one, pistols and submachine guns cased in the next, bows and crossbows in the third. The next to last was empty and a broken shutter swung and banged against the further wall. The window had been boarded up. You didn't have to be a private eye to guess someone had broken in and stolen the contents, but it helped. The last contained heavier machine guns. One wall was filled with looped chains of ammunition, some of it large calibre.

The three rooms on the second side, the one facing the gates and the tank in front of them, had been properly modernised and were, China told me, used by Jerry Lennox when he stayed at Homage. They were linked to each other as well as having their own doors onto the verandah. We entered the suite through the first we came to.

It was a bathroom. The bath was a sunken jacuzzi. At that moment the only living thing in it was an eighteen inch sienna coloured centipede with jaws big enough to crack a nut. The whole room was done out in patterned mosaic, mostly blue but with quite a lot of gold. China flicked on spotlights to get the full effect.

'Nice, huh?'

The next was a bedroom, with a king-size, curtained in muslin. It occurred to me mosquitoes might be a problem, with the pool so close, and indeed the windows were shielded with heavy duty net. Again, no glass, just louvred shutters on the inside. I peeped through. On the outside a high security fence about ten yards from the building then the desert climbed to a visual ridge maybe half a mile away. Inside there were a lot of mirrors, including on the sliding doors of the closets. Not on the ceiling though, so not totally decadent.

Finally a long living room which had, I reckoned, originally been two rooms in the old *finca*. A self-consciously male room, this: rafters left exposed above, animal heads on the white, rough-cast walls, a mountain cat, a bear, and a mountain goat. Beneath them a pool table, a bar, leather furniture with animal skin throws. Board floor with Indian weave rugs. At the far end a wooden desk with PC, telephone and so on, a dark-stained bookcase, and a filing cabinet.

One odd thing. It stank of cigarettes. The heavy acrid smell you get in a room that has been smoked in for twenty years. Yet there were no ashtrays.

A large alcove where an old fireplace had been taken out so it could be turned into a shrine was what an estate agent would call a feature. It was dominated by a flag pinned to the back wall, the Stars and Stripes, but, superimposed on it, a black circle filled with white SS lightning flashes.

There was also a big photograph, black and white, landscape, poster-sized. It had been faked using Photo-shop or something similar to show Hitler, in an open Merc, the one he used to enter Vienna after the Anschluss, driving up Whitehall, London, giving the Hitler salute to massed and cheering crowds. On the table there was memorabilia — tacky statuettes of the Fuehrer, an iron cross in its case, an SS or Gestapo dagger. I pretended not to see all this, the way one ignores a loud fart.

'Yeah. OK. So he's a nutter.'

I turned.

'Why don't you sit down and tell me about him?' I suggested.

She made a move, waited. I got the message and pushed a heavy leather armchair up near the desk and then sat myself in the bucket-like affair that went with it. She put her knees together, swung them to the side, crossed her ankles, sat up straight as if she'd been told to.

'How long have you got?'

She shrugged, looked at something tiny and glittery on her wrist.

'Plenty. Two hours be enough?'

'Don't see why not.'

She sighed, put her left arm across her diaphragm, propped her right elbow on her left wrist, and made a question mark of the index finger against her lips.

'Jerry is forty-years-old,' she began, and dropped her right hand so it clasped her left upper forearm, 'son of Pa's third wife. She now has a cattle spread in Costa Rica, a fancy man to look after it and a fancy house to live in. My Ma, who was number two, only got a condo on Miami Beach when they were still fairly cheap. Of course I hated Jerry to begin with...'

'Hang on. I take it he is the general's natural son. I mean he didn't come with number three as part of the package?'

'No. He's his. Born in wedlock.'

She went on.

'But I got over the hate pretty quickly. I was four when he arrived, about six months after the wedding, and since his mother was a lush and I had nothing much to do, I spent six months a year here, six in Miami and I got to play with him quite a bit. Only when I wanted to. Other times there was what Pa called a 'nigger woman' who was actually a very well-trained nurse. Anyway, Jerry was a doll, a real-life living kewpie doll, who soon took up walkin' an' talkin' too. He played cute right through until puberty set in and we all loved him for it. Blond curly locks, freckles... I guess he was spoilt rotten; even his Ma loved him when she was sober. Well, drunk too I guess. Then Pa fell for number four. Bad scene.'

Her eyes went dreamy and fixed on something beyond the focal plane of the wall behind me. Then she snapped out of it and went on.

'For all the wives he had we were the only two kids. Born in wedlock anyway. I was a bitch so didn't count. Oh, Pa would see me comfortable, and prop up Mr. Right if his bank account didn't match up, but Jerry was the heir apparent. So no way was he going to be allowed to go off to Costa Rica with his Ma. Now, it turned out Jerry was a lot fonder of his Ma than anyone had thought and he kicked up no end of a fuss. By now he was sixteen going on seventeen. There were terrible rows. Both sides appealing for allies. What was a girl to do...?'

Again, she took time out, this time to look over her nails, found nothing wrong there, looked up at me, found room for improvement but didn't say so.

'Mind you, by then I was within spitting distance of twenty, and already widowed, so I guess I was in a pretty emotional state too. Lyle, Lyle Heart, had been two-timing me from the start with a widow woman in Yuma and when Pa got to hear of it he chased him all over the spread in his 1955 Corvette convertible and eventually squashed him between the fender and a cottonwood. But all that's another story.

'Meanwhile, Jerry went all quiet and reserved on us for, oh, five or six years. Seemed to be going through the motions, you know? Dutifully went to a private college in South Carolina where they played soldiers in fancy uniforms a lot, then on to West Point. And there he hit trouble. First we knew, though I reckon Pa had been warned in advance, he turned up here with a discharge in his pocket. Mentally unsuitable to serve as an officer in Uncle Sam's armed forces. Why? On what grounds? He'd arranged for a jeep full of automatic weapons and live rounds to be left where members of the Army of the American Republic could pick them up. First cousins of the group behind the Oklahoma bomb.'

Long pause. More nail inspection.

'And now he's gone walkabout,' I offered. There was more. I could tell. 'So?'

'With, item,' she ticked them off on her fingers, 'an M60 heavy machine gun with six five-hundred-round belts, a five-point-five six millimetre Colt M4 carbine, six frag grenades, a German Walther P five compact pistol, a Purdy hunting gun, a standard police issue pump-action shotgun and a crossbow that can pierce medieval sheet steel armour at a hundred yards. There may be more but that's all that's been found to be missing so far. He left, oh, just over a week ago, no it's more than that, in his Chevy 4x4 pick-up, one of the big new ones, not been seen since.'

'He took the hardware from the stores outside?' I nodded my head towards them. 'Why's it there? Is it legal?'

'It's legal. Pa's a weapon freak. He collects. Not just antiques but the latest technology when he can get hold of it. And three star generals have their sources.'

I thought for a moment.

'I must,' I said, 'be just about the most unsuitable person you and your father could have picked on to find him. Except possibly Jefferson himself. I don't know how well you know, knew Jefferson but he would have hated...,' I looked around me, at the fascist shrine, the dead animal heads, the weaponry outside, the whole ambience these absurdly rich people lived in, 'all this.'

Her eyes went cold. Her nails pressed into the leather arms.

'He came recommended. He took the job. And you? You were his friend. What do you think about it all? You can still quit if you want to.'

I thought.

'Lady,' I said, 'in a good year I make an annual profit in pounds sterling equivalent to about twenty-five thousand dollars. I have an ex-wife who won't work. She, we, have two kids. She has the marital home on which I have to pay the mortgage. I live in a room a quarter the size of this. If the money's right,' and I patted the Wells Fargo bag on the desk beside me, 'I don't think. But there are other problems I didn't like to mention to the General.'

'They are?'

'I've never even been to America before. I am not licensed to work here. I know nothing about the weapons you've mentioned. I'm fifty-two years old and though I'm tolerably fit for my age, my knees creak, my eyes don't work below three feet unless I put on reading specs, and I'm all but deaf in my left ear.'

'On the plus side you don't drink, you don't drug, you don't over-eat and you look like Sam Spade.'

'Be serious.'

'I am. You're a trained detective and, according to Wilbur, a very good one. If you're killed or disabled you'll have the satisfaction of knowing your wife will have to get off her butt and work —'

'You expect me to be killed. That's a great incentive.'

'No. But if, when, you've found Jerry you have to talk him down, as it were, you'll do it with a bit more cool than most people could muster.'

'Just what are you afraid of? A shooting spree? Like those kids in Columbine?'

She shrugged. But it was a very affirmative sort of a shrug.

'Frankly, yes. As for being unlicensed, that only counts when someone, and it has to be you or me or Pa, lodges a complaint that you're working as a PI for us. But above all there's this. There's Wilbur. Jefferson. Your friend. He wanted you here helping him. And that's what you're going to do.'

She paused, looked over towards the windows. Almost I thought there was a tear in her eye. A moistness anyway.

'I want him back. Jerry. Unharmed.'

She turned her head. Her eyes found mine, held them. Damnit there was a moistness. Her voice dropped to a whisper.

'Don't tell Pa this. But get him back in one piece and I'll pay you a bonus. Fifty.'

'Grand?'

'You think I meant elephants?'

We sort of laughed. Intimacies had been exchanged on both sides. Soon we'd be buddies.

There was something there she wasn't quite getting to. I had a stab at it.

'You want to keep him out of trouble. Unharmed. Because... you were a mother to him? He'd been your baby doll, and your best friend. In effect you were big sister to a guy who had no mother?'

'That and because when the rows started when Pa booted his Ma out, which was just when I discovered Mr Heart wasn't bolted to the floor, we did some fucking together.'

Half-siblings and she four years older than he.

'Oh,' I said. Nothing else seemed adequate. Fortunately my stomach rumbled. She took the point.

'I'll get them to send you a sandwich,' she said, pulling herself out of the deep chair. 'Pastrami on rye?'

'How did you guess?'

'Standard fare for private dicks. Coke?'

'Diet. Cold but no ice.'

Chapter 6

I let the silence settle in behind her. Then I found a wall thermostat with a switch. It was set for sixty-eight and came on when I pressed on. The system dropped the temperature within minutes.

Where to start? Get the easy stuff out of the way first. The bathroom had a complete set of toiletries, a flannel, sponge (real of course), toothbrush, but all dry, crisp, new, some of it still wrapped. I guessed he'd taken the ones he currently used, which indicated I supposed that he'd had at least a measure of say in his going. Not that there had been any suggestion of kidnap or coercion, but you never knew.

The bedroom drawers and closets were neither as tidy nor were the clothes as uniformly clean as Jefferson's had been, but it was easy to guess that a fairly rapid gathering had been made of basic items. I'd guess from the way things were disturbed and hangers left empty that he'd taken a fair selection of ordinary casual clothing. The really expensive and formal wear had been left behind — unless of course he had a very extensive collection of such stuff. Which, considering the apparent wealth of the whole set-up, was not impossible. Still, looking at what he had left behind, I'd guess he wasn't about to go to gala performances at the opera, nor, judging by a heap at the back of one closet, get under a car engine and fix it.

Back to the living room. Here life for the private investigator was going to be a lot more difficult, especially if access to files on the computer was protected. It was a conventional IBM compatible, not particularly new. I watched the screen change as it booted up and surmised that whatever else he was Jerry was no computer freak, into the latest gizmos and wrinkles. The desktop was a Hitler Youth poster of an Aryan blond facing a future which belonged to him. Jerry was on the net of course and had a list of websites and email addresses he used most: specialists in Nazi memorabilia, organisations for American racial purity, a society for the castration of homosexuals and pedophiles, about a dozen dedicated to the destruction of Washington D C and all its works. And so on.

One thing came clear. While it remained a mystery why this family should have hired Jefferson it was obvious why he took the job. He'd have seen it as a duty to get a guy like this off the streets if not actually locked up before he could harm anyone.

Then I tried to get into the personal part, correspondence, accounts, and such like and here of course it was all protected. Password Please.

For the rest the computer was an everyday tool — and source of minor recreation. He hadn't even bothered to update from Windows 95, which was a relief, since I haven't either. I found he had most of the commonest games, including mah-jong which tempted me for a moment, as well as the violent ones. Someone who has mah-jong on their computer can't be all bad, though probably it came with whatever package he had bought. Finally there were twenty-odd files identified with letter and number groups which looked like first letters or initials, and, as often as not, dates. TRA9900 might well be travel for the current year. I decided to give it a go when I sensed a presence behind me. Actually I smelled Cacharel for Men, which was one of the after-shaves left behind in the bathroom.

I stood, turned.

He held a chrome-plated Colt .44 automatic, Dirty Harry's Magnum, but loosely, swinging at the end of his right arm, pointing at the floor.

Inanely I muttered:

'Have a man come in with a gun.'

'What!'

The 'a' flat to rhyme with hat.

'Have a man...,'

Using his left fist with the easy skill of a professional boxer he jabbed me firmly on the nose.

I deserved no less.

*

From my new position on the floor, holding the injured article, which was already bleeding, I looked up at him. He was a fat slob. A big fat slob, who may once have fought in the ring and who packed, as they say, a mean punch, but now definitely a fat slob. Lank red hair was smoothed in thin strands over a salmon-pink dome, pale blue eyes gleamed maliciously from beneath yellow brows, the fat on his face pushed up round them enough to give them a piggy look. Meagre eyelashes. A neck like a tree-trunk above a check shirt and jeans which must have been a bother to do up over a stomach like the dome of St. Paul's and elephant legs. As is often the way with such monsters his hands, though puffy, looked small.

'The fuck are you. You ain't got no right to be here.'

The accent was southern, Texan maybe.

'I'm sorry. But that's precisely what I do have.'

I sounded petulant. Damnit, I felt petulant. This was the second time that day I had been floored for no apparent reason by a complete stranger.

'Whaddya mean?'

'General Lennox has employed me to find his son Jerry.'

'He ain't hidin' in this computer. Get up.'

'Not if you're going to hit me again.'

'I don't incline to such an intention right now.'

I got up. He gave me a handful of tissues dragged and shaken one-handed out of a box on a table by the desk. Then he stuck the Magnum in the waistband of his jeans. It was a tight fit, a bit of a struggle, but he managed.

'Thanks.'

I dabbed and wiped. Not as bad as I had expected.

'Ma name's Jake. Jake Carson. What's your'n?'

I told him.

'You speak kinda funny, Christopher. Where you from? Bowsteown?'

Boston?

'No. England.'

'Bowsteown surely is in England, aint it? New England?'

'I come from old England.'

'There's another England?'

'The one with a Queen.'

'Oh. That England?'

The silence lengthened. I tweaked its tail before it could get settled.

'What do you do, Jake?'

'Me? Oh, I just look after things? Like I'm Mr. Lennox's bodyguard?'

Clearly he had that infuriating affectation of giving everything he said an upwards inflection. I wondered. Did I dare go back to the PC? Did he read my thoughts? Or had I glanced in its direction? It's catching.

'How was you reckoning, Christopher? I may call you Christopher.'

'I prefer Kit. It's short for Christopher?'

Fuck. There I went again.

'Kit? How was you reckoning to find Jerry Lennox through that there computer?'

'Most people these days keep all their documentation on their computers. I thought maybe —'

'I know where Mr. Lennox is. You shoulda asked me.'

'I didn't know you. Till just now.'

'Mr. Lennox lives in San —'

San? Santa? Barbara, Monica, Francisco, José, Diego?

We both heard it. The slap of a leather shod foot stamped on the wood floor in the doorway.

'Jake? Shut the fuck up.' China came in. The sassy black help behind. 'Pastrami on rye. Diet Coke. No ice. What happened to your nose?'

'He hit it.'

'Jake? That was naughty, Jake. Very naughty. The General wants you poolside. There's an insect floating in it. He wants you to get it out, then he'll need you to help him get in. Run along now.'

'Running' was not on the menu, but Jake moved quickly enough, padding up into the garden, round the armed and armoured vehicles and out of sight. He used the same ability to be quiet about it that had brought him close to me before I realised he was there.

The help put the small tray down on the table next to the box of tissues. The sandwich was garnished with lettuce with a relish made from fresh horseradish on the side, and came with a linen napkin. The Diet Coke was still in its tin, can, though the ring-pull had been pulled. Both the can and the glass beside it were beaded and frosted. It all looked very attractive.

'Thanks... Sambo,' I murmured.

He grinned. White teeth, expensive orthodontics.

'You fulla shit, tight ass,' he whispered back, and went.

China didn't hear, or pretended not to.

'I'm sorry about Jake. He's a rough diamond and a bit simple with it, but heart of gold. And very loyal. Did you find anything?'

'Not yet. Your brother packed a few clothes and his current toiletries so it wasn't a completely unplanned, spontaneous departure. The PC's not much help. Most of what's on it's protected. Probably encrypted too.'

I felt my nose again, gave it a waggle, testing for a break. It seemed

OK, just sore. I took a bite of the sandwich. It was as good as it looked.

She hitched her butt on to the edge of the table in front of the fascist stuff, hands gripping the edge on either side.

'So what's the next step?'

'Why don't you just tell me how and when he made this disappearance?'

'You know most of it already. Two weeks ago he drove off from here in his new Chevy pick-up —'

'Tell me about that.'

'The Chevy? It's new, black apart from a lot of chrome, big, fast, powerful, can carry four people including the driver across the front seat. Behind, the truck part is normally open but there's a tarpaulin. It can carry a lot, I don't know how much, maybe a couple of tons. Although they're built for work a lot of kids buy them as fun vehicles. Four by four they can go just about anywhere a jeep can, they're fast, they're high up off the ground, you see one in your rear-view mirror, you get out of the way. And when it's gone past you, you read the word Chevrolet in big chrome letters across the tailgate.'

'Registration number?'

'Blitzkrieg.'

'I beg your pardon?'

'Blitzkrieg. Surely you've noticed you can have anything on California plates. If you can pay, and so long as no one else has had the same idea.'

Well, I thought, he'll have changed those if he wants to remain anonymous.

'He drove off...?'

'Early Monday, fifth of July. We'd had a party the night before, most often we do on the fourth, we had guests sleeping over, and only the servants were up. Jake amongst them. He helped load the weapons and the ammunition. That only came out later in the day. He said it wasn't his place to tell us before. Up till then we hadn't bothered. We reckoned Jerry'd got a bit of a hangover and had just gone up in the hills to work it off. But after three or four days we guessed he may have gone further, though at the same time we didn't want to alert the authorities, so we called in Wilbur. Jefferson.'

All through this I had been munching my way through the first quarter of the sandwich, but now I didn't want her to move on to the next stage until I was sure she'd left nothing important out so far. I shifted a smear of horseradish from the corner of my mouth.

'Cook said you'd like that. Being English.'

'She was right.'

'He.'

'So why the panic? Even with the weapons couldn't he have just been planning a hunting trip? Up in the mountains? There must be game up there, deer perhaps? Surely, if it were a hunting trip he could be away a week or more?'

'Elk and big horns, bear, of course, if you get high and into the wilderness. But no. Wrong weapons. He'd have taken a long-range hunting rifle if that was what he was planning. Thing is, there'd been a discussion, sort of, the night before...'

That lengthening silence again.

'Are you going to tell me about it?'

'Yes. Sure.' She sighed, got a grip.

'As I said, it was the fourth of July. People got talking in that serious, slow, concerned way you sometimes do when you're drunk but not drunk enough to enjoy yourself. About the American way of life. The frontier spirit, the last frontier. What makes Americans American. Shit like that. Then they, we, moved on to immigration, race, and so forth. There were a couple of Klansmen there but Jerry said negroes are all right. They've been here a long time, they win us medals at the Olympics. Jews are OK too so long as they don't wear silly hats and bang on about the Holocaust all the time. Latinos? Well, there are a hell of a lot of them, but then after all, in these parts anyway, weren't they here first? All, each, in their own way as American as apple pie, as chilli con carne anyway. Do you mind?'

She reached forward and took the last quarter before I could. She'd changed her nail varnish and lipgloss during the morning to a bright carmine with a subtle hint of blue in it, not enough to be purple but went well with the dress. She chewed and swallowed.

'Then it began to get silly. San Francisco Chinese are OK, they built the railways and so forth and most stayed in Chinatown. But not the Japs nor, and these were worst of all, the Koreans. The drunkenness shifted. Exaggerated tales got told. How in LA whole suburbs had been taken over. Jap money owns the Rim, movies, would have bought up San José, Silicon Valley, but they had this economic hiccup. The Koreans are worse. Korean is the first language in LA's public school system. And is it true Asiatic women have slanty cunts, like their eyes?'

She took one of the tissues and wiped her mouth, drank cola from the can, not the tumbler I was using.

'And Jerry just sat there looking more and more bad-tempered. He didn't say much, but in the end he walked away — we were having a barbecue on the other side of the spread — out into the desert. He came back a couple of hours later, just when you could see there might be a dawn and most of us were drifting off to the pool, or bed, and some to their cars to go home. And all he said was: 'Someone's got to do it. Someone's got to make a start cleaning the shit out of the Coast.' And that was the last any of us saw of him. Apart from Carson. Like I said, Carson helped him load up.'

'Carson?'

'Jake.'

She walked slowly down the room and into the sunlit doorway, spoke over her shoulder.

'None of us worried much. Till we realised he'd taken enough hardware to start a war.'

I sensed she'd said as much as she wanted to say but I still had a question or two needed asking.

'There's still a hell of a lot needs explaining.'

'Like you saw Wilbur's body and it disappeared?'

'For starters.'

She sighed again.

'Well, I wish I could help you with that. But I don't think I can.'

The body language was saying it now: shut the fuck up I want to go. 'Look, I have to be back in San Diego by five. And you've hardly started in here yet.'

'One last thing.'

She sighed. 'Yes?'

'A photograph?'

'I'll see what I can do.'

And with that she was gone.

*

I went back to the computer. I played three games of mah-jong, not wanting to stop until I had got out. Congratulations and fireworks. It felt like home. Then I flicked through the very few open files. There wasn't a great deal in them, often only four or five items in each. An attempt to keep accounts; an attempt to catalogue the armoury; letters to newspapers or radio stations grumbling about the amount of state and federal money spent on immigration and immigrant chasing with no real results: a small army of airborne vigilantes patrolling the borders and viable coast-lines would cost less. Four letters to a lady I took to be a Spic whore who had taken his fancy: they were part romantic slush, part S and M porno. A picture was emerging: a guy frozen emotionally at age fifteen, a social inadequate, an obsessive. Yes. Just the sort for a spree-killer.

I closed down the machine and began to look about for paper. Bugger all. But almost I made the classic mistake: the one that gets you drummed out of the Royal Society of Private Dicks. I nearly forgot the waste-paper basket.

It was a big square container, black with a chrome trim, tucked under the table in the alcove, the table China had perched on. She'd even banged her heel against it. It looked as if it hadn't been emptied for a month.

Most of it was junk mail, but even that can be revealing: circulars from gun dealers and purveyors of military, mostly fascist, memorabilia; publishers of kinky magazines and video tapes; the chess-freaks' book club. No charities apart from Vets', no Oxfam, Save the Children, or Amnesty International. But a reminder that his Mensa subscription was due.

There were gum wrappers, some holding used gum, as hard now as little grey pebbles, and there were empty foil pill or capsule holders which claimed to have held Duraphet-M. Great, I thought, a potential spree-killer with a speed habit. There were downers too: Diconal and DF-118. There was a paper-bag with a green cross on it. Tijuana. My spirits rose then crashed. Not, after all, Farmacia San Cristobal but Farmacia Francisco Xavier. Were these what the General had been thinking of when he warned me against going to the police about any of Junior's activities? Up to then I had had just straight racism in mind, but it seemed unlikely Pa would judge that to be criminal.

And there, amongst all the rest, was it. A crumpled letter, or note. Good quality fax paper, not the old crinkly stuff, laser printout. The header said Handlery Union Square Hotel, 351 Geary Street, San Francisco, with a fax number. The date was 02.07.99. There was no footer.

J.

I'll meet you at Da Vinci's (B H) seven, the 19th,
until then, *ciao and con amore*

J.

I looked at my watch, did the mental arthmetic. Not quite the nine-
teenth in England, still eight and a half hours to go in California. J for
Jerry? But who was the J who sent her love?

At that moment I heard a very faint squeak, the sort an amorous
mouse might make, and gliding past the window saw the head of the
general. A moment later his electric wheelchair filled the doorway.
He was now robed in a pure white bathing wrap that set off the tired
ochre of his seamed and gullied face.

'How you doing, boy?'

'Not bad, sir.' Hell, I could not stop that sir from slipping out. 'It
seems he intends, or at any rate intended to meet someone tomorrow
at a place called Da Vinci, B H.'

'That would be the restaurant in Beverley Hills. Wop place, but
some class. You'll be heading in that direction, then.'

'Yes... er, yes.'

He engaged reverse, left me room to get out. Blinking in the still
piercing sunlight I joined him in the old garden. He looked around
with pride.

He set the chair going again, clearly expecting me to follow him.
The long leafy streamers of a pepper tree brushed my head as I
caught up with him. We passed the dark rooms where guns stood in
racks as if held to attention by shadows formed up in files immacu-
lately dressed.

'What do you think of my collection, boy?'

'Very impressive... general.'

He stopped in front of the empty room, the one with the broken
shutter and the roughly boarded up window.

'Lost a company's worth of AKs a month or so ago, and the ammo
too. Made to look like a raid, but I reckon it was an inside job.'

He cruised on ahead of me. In front of the tank, under its long
barrel probing the spaces in front of it, he turned the machine again
to face me. He jabbed a crooked, arthritic finger at me. Shadows from
a cork oak mottled his robe with violet.

'They also serve,' he rumbled, 'who only stand and wait.'

The breezy laugh crumbled into a cough and he spat into a clump of desert lavender.

The chair purred up the ramped paths with me in tow. We followed the sinuous deck round the pond where the nubile maids still waited for the lads who never came. The long-legged fly though was nowhere to be seen. I wondered if Jake Carson had treated it gently. For all my nose still felt sore I thought he might have done. China met us on the terrace. She took the chair handles, pressed a button so the purr died, put on a brake.

'I take it you're through for now.'

'I reckon.'

'What next?'

'Like I've just told General Lennox.' I glanced at the old ruin. He seemed to have nodded off, head lolling forward. I turned back to China. 'I dug up a lead.'

I spread out the note, handed it to her. She read it, read it again, turned it over.

'Is it from Jerry or to him?'

I shrugged.

'Since it was sent from San Francisco, I guess it's to him.' I took another close look at it. 'Odd the footer's been sliced or scissored off.'

She didn't comment on that.

'Pa. Say goodbye to Mr. Shovelin. He's going.'

The granite head came up. There was a bubble of spittle in one corner of the thin, evil mouth. He wiped it on the back of his scaly claw.

'Guess it's time he went. I caught him snooping round old —'

'Pa! That's enough. It's what we're paying him to do.' This was sharp. I'd heard the tone before, when she spoke to Carson. She took my elbow and almost pushed me through the glass doors, lifting the muslin curtain over my shoulder, and into the circular hall with its mast-like palm. 'He's getting old. Forgets things. Felix is bringing your car round. In the meantime here's a photo. It's a good likeness, though it was taken, oh, five years ago?'

She handed me an unframed 6x4. Taken outdoors, half length against a background of shrubs and a clear blue sky it showed a tall handsome preppy-looking guy with a blonde quiff, thickish lips, wearing a jacket and a silk scarf. There was something just a touch old-fashioned about it, but then that went with a lot of things about the Lennoxes. The paper, the finish and so on, looked new.

'Can I keep it?'

'Yes. I've got another copy in a frame upstairs.'

I slipped it into my inside pocket.

'Felix has your car waiting.'

'Felix?' I asked

Out on the gravel I walked round to the right while Sambo/Felix opened the left-hand door.

'Checking for scratches? Sir?' And he grinned. Fucking bastard. China's expression said: Maybe this guy's mad and not the best choice for the job we're asking him to do. But she caught my elbow again before I got in.

'Listen. If, when, you find him, if he's got the Chevy and the weapons are in it, just call in the police. If he hasn't got the weapons, then report back to me.'

She pulled a tiny pad from the kid purse. It was attached to a slim gold plate for backing and had a little gold pen tucked in the spine. She scribbled three numbers on the top sheet, tore it off. 'One of these'll find me. Right. Good luck then. You can kiss me if you like.'

Shit.

I did so. On her cheek. Soft like petals.

'Properly.'

She put her arm round my neck and pulled my head down, made a deal out of it. I could feel her teeth. Harder than petals.

'I could get to like you, Kit. You're nice.'

Like the song says a kiss is just a kiss, but if it's thrust upon you by the sort of woman China is, it makes you hers if not for life then for at least an hour or so. That, at any rate, was what she had in mind.

I drove off, with the taste of blackcurrants on my lips. I didn't dare look back to see what Sambo had made of it.

*

Two other things I should mention. On the way out, while redneck was checking I wasn't making off with the family silver, the Lear appeared again, or its twin, roller-coasting over the gritty dunes, between us and the wind-pump, never more than a hundred feet above the brush. Just before it crossed the track it loosed off a small black object from a mounting tucked up under the nose. The missile hit a rusting wrecked jeep and immediately mushroomed into orange flame and black smoke.

'Shit,' I said.

'Napalm,' said redneck, straightening and hitching his belt. 'No luck today then.'

'What do you mean?'

'He come back still armed, means he ain't found nothing nor no one to slot.'

I suppose I looked puzzled. He went on.

'They go out every afternoon. Mr Heart and the General if he feels up to it. They got cannon concealed in the wings too. Taken from an old Mustang the General got.'

'Why?'

'Hunting for what they call wetbacks further east, where the border's the Rio Grande.'

'Illegal immigrants?'

'Some call'm that. Some say vermin.'

'And they drop bombs on them?'

I couldn't keep it out of my voice. Shock, horror. It got through to him, he took a step back and the pump-action shotgun came up to his waist, held in both ham-like hands.

'Now I never said nothing like that, mister.'

I looked into the pale blue of his red-rimmed eyes.

'No, of course you didn't,' I said.

I got back inside the Grand Am as quick as I could and I didn't think about the actual words he'd used for an hour or so. Mr Heart? But the only Mr Heart in the story so far was the philanderer who had been squashed between a cottonwood and the fender of a Corvette. Perhaps I misheard him. Perhaps he said Mrs. But she and the general had just said goodbye to me. Must be a third party I hadn't met in the plane. Anyway. Mrs China Heart swooping about the desert with her mad father napalming Mexicans? I didn't think so. I hoped not. I really did hope not. Shows what a kiss can do.

And the second? A mile or so down the road to San Diego I met a convoy of campers, the big ones, recreation vehicles they call them, I think, Winnebagos and such like, trundling towards me through the heat-haze, seemingly floating on pools of miraged water above the blacktop. There must have been twenty, with what looked like Hell's Angels on Harleys as outriders. Some of them flew flags, big banners ironed smooth by their slipstreams, Confederate flags, the

Californian Republic bear, and one at least an Old Glory with the double S lightning flashes sown into the centre that I had seen in Lennox's room.

Chapter 7

I was back in La Jolla, in Jefferson's apartment, by five. I stood on the threshold and sniffed, the way bloodhounds are meant to. Couldn't be certain, but I sensed someone had been in during the day. Taking the opportunity for a final clear-out of anything that might give me a line on just what the hell was going on? Did that imply they knew where I was going, how long I'd be? If so that presumably meant someone, and I need not be absolutely certain it was China Heart herself, had told them the coast was clear, would be clear for some time.

Nothing drinkable in the fridge of course, I'd drunk it all the night before, but I managed to get together a coffee with Half and Half. I took it into the living room and sat in the tan armchair, facing the faux fireplace and the Johns litho of the Flag, fiddled with my tin of tiny cigars, put them back in my pocket, drank the coffee.

What a crew! That monster of a general cruising the desert looking for peons to kill, the fascist son, the killer queen of a daughter — Snow White's step-mom dressed in Versace. How could I consider getting mixed up with a mob like that? Was it just the money? No. It helped though. Find Jefferson's killer — but surely that's homicide's job. Don't call me Shirley. Confess it Shovelin, it's the glamour too, the charisma of extreme wealth, the sick, slick style of a bottomless money pit. And a kiss? A kiss is just kiss, what a silly bugger I was to be caught with a kiss.

Time to do a bit of sleuthing. I finished the coffee, took the mug back to the kitchen, washed it up, mopped down the surfaces. You do when you live alone, otherwise you end up in a tip. Jefferson had been the same. Worse actually, almost obsessional in his middle age. I could see where something had been moved and then put back not quite as he would have wanted it, which confirmed my suspicion — they had been there during the day. I wasn't optimistic anyway. Business happened downtown in his office, not up here in La Jolla. But I remembered the headers and footers on the two emails he'd sent me had carried the La Jolla address and numbers and I got them up on the computer without too much difficulty. In fact I tell a lie. I found them a sight too easily. At the time that seemed a bonus. I was still tired. Disturbed. Didn't question what normally would have niggled.

My Bournemouth address was in a data base of personal numbers and addresses and in the personal organiser, too. I searched for any other references to anything to do with Homage, the Lennoxes, Tijuana and the Farmacia San Cristóbal and of course drew blanks.

Then I had a look through his other stuff. About five hundred shelved books, two of the shelves legal stuff, two criminal sociology and psychology. Clearly he took certain aspects of the job a lot more seriously than I did. Three more reference shelves, which added up to a lot when you considered he had internet access, too. Novels. Not far off complete Burroughs and the Beats, many of them first editions published by City Lights, San Francisco, some of the poetry autographed including a copy of *Howl*. There was a first edition of *On the Road*. There was Genet too, also Baldwin; the more recent stuff was mainly by black writers though there was a lot of Edmund White too. Some politics and philosophy but not much new: the stuff we read in the late sixties: *Reason and Revolution, The One Dimensional Man, The History Novel* — I pulled that off the shelf and yes it was the copy I'd sent him — also Adorno and Benjamin.

Art books: mostly American abstract from de Kooning onwards and Pop-Art, but Hockney too, Chuck Close and Louise Bourgeois. Photography: Capa and other Magnum productions, Mapplethorpe, Annie Leibovitz. CDs: MJQ and Miles Davis of course, and a lot of other jazz I'd not heard the names of...

He chipped in here, growling in my ear: 'Man, you don't know Keith Jarrett, where you been these last twenty years?'

Classical too — mostly keyboard, a lot of Bach including three versions of the Goldberg Variations, one of which was Keith Jarrett again, Beethoven sonatas, two complete sheets, one Backhaus, the other Brendel, the Diabelli Variations, and modern American: Reich, Glass, Adams.

Very much what I expected: cool but already looking a little dated, but then he was, had been, my age, and after forty-five or thereabouts you settle for what you've got, you stop trying to keep up. And with no children to keep you in touch...

Was he... had he been gay? Not with me. Oh, we loved each other. You could say that in 1968. Maybe we were queer in our love, though we never did it together. But we touched a lot and hugged when meeting or parting. Partly that was because he was black and I am white and we felt it necessary to show the world we didn't care about that at all. Though in those days it was always in your mind — you couldn't quite forget the guilt on one side, the ingrained knee-jerk hate on the other. That is, he couldn't forget the racial guilt I might have felt, and I couldn't forget the unindividuated hate I thought might fester in him. So... well, yes. Already, just looking through the rooms he had made his own, for the first time in my life I had to say, yes, this guy's gay. Was. But no sign I could see of an ongoing relationship.

Now, dear reader, that was where I made the next in a chain of errors. I didn't know what I was looking for. But I was not looking for his personal life. It did not occur to me that the lack of anything pointing to an ongoing personal relationship might mean that that was precisely what 'they' had been at pains to remove, obliterate.

OK. Let's move on. The one copper-bottomed, unsinkable, real McCoy coincidence in this story is that independently we, Jefferson and I, both ended up making more or less respectable livings as private eyes. Gumshoes. Inquiry Agents. Perhaps not all that much of a coincidence. When you find you can't after all save the world, but you still feel you ought to do your bit, and you lack the faith to be a vicar, the conformity to go into school-teaching, the dedication to be a nurse or even a doctor, and you know politics are crap, there are worse things to be, worse ways of lending a hand. Particularly if you stay picky about what you take on. And that doesn't mean turning down divorce cases. If some poor guy is being two-timed by his or her spouse, there is some good in helping them get shot of a bad domestic scene. More suffering in a bad marriage than in most prisons. But anyway, with the changes in the law in both countries the divorce market bottomed out early in both our careers.

He did better at it all than I did. Started in L A, his first address was Westside, mine was Camden Town, then San Fernando Valley and finally south to San Diego and La Jolla. Bournemouth is OK, but La Jolla it is not.

By now I was standing in his study window, a faux door onto a faux balcony, looking down into the street. It was a fuck, it really was. Four times he'd come to Yurrup to see me and we'd had good times, quiet but good. Once we went back to Paris, and another time we did Rome and Athens, and every time I'd promised next time I'd come out and see him. So when finally I *do* do it, I find him with a hole in his head...

'Can it, Kit. Just find the fuck who did it.'

I went back to the study and had another look round. Something bothered me. It took a minute or two to realise what. Amongst all the other furniture that Chinese cabinet stood out like, well, as the man said, a tarantula on a slice of angel-cake. I mean it just didn't fit in with the rest of Jefferson's furnishings which were all modern, very modern.

It was a near cube set on tapering legs, basically lacquered black with a shine like glass but painted with Chinese dragons, red and gold. There were three drawers with a space above them about three inches deep which it took me a minute or two to realise, so fine was the join, was a lid.

I held my breath before opening it. This was surely it — the reason why he'd bought it. A secret compartment.

But no. It simply became a writing desk. Three empty matching glass ink bottles, each only an inch high, with milled brass tops, set in square sandalwood compartments, shallower rectangular places for pens and so forth, an unused stick of sealing wax and a small brass seal, like a chess pawn, with a raised monogram, W J, in a circle on the base. The inside of the lid was green baize with half an inch of leather margin decorated with gilded scrollwork. I guessed the whole thing wasn't Chinese at all but English eighteenth-century Chinoiserie.

Nice. Still, it did not fit. And it was no heirloom either. If Jefferson had an heirloom that old it would be a manacle. Irony here perhaps. If it was English then maybe its making had been paid for by the labour of a West Indian sugar plantation slave.

'Come on, Jefferson,' I murmured. 'Lend a hand. Give a guy a break.'

I made the balls of my fingers sensitive. You can do that. Just a little mental effort. And I ran them over every inch of the top, and down the sides, like I was loving it up. And I found it. A raised circle of lacquer, on the left hand panel, near the bottom, less than three millimetres across, less than half a millimetre thick at the centre. You'd think the guy painting it had let a tiny drop fall unnoticed from his brush and let it dry. I felt it before I looked at it. It was red, the eye of a dragon. None of the others was raised that much. I pressed it with the fingernail of the middle finger of my left hand and a small drawer sprang open just below it. This time the joins were so fine you couldn't see them when they were closed. Small. But big enough to hold a small 9mm Beretta, the 1934 model, and a Microcassette.

The answer machine used Microcassettes.

This was where it got to be really spooky, sitting in Jefferson's study, at nearly eight o'clock in the evening, almost dark outside, with my body-clock still playing up so my ears buzzed and all those feelings you get when you're exhausted — a combination of déjà vu and a sense at the same time that catastrophe is two minutes away, like the moon will crash into the earth, all playing hell with my psyche.

First of all a woman's voice. Almost a caricature of southern black serving girl.

'Crabwise here, Lo-lee-ta speaking, Jefferson, Mistah Jefferson. The boss want to know you want chilli in your crab chowder, he recommend a nice coriander butter he just whipped up, but I tell him you like chilli, a nice tabasco. An' he don' know whether you coming for it or you want delivery. I tell him you coming for it, but he say why you phone for it if you coming for it. Anyway, you give us a call right now and tell us, huh?'

Then:

'Kit. How are you man? They told me this morning you are on your way. Man, I'd like to warn you off the whole business, say go home, get back to Lindbergh Field and get the first plane back out. I've got no time to spare, so I'll have to cut a few corners. The first thing you've got to know is that the Lennoxes are... Shit! Listen. If I don't finish this, ring Crabwise, ask for Lola...'

What had interrupted him was the door buzzer, I could hear it on the machine. And before he answered it he had turned off the machine, taken out the cassette, replaced it with a blank, put this one in the secret compartment of his Chinese box. Knowing his way round what he was doing, all that would have taken less than twenty seconds. Then he opened the door or activated the downstairs entrance. To the person or persons who killed him.

What he had not done, which was bloody foolish of him, was take the Beretta out of the drawer when he put the microcassette in. He wasn't a gun man. Either that or maybe he knew who was calling and felt he, or she, was not a threat he couldn't handle without a gun. Maybe he looked through the spy-hole and saw Lolita with a crab chowder.

Anyway. Whatever. The gun was clean, the magazine full but no round up the spout, and the safety catch at 'on'.

Which left me where? Shivering, in a cold sweat. Knowing a good place to get a crab chowder. Well that's OK. I like crab.

Oh yes. One other thing. I had a gun. I could use it. I mean I knew how. Ten years ago I joined a club for a couple of months, so I knew my way round it. Could. But would? I sensed I might. Something to do with being in California rather than Bournemouth. One thing though. That club taught me the mechanics but I'm still a lousy shot. Anything over five yards away is pretty safe where I'm concerned.

I looked up Crabwise on his computer, walked round, via the seafront. Four or five groups of people and as many pairs had tables and chairs out on the grass among the cedars, there were even a couple of portable barbecues. They were watching the sun sink into a bruise-coloured haze on the horizon, the Pacific. Leaning on the rail I promised myself I'd have a swim before I left in the morning. After all, I didn't have to be in L A, at the Da Vinci until the evening, and I guessed it wasn't much more than a couple of hours drive.

Crabwise turned out to be a middle-of-the-range restaurant. I had a crab chowder served in a loaf of sourdough bread, very creamy and filling, virtually comfort food, which I needed. I went for the coriander rather than the chilli. Two of the girls serving table were black. I didn't work out if either was Lo-lee-ta.

Chapter 8

I slept badly again, woke with the dawn, stiff from the settee, with a bad head and a throat that felt like oily emery paper. For forty years I had promised myself I would go to America, to the West Coast, and swim in the Pacific, and at that moment, tired, sore, deeply confused and mourning I needed to be doing something cleansing and elemental. And at that moment only the lack of swimming trunks stood between me and the ocean.

Jefferson had a pair, three actually, why does a guy need three garments to swim in? I chose a pair of skimpy Speedos. If I can't swim naked I prefer what I'm wearing to be as minimal as possible. Dead man's shoes? What about swimming trunks then? But I heard his voice: 'Go for it, Kit. Why should I mind? They're clean. You won't get crabs.'

The more southerly of the two tiny coves had less in the way of rocky reefs and kelp. The sun hadn't quite reached the beach, which was chilly, and had a used look above the high-water mark: footmarks, the odd gum-wrapper (though nearly all the litter had been cleared), a sandcastle that looked like a World War II German bunker built the day before above the high tide line. With my back to the rocks that climbed to the prom, I performed the English Crane Dance as seen on English south coast beaches between Bognor and Swanage. Since it's only performed by middle-aged to elderly men, it's on its way out.

First the performer gets his shoes and socks off and loosens the belt round his trousers. He then wraps a bathing towel round his midriff, above the trouser waist-band and fastens it with a tuck. Using one hand to keep the towel in place, the performer uses the other to lower his trousers and kick them off, followed by his underpants. Now comes the difficult part: he threads one foot into the leg of the trunks, hoists that side of them above ankle height, then attempts to get the second foot in the second leg-hole. It is at this point that the towel should come loose. But it never, never falls.

The trunks are now hoisted within the towel, the towel is released, and finally, after a check that no adjustments are needed, the shirt and vest (by which, dear American reader, I do not mean waistcoat) are removed.

The performer will welcome a small spatter of applause from

nearby members of the audience, but money should not be offered. Art is its own reward.

The Pacific was colder than I had expected, but the clearness of the water was a marvel, and the surf an adventure in itself. No one attempted to steal my clothes or Jefferson's towel. The sun hoisted itself above the tops of the palms and the buildings behind and turned the grey to deepest blue and emerald. I swam beyond the breakpoint and for a time lay on my back rocked in the cradle of the swell, my body, apart from my finger-tips, now happy with the temperature. I kept the Lennoxes out of my mind, let it brood like the spirit on the waters. I was there. Doing it. Swimming in the Pacific. As new and wonderful and as huge and limitless to me as it had been to Balboa or stout Cortez.

Then I got a mouthful. I turned on my front, my signal swim spoiled, and the horror and loneliness of it all flooded back. I wanted out. I wanted normality. I wanted home. I headed for the shore, almost certain I'd phone the police just as soon as I got back to the apartment.

I came out, pummelled my head with the towel. My hair is short, sparse, and dries quickly. I spread the towel in the sun which had now reached the sand, and was already hot, and lay on it, making a mental note that I must avoid both sunburn and lumbago by giving myself not more than ten minutes. Then I'd phone.

A young woman had been watching me. I took to watching her. She was tall, had full, dark hair tied back with a pale blue scarf, was wearing denim dungarees over a coffee-coloured t-shirt. She was about nineteen or twenty and in the full glory of Californian female loveliness. That is: perfectly proportioned, by no means fat but not thin either, athletic without being over-muscled, with a tan like dark honey. She seemed restless, paddling at the edge of the water, having first rolled up the wide bottoms of her dungarees. It was not difficult to guess that she wanted to swim, but had no costume with her.

I was right. Suddenly, with a what-the-hell shrug, she unfastened the straps of the dungarees and stepped out of them, leaving on the t-shirt and plain fitting briefs. With scarcely a backward look she now ran down the sand which shelved abruptly as soon as she was in the water, and with a little dive that flashed her white rump, was off with an easy, fluid crawl that took her through the surf and into the middle of the tiny bay. She played there for maybe five minutes, as easily and voluptuously as the seals just round the corner, riding the swell, letting it take her inshore, turning to dive beneath the breaking surf again, scattering nimbuses of scythed water from her hair as she shook her head coming up again. She was a deal more graceful about it all than I had been. Finally, she picked a big one and rode in on her tummy which allowed her to dismount and walk or rather wade, as it rushed on up the beach ahead of her.

The t-shirt clung to her breasts which were perfect and considering the healthiness of her overall build, not large. The briefs remained almost as white and opaque as they had been. At this point a cloud briefly covered the sun, casting a chill, and I quite quickly ran through the second half of the Crane Dance while the cloud moved on. She must have felt the same chill, but had no towel, and no dry warm clothes to change into. Except her dungarees. And as I towelled the sand off the soles of my feet, prior to reassuming my socks and shoes, she did it.

First a glance around her and behind checked that I was the only person between her and the rising slabs of rock while in front of her there was the ocean. Then, quite briskly but without undue hurry, she dropped her briefs, and stepped out of them, first one foot and then the other, swaying a little and giving her body the twist classical sculptors gave to their Aphrodites. For a small moment her waist, buttocks and legs were there like an epiphany, a revelation, a glory. Honestly, what I felt was closer to reverence than lust. Then she hoisted the dungarees to just above waist level, contrived to hold them in place with one elbow, and peeled off the wet t-shirt. I saw one breast in profile and felt a wave of dizziness. Then she re-fastened the sliding brass buckles of the straps and tightened them.

She gave her hair a shake, pushed it up off the nape of her neck, retied the scarf, turned, and looked down at me across the five yards or so that separated us.

'Say, Mister, could I borrow your towel for a second?'

*

California girls. Why can't they all be Californian...?

*

She rubbed her hair and then paused.

'English?'

'Yes.'

Rub-a-dub-dub.

'Kit Shovelin?'

'Yes.' Determined not to show how surprised I felt.

'Hi. I'm a friend of Wilbur Jefferson's.' She sat down beside me, on the sand, knees up, forearms resting on them, face turned towards me. Her eyes, a dark amber, were frank and open, her full lips promised the smile that was on its way. 'He told me you were coming. Said to keep an eye out for you. Said if he wasn't around, I was to look after you till he came back. My name's Lola. Lola Winter.' Rub-a-dub-dub. 'So. How's Jefferson? Giving you a good time? He's a helluva guy. I love him.'

'Jefferson's dead.'

It was the only way to do it.

A couple of lines sank into the skin between her brows. Then her bottom lip trembled.

'Shit,' she said. 'You mean it.'

She looked out at the horizon for a moment. When she turned back there were tears unspilled in her eyes.

'How? How did it happen?' Her voice had sunk, sounded lost, like a child's, a child suddenly lost in a dark cave. 'An accident?'

I shook my head. Faced with her shock, and, I sensed, grief too, my own, which I had suppressed, rushed back.

'He was shot.' I fumbled for words. 'It's a... No it isn't. I was going to say it's a long story. But it's not. So far it's a short story. I had a set of his keys which he sent me. I let myself in. This all happened day before yesterday. He was there, in his study, on the floor, head against the settee, shot, in the head. After a time I went out, came down here. Then I went back. And he was gone. His body was gone. That's about it. At least, as far as I know for certain.'

'You went to the police?'

Put like that it seemed even more crazy than before that I had not. I tried to explain.

'I didn't think they'd believe me. Whoever took him away cleaned up very thoroughly. They even swapped the settee for another one. It would be difficult to believe there had been a body there. At the very best I felt they would have treated me like an imbecile who had had a hallucination. I just felt I stood more chance of getting to the bottom of it on my own.'

'Have you?'

'No.' I thought a bit more. What had I achieved? Bugger all, really. I was not one whit wiser about Jefferson's death than I had been when I first saw his body.

'No,' I repeated. 'Not at all.'

Something in my tone must have touched her. She reached across and squeezed my wrist.

'Where are you staying?'

'In his flat. Apartment.'

She stared at the ocean for as much as a minute. A distant wall of haze was forming between us and the horizon. Then again she turned her liquid eyes on mine again.

'Can I come back with you?'

'Of course.'

We clambered up the footpath that threaded through the rocks and on to the sidewalk. It was busier than it had been when I came down, a roadsweeper worked along a gutter, chaps in suits, one with a doughnut wrapped in a tissue half in his mouth, hurried by. A garden worker sprayed a bed of sub-tropical flowers whose brightness was already a pain in the retina.

'Were you...?' I began, then, 'I think you were waiting for me.'

'Yes. I wasn't sure you were you. So I followed you down to the sea.'

'Where were you?'

'There's a seat under the jacaranda opposite Jefferson's place.'

'You were there that early?'

'I missed you yesterday. I had a full day at Crabwise with just a short break in the afternoon. I came round then but no one answered.'

'You work at Crabwise? I had a crab-chowder there last night. I didn't see you there then.'

'No? Nor I you. But I work at the take-out counter.'

The voice didn't sound the same. But then, if she was that friendly with Jefferson the southern black could have been a put-on, a joke between them.

We crossed Silverado, took a left into Jefferson's street. I fumbled out his keys, let her in in front of me, followed her up the stairs. As soon as we were in she looked slowly round his study, then looped her arms round my neck, put her head on my shoulder, she was almost as tall as me, and began to cry, quite gently, her body warm against mine. I patted her back, slowly, ineffectually.

She pulled away, wiped her cheeks on the backs of her hands. I gave her the towel again.

'I'll make some coffee,' I said.

'Have you had any breakfast?'

'No.'

'Let me fix something.'

While she worked at it, she seemed to know her way round the kitchen, I gave her a very brief resumé of what I had done since I had arrived: how I had gone down to the office in San Diego, met Mrs Heart, then the General out at Homage, accepted the job Jefferson had been doing; how I had discovered Jerry Lennox was meeting someone, someone if that 'con amore' meant anything, he was having a relationship with, at Da Vinci's in Beverley Hills; how I intended to drive there in Jefferson's car. I didn't mention my trip to Tijuana. Not easy to explain why not except that it seemed a long time ago, a lot had happened since, and, apart from old man Guzman's reaction to the name Jerry Lennox, it did not seem that relevant. But there was a wariness there too. After all, it was the one thing I'd done no one knew about, and I still had no idea where this girl was coming from.

She fixed us two eggs each, over easy, or easy over, whatever, and pancakes, using a mix from one of the kitchen cupboards, coffee and orange juice. It meant opening another carton of Half-and-Half long-life. We had it all sitting at the breakfast counter.

'And now,' I said, when I had finished, 'I think I'd better ring the police after all.'

She reached across, grasped my wrist lightly. Her short nails were painted metallic pearl, her fingers were long, her wrists thin.

'No,' she said, and shook her head so the hair swayed as if to confirm her certainty. 'Don't do that. Not yet anyway. Believe me, I know what I'm talking about. They're not equipped for this sort of thing. The wrong mindset. They're not detectives, not even in homicide. They're enforcers and good at it, but this is not their ballgame.'

She swung herself round on the stool so our knees briefly touched and she took my other hand too.

'What will they do? Like you said, not even forensic will find anything here. They'll bully you, maybe lock you up for a day or two while they check you out. Then they'll file the whole darned caboodle.'

71

You know, when she said that, my main feeling was relief. Life would, I knew, get impossibly complicated if I called in the police and possibly worse than complicated. From that moment I did not give the possibility another thought.

She finished her coffee, stood, sat down again.

'Another?'

She nodded.

As I poured it I asked her: 'What was it Jefferson wanted you to tell me?'

She looked up at me.

'I was to tell you he'd be in LA, today, staying at the Golden Gateway Inn on Westchester, near LAX. He wanted you to meet him there. He even said that if I was free I should come along too, show you the way, that sort of thing. I think we should go. Something may turn up. And, if nothing does you can check out the Da Vinci in the evening.'

Chapter 9

My main feelings were of relief, but there was some excitement too — that this gorgeous creature was not about to go out of my life as suddenly as she had entered it. Relief? That I wasn't alone any more in all this, relief that someone was backing my strong disinclination to get the police involved. And relief too that there'd be someone with me who knew the place when we got to LA. She said she'd go and get some things to bring with her, back in twenty minutes. I went to the bathroom, had a shower and a crap. I was still shaving in my underpants and cotton dressing-gown when she rang the buzzer. I released the outer door, let her in, took a quick look through the spyhole when she arrived at the inner door. She was carrying a backpack apparently stuffed with clothes and no large pistols that I could see. She was still wearing the dungarees, but had a different t-shirt under them, a green one this time, and later I saw it had the San Diego Zoo pandas on it. I began to stuff the few things I had back into my holdall. I had a largeish holdall and a smaller shoulder bag. Then I began to pull on my trousers. She gave me a look from the kitchen where she was washing up.

'Don't you have a change of clothing? Those pants are a mess, need valeting.'

I went to the bigger of my bags, pulled out a pair of off-white jean-cut whipcords with buttons instead of a zip, and pushed the offending trousers back in their place. Skillet in one hand, drying cloth in the other, she watched me through the doorway. I became a touch over-conscious of varicose veins, unevenly hairy legs, socks that went half way up my shins. But what the hell, I thought: this twenty-year old goddess is hardly going to feel impelled to bed me anyway.

'Clean shirt?'

Choice of T-shirts. I took the Longleat Center-Parc one. I'd taken the kids there the previous Easter holiday. Daughter made me buy it. Thinking, this way I'll remember to get it laundered or wash it myself, I stuffed the soiled but proper shirt in the smaller bag.

'I'm keeping the jacket,' I said. 'I need the pockets.'

The Beretta, small though it was, bumped the top of my hip bone as I slipped it on.

She finished the dishes, then turned to me and said: 'OK, pardner, let's go.'

Down in the tiny parking lot I gave her the keys.

'You drive,' I said.

'Why?'

'Driving over here scares me.'

A short climb through suburban hills took us on to Interstate 5. We stopped for gas at a Mobil filling station just before joining it. Then it was the freeway all the way to Los Angeles.

I was glad she'd agreed to drive. There were aspects of the whole business that had caught me out the day before, even terrified me. Get into a right-hand lane and suddenly you'd find leaving the freeway was not an option, it was mandatory; road signs across the highway indicated not what you were on, but what was about to cross you — a system that is logical, assuming you know what road you're on, but had me confused in urban situations as well as outside. Then for much of the way the outer left hand lane was for pooled cars only — vehicles carrying two people or more, which included us, and gave us a fast uninterrupted run for much of the way. Too fast, with, if you were in the driving seat, a brutal concrete central division just below the window level.

The terror? The trucks, of course. They were huge, and nearly all had those squared off, heavily chromed, portcullis like radiators in front of long hoods, which, bearing down on you from behind looked like shiny metal walls hurtling through space in some glitzy sci-fi fantasy. Remember Spielberg's first real film, *Duel*?

And everything was so bright. The very air was bright, the sky was bright, even the thorn-dotted hills to the right glowing in front of distant blue mountains, were bright. There was no haze and the sun bounced off windscreens and chrome, gleaming paintwork and the glass sides of buildings, as if aimed at us personally from a million laser guns. And the traffic was relentless. Never less than three lanes each way, often as many as five, it all moved at the same speed, seventy miles an hour, exactly five above the speed limit, but there was no sense that the central lanes were fast lanes, the outer ones for slower traffic as there is in England, all moved at a uniform speed as unvarying as that of a river running between concrete embankments.

And over to the left, for two thirds of the way, the Pacific — the reason why there was no haze and the sky was so bright — deepest, blackest blue except for the occasional glimpse we caught, beyond the dunes and the old Highway One that the freeway had replaced, of chalkier blues and emerald, and white lines of surf.

A rest area was sign-posted.

'I need a pee,' I said.

'I could do with a Coke.'

Low, quite pleasant buildings in a small copse of pines, drink machines and rest-rooms which turned out to be toilets, nothing more nor less. Pardon me, but a Brit like me expects a rest-room to have at least a chair to sit on. Outside, a low parapet above thorny shrubs crowned a ridge of sandstone and sand that fell away towards the ocean but obscured the actual beach. A cloud of kids were standing on the parapet or leaning over it. I joined them. Seven or eight little squirrels, grey, with neat markings not unlike a short-haired silver tabby, scurried about in and out of tiny burrows. There were also a couple of birds, black but with bright orangy-red flashes on their wings. I looked around for Lola wanting to ask her about them. She was coming out of... or was she just passing, a telephone booth?

I turned back, felt her presence behind me.

'What are they?' I said, pointing at the squirrels.

She frowned, puzzled at my interest.

'Ground squirrels, Californian ground squirrels to be exact. They're everywhere.'

'And the birds?'

'Blackbirds. Redwinged.' Again dismissive, as we made our way back to the car. 'Do you want to drive now?'

'I'd rather not. If you don't mind.'

Back in the car she drank some Coke, shook the can at me.

'Want some?'

'No thanks.'

She crushed it, lowered her window, tossed it towards a garbage bin. It missed. She left it where it fell. Back we drove, into the maelstrom.

'Did you know Jefferson well?' I asked.

'What's well? Do you mean did we fuck? Were we an item?'

Agression there. Attack the best means of defence. I tried again. 'OK. How long had you known him?'

A huge sigh this time.

'I hate that 'had'.'

She glanced at me, pushed a thick lock of hair off her cheek, went on.

'About three months by sight, like he was a customer at Crabwise? From the start he'd chat me up but always in a nice way. Sort of flattering, you know? Like sexually aware but not sexually harrassing. Sometimes he ate in, mostly it was to go. Then one evening, maybe, let me see, oh about five weeks ago, he rang for delivery which we do. Fred said, now's your chance, go for it, that guy's loaded, something like that. Usually his son did the deliveries.'

'Why did he want delivery?'

'He said he was too busy to come out, had a deadline. I could see from the door he had a lot of papers out, the computer on and such like. He offered me a drink but sort of off-hand like he really was busy and didn't want me to say yes. So then I reckon he realised he'd sounded well, you know, a bit abrupt, so he said he'd be through in a couple of hours and if I liked I could call back then. Maybe we'd go out for a drink. He didn't expect me to. Call back, that is. But I did. After that we went out three, four times a week? Mostly in the evenings. But one afternoon I told him I'd never been to the zoo, and he said that was a must and we spent the rest of the day there. He bought me this t-shirt. And that night I stayed. That's what you want to know, isn't it?'

'I want to know how well you knew him. I wasn't being prurient, or anything,' I lied.

'Course you were.'

'OK. But since I'm trying to find out who killed him, it's important, it could be important to know how you got on with him, how well you knew him.'

'You think I could be involved? In his killing?' The anger flashed again, but I wasn't going to back off. I shrugged.

'What do I know?' I said.

She didn't like that, drove on in silence for a bit.

Presently she pressed the audio-cassette button, happy to go along with whatever Jefferson had left in. A Soul compilation. Marvin Gaye 'Heard it on the Grapevine'. Aretha Franklin 'Son of a Preacher Man'.

'I prefer Dusty Springfield.'

'You would, wouldn't you?'

'It's the version Tarantino used in *Reservoir Dogs*.'

'*Pulp Fiction*.'

A memory jogged my mind. When Jefferson and I were lads, when we first knew each other, Soul and Tamla Motown were just coming in, just getting needle-time on the channels white kids listened to. And Jefferson affected to hate it all, said it was Uncle Tom music, blaxsploitation at best, and grew out of Gospel, which, as an atheist, he really did hate. But we change. We grow up. If that's what you call the accommodations we all make.

Carlsbad, Oceanside, San Clemente, then the freeway headed inland and the industrial wasteland on the edges of Los Angeles closed round us like a sponge — flatlands, drained marshes, shanties and old plant amongst new developments. There were roadworks, huge new flyovers going up, spaghetti junctions in the making, the concrete poured into vast timber cradles of form work, so much timber used. Did it ever get used again? No shortage of lumber in the Sierra Nevada.

On the way she told me a little bit more about herself. She said she'd dropped out of U C Berkeley the year before, served table here and there since, done a bit of child-minding. Her full name was Maria Dolores Paz y Winters, Winters being her mother's maiden name. Her father had been a wine-grower with land of his own in Napa Valley, bought out by one of the big firms for a lot of money not long after she was born. He was dead before she was six. Her mother lived in a big house outside Carmel on Seventeen Mile Drive, drank Beefeaters and played bridge.

The city was closing even more closely around us.

'Do you know the way?'

'Sure I do. We take a left on to 405 which becomes the San Diego Freeway. Then another left on to Highway One. Westchester runs off it, just after the terminals.'

She was right. Of course. We pitched in just before one.

The Golden Gateway was a big block of a hotel, shoe-box not upended but on its side, concrete frame with brick-facing between the beams, a good ten storeys high, set back off the boulevard with its own parking lot to the side. Opposite, the environs were seedy: cheap motels, strip joints, porn cinemas, fast fooderies, partly masked by a huge billboard, at that time advertising Austin Powers advertising Virgin Atlantic, two flights a day to Heathrow: Powers saying something like 'I'm the only virgin you'll find on this baby.' There was a big marquee with shuttle buses pulling in and out and a small crowd of travellers coming and going. We parked down the side.

The foyer, welcome area, whatever, was huge, a marble-floored, marble walled, marble pillared, two or three storey high atrium with carousels of leather furniture round low tables, a yellow marble fountain, and some classy modern art, real art, hard edged abstracts and sculpture that recalled early Henry Moore before he got monumental and mother-obsessed. The desk at the back looked a mile long behind a silky looped rope, but was probably no more than thirty yards. Yet it was busy. There was a crowd of Japanese tourists pulling out, another of Germans coming in, families unattached to anyone but their own members, and lots of single business persons, male and female. For the most part California dresses with self-conscious informality, though expensively, certainly that went for the tourists. Many of the men were in shorts and sneakers, the women in trousers or jeans which generally supported rather than clothed giant buttocks, but none of it cheap and all of it spotless and pressed.

I began to feel my clothes were wrong on two counts — the jacket too formal, but not pressed, grubby even as well; the jean-cut whipcords cheap looking.

I was about to join the queue, line, behind the Germans, when a tall coloured man, wearing a combat-style vest, ten pockets at least, and a straw hat which hid most of his face from me sidled in two places in front of me. He was carrying a single leather holdall. From behind I could see that his hair, beneath the brim of the hat, was grey. I never got to see his face properly though caught his profile for a second. I'd like to say he looked like I'd seen him before, but that would be a lie. The Germans suddenly evaporated, shepherded away by a courier who had done the paperwork for them. The coloured man got to the desk.

'I checked out this morning,' he explained to the oriental receptionist, a pretty girl whose make-up was so severe it said 'I will not get rattled, I will smile at all times, but distantly, not encouraging loitering or unnecessary conversation'. He went on, his accent Caribbean: 'But I left a bag in the luggage store. I have the ticket right here.'

And the oriental lady called up a bellboy who took his ticket while he wandered off towards one of the fountains, presumably to wait for his bag. Meanwhile, we checked in. No problem. The reception clerk took my name, made me sign a document, fed my Visa card through a scanner, put two plastic key-cards through another scanner and slipped them into a card wallet embossed with the name of the hotel.

'Room 538, Mr Shovelin. Enjoy your stay.'

I looked round for our bags (all through this Lola had been behind me) and she pointed at a bellboy who was already pushing a fully loaded trolley across the floor.

'He already took them.'

The receptionist added her tuppence worth.

'Your bags will be waiting for you when you get to your room.'

Except they weren't. The bellboy was coming out of room 538 just as we arrived. I tipped him five dollars and went in. Lola's backpack was there. I should have had two: like I think I've already said, a matching pair of black soft leather, one largeish the other little more than a shoulder bag. Free offer with cheap house insurance. The larger was missing, the shoulder bag still on my shoulder.

Chapter 10

I looked round the room. Pale coffee textured wallpaper, a framed reproduction of Renaissance architectural drawings pushed together in a sort of montage, a pair of queen-sized beds, TV, coffee-maker, bathroom with shower, all the usual stuff, but ever so slightly tired, not quite matching up to that atrium. And no bag. I even opened the wardrobes. Closets.

'Shit,' I said.

Lola was already on the telephone to the desk.

'They say not to worry, they're on to it. No doubt the boy took it to the wrong room.' She cradled the handset. 'What was in it?'

'Just clothes.'

'Toiletries? Personal stuff?'

'In this one.'

'Not a huge worry then.'

'I suppose not.'

'Look on the bright side. It'll turn up. Bet on it. OK. What next?'

'See if anyone calling themselves Wilbur Jefferson has checked in.'

Again she lifted the handset, passed on the question, came back with an answer.

'This is strange,' she said. 'He was here, a man called Wilbur Jefferson, but he already checked out.'

'Here today?'

'I guess. That's what she said.'

I went over to the window. It faced south. Behind the hotel there was a narrow strip of low-rise air-travel related factories and workshops, then the departure runways of LAX itself. A plane took off left to right, from east to west, getting airborne a quarter of a mile back and then soaring at forty-five degrees past us and only about three hundred yards away, maybe less. They were over the ocean in seconds, though I couldn't see it from where I was standing. Facing back into the room I watched the reflection of the next in the glass of the architectural print. It followed the diagonal from bottom right to top left almost exactly.

There was a very slight smell of burnt kerosene in the room. It had been stronger in the corridor. With the fourth busiest airport in the world on the doorstep, and a town with a smog problem almost as bad as Mexico City's outside, not a surprise really. Even though the windows were sealed the air had to come from somewhere.

'So what now?' she asked. She was still holding the phone.

'Hang about until it's time to go to the Da Vinci. Is it far?'

'Half an hour. No more.' She joined me near the window.

'If,' she said, 'you believe everything you see at the movies, down there, where the runway ends and the grass begins, is where Robert de Niro and Al Pacino shoot it out at the end of *Heat*.'

There's a thought, I thought, as she turned away. Maybe this is the airport hotel Pacino hunts de Niro out of.

'Do you mind if I have a shower? I feel the need to freshen up after that drive.'

'Of course not. Do you mind we're sharing a room?'

'No. I guess I can handle any move from you I don't welcome. Not that I think there'll be one. You English. Always the parfit knyghtes.'

She pronounced the K. Why not? Chaucer probably did. She was right of course. She had age and fitness on her side and I doubt she was more than twenty-five pounds lighter. Anyway, a 'parfit knyght' is what I am.

I took my jacket off, hung it in one of the closets with the pocket holding the Beretta furthest from the door, then I turned on the TV, surfed the free channels. The Kennedy thing everywhere, interviews, the bodies found in the wreckage. His wife's and sister-in-law's too. It was late afternoon Eastern Standard Time. Plans for the funerals. Appreciations of the man he might have grown up to be. That little boy's salute behind the gun carriage at his Dad's funeral. Wearing a bon ton camel coat with leather buttons against the Washington November not far off forty years ago. A nation mourns. Except that it didn't. In the two days since I'd arrived nobody I had spoken to or overheard had mentioned it at all. An opinion poll had already found a large percentage saying the media coverage was excessive. Eventually I found Scooby-Doo and they weren't mourning either. I gave them five before I turned them off too. Seen one, seen 'em all.

Half an hour went by before Lola came out of the bathroom. She had wrapped a hotel bath towel round her body, tucked it up under her armpits, and made herself a turban with another. Her skin, with its California tan, glowed like a ripe peach.

'Make me a coffee,' she said, 'while I dry my hair.'

Standing in the bathroom doorway she unwound the turbanned towel and used the hotel dryer. I watched her arms, curved like the branches of a birch tree, twisting and turning above her shoulders as she fluffed her rich hair out and swayed it this way and that with easy, familiar movements, performing in front of a mirror a task she enjoyed, a task she must have done several thousand times already in her shortish life. A line of Robert Frost bounced about in my head but wouldn't come quite right: *A man can do worse than be a swinger of birches*, something like that. I made two cups of coffee using a Starbuck sachet but only three quarters the recommended water, and tipped in milk from tubs which peeled a hell of a lot more easily than English ones do.

Then I sat on the bed nearest the window, but the inside edge, and drank mine. When her hair was dry and her coffee drunk she came and sat on the edge of hers so her knees were close to mine, but pushed to the side.

'I didn't get it off with Jefferson.'

'No?'

'You knew him so well, how come you didn't know he was gay?'

'It just never came up.'

'You're not gay then?'

'No. No more than the next guy.'

She frowned.

'Bisexual?'

'No more than the next guy.'

This time we said it together, in unison, then laughed and she leant forward and stroked my knee, gently, naturally, it came with the laugh. Then she knelt between my knees and began to pull the bottom of the Center parc T-shirt out of the waist-band of my trousers.

'You don't have to do this,' I tried.

Her face came up, close to mine, I could smell the slightly fruity, warm scent of the shower gel she'd used. She kissed me. Blackcurrant again. Maybe it was the lipstick, the same brand.

'Oh come on,' she said, still very gently.

Well, what can you do? I came on. You do, don't you? She had a lovely body. On the beach it had filled me with awe rather than desire, the glory of young, healthy womanhood. Make no mistake — thirty years earlier I'd have had no qualms. When you're just out of your teens you go to it like gilded flies. But then, with Lola, it felt... mechanical, like automata going through the motions. She was athletic, found a position or two I'd seen in porn films but never experienced, like, while I was still sitting on the edge of the bed, she sat across my thighs, legs on either side of me, breasts crushed against my chest, arms locked behind my neck and somehow got it inside her.

'You can't do this with fat men,' she said, her breath hot in my ear.

Of course, I nearly dumped her on the floor, but managed to hold on. In more senses than one.

Oh, I enjoyed it, more the sight of her, the touch of her, I'd have liked a lot more of all that, than the actual moments that are meant to mean so much, the getting inside, the coming.

Not much later she got off me, then off the bed too.

'That was nice,' she said. 'Not absolutely the most earth-moving occasion of my life, but very nice. Now I'm hungry.'

If it wasn't that brilliant, I thought, you have only yourself to blame. I had done very little towards organising the event beyond holding on for as long as I could.

She put the room service menu across my blotched, moist thighs.

'I'll have a cob salad with sparkling mineral water, Perrier preferred but that Italian one will do. Pellegrino. Room service always takes an age so I'll have another shower while we wait.'

She had nothing on now and posed in the doorway for a second, backside towards me, hand on her hip, looking over her shoulder.

'You liked it when I flashed my butt at you on the beach. Yes? Course you did. I have a great butt.'

I rang for room service and added in a Caesar with prawns. I lay back on the bed and wondered if I'd ever get into the bathroom. I'd read how American girls are crazy about personal hygiene. After a time I gave up on it and got dressed. The faint taste of blackcurrant lingered and while it did it bothered me. But I soon forgot it.

I watched the reflections of the planes in the picture glass, one every three minutes or so, and wondered about it all, where I was, what I was doing, what I had done. These things don't happen to private eyes in England. Not in Bournemouth anyway. The salads arrived. I toyed with mine, hungry but thinking I should wait until Lola emerged again from the bathroom. It was very good, the salad I mean, the croutons crisp, the prawns large and succulent, the lettuce a proper Cos and that-day-fresh.

Lola came out of the bathroom in clean T-shirt (Lucky Strike — the red-circled logo) and briefs. Once I'd got over that I speared a prawn with my fork, chewed and, as they say, enjoyed. I watched a United Airways Boeing 757 climbing across the diagonal of the architectural montage. When it was just about in the middle, it blew up.

Chapter 11

First a star-shaped hole like a black flower with an orange centre appeared in the fabric just above the line of the passenger windows, and behind the wing. Shreds of fuselage skin, no more than specks at that distance, whirled away. The blackness of the hole filled with orange flame, which pumped out white smoke or vapour, also, like the fabric, shredded by the slipstream, and then, within only a second or two of its first appearance it spread and blossomed like a nova or even a giant dahlia. The body and wings of the plane began to thrash in the air, like an animal trying to shake off a predator. The tail flapped like the tail of a big gaffed fish, following the main body, which was still hurtling upwards driven by engines opened to full throttle for take-off.

The rest of the plane now acted like a faultily folded paper-glider. For a moment it stood on end, nose in the air, then the nose dipped and it fell, both spinning and turning, shedding the tail as it went, until it hit the dried up grass beyond the end of the runway, between two banks of lights. Just about where Al put the final shot into Robert. The front crumpled back to the wings before the whole thing crashed over and forwards onto its back. There was a moment when nothing happened — almost as if the collapsing systems were wondering what to do. Then its full fuel tanks blevvied. The hotel windows shook but held and the triple-glazing reflected back most of the sound.

The fire-ball rose to a thousand feet, or so the media said later, black smoke and white kerosene vapour with balls of fire spinning within it mushroomed like a mini-Hiroshima and then settled into a much higher column, pumped out by the flames below.

It all happened in seconds. Eight. From initial explosion to blevvy. Just enough for me to turn from the reflecting glass of the print, stand up, rush to the window. Before it hit the grass I felt Lola's breasts pressed into my back. As the tanks went, her nails sunk into my upper arms, and her chin dug into my shoulder.

We stayed and watched. You have to, don't you? Though the blazing wreck was now at the limit of our vision on the right hand side of the sealed window.

A thrust of terror, a surge of relief: at least this isn't happening to me. Then a wave of panic and anxiety, a hollow, untethered feeling, perhaps what you would feel if gravity was suddenly switched off. Excitement. Awe. Pity — when one thought of it — for the people who had known for a few seconds that they were about to die, but not for the bodies now vapourising in the holocaust. A hope that one wouldn't see anything too nightmareishly beastly in the aftermath. Of course one wouldn't. Not at this distance. Not without binoculars. Then — I wish I had binoculars!

'Shit,' Lola cried. 'Jesus!' Then: 'I wish I had a camcorder!'

The smell of used kerosene was stronger, and soon tainted with something more evil: burnt fat.

Of course there were camcorders in the hotel, and in the other hotels on Westchester, and within forty minutes the more competently recorded tapes were being shown on all the channels that carry news and some that don't. We stayed in room 538, alternately at the window looking at the emergency vehicles that swarmed round the blazing wreckage, pumping foam into it, taking the black out of the white vapour, or surfing the TV channels for close-ups.

Soon the speed at which things were happening decelerated and bit by bit chat, feverish, gasping at first, later with the spurious urgency commentators and link-persons feel they have to inject to keep interest alive took up as much, then more of airtime. Then came an endless round of interviews with airline and airport staff, security employees, experts on air travel and all the rest.

Over an hour or so theories were bolted together. First, terrorism could not be discounted. This hardened into the near certainty that terrorism was surely at the root of it. Although no camcorder had caught the moment of the first explosion many eyewitnesses agreed that there had been an explosion. The LAX control tower confirmed the pilot's last recorded words had been: 'Christ and Holy Shit, we've been bombed!'

The flight had included a party of Japanese nuclear scientists who had been attending a conference at UCLA dedicated to finding means to wind down Japanese dependence on nuclear power. Japanese groups both from the left and the right, many of them extremist, had already protested these meetings and had been joined by workers in the the U S nuclear industry. The explosion may well have been set up by what one Republican senator called 'an unholy alliance'.

86

But there again it might have been North Koreans.

The Governor said that although he did not wish to stir up trouble for the respected citizens of Koreatown in east Los Angeles, every one knew that many so-called south Koreans originally, and not so long ago, came from the North. A Korean businessman accused him of racism, and three Korean-owned corner shops in South Los Angeles were torched by nightfall.

Through all this, especially during the commercial breaks which were as unrelenting as ever, Lola shifted about restlessly, ignoring my questions about what we should do. She was, no other words for it, in a state. Not distressed, not shocked, not anyway in the conventional sense, but high. I've seen people on serious cocaine highs behave in similar ways. She could not keep still, she dashed between TV and window, eventually trying to shift the set so she could watch both at the same time, but it was bolted into its cabinet. A lot of the time a red flush appeared on her sternum just above the top hem of the t-shirt and she began to sweat in the armpits. Occasionally she grabbed me again, usually from behind and ground the front of her body into my back.

She attacked her salad, first with her fork, then as tuna and greenery sprayed about the room when she waved it, with her fingers. She knocked over the Perrier bottle, opened the mini-bar and drank off, out of the bottles, the two quarter-pints of champagne before attacking the beers. But for a lot of the time she stood in front of the window with one hand pushing convulsively through her hair while the other appeared to be thrust down the front of her briefs. The one thing that pulled her back from the window was re-runs of the actual crash on the TV, especially when yet another amateur video was shown for the first time.

She went to the bathroom, two, three times. Yes. perhaps it was a coke high fuelling what the crash did to her.

Shortly after four she suddenly breathed out a long, deep sigh.

'Kit. Come here.'

I stood behind her.

'It's just about over now, isn't it?'

'I'd say so.'

Again the sigh, then reaching behind she grabbed my wrist, pulled my hand in front of her, pushed the middle three fingers into her groin.

'Feel!'

The cotton triangle was soaking. Her head fell back on my shoulder. I could feel her hair again in my face, her temple against my cheek.

'I've never,' she murmured, 'never been so wet.'

Outside, a quarter of a mile away, on the oil-smirched, singed grass, in front of the steaming, smoking wreckage, now a huge pile of shapeless twisted black metal, you'd never imagine it could ever have been an airplane, ringed with emergency vehicles, paramedics in space suits, orange and white blackened with smears, transparent visors, were awkwardly zipping what looked like charred twisted branches into black bags.

I pulled back from her, and went to the bathroom. I was sick. Prawns and croutons.

By six o'clock most commentators were buying the left-wing anti-nuclear industry terrorist theory, while sabotage experts were demonstrating with diagrams and graphics where the original bomb had been, and whether or not there had been other stashes of explosive on board. Detonation was becoming a central point of discussion too, with the commentators desperately trying to fill time and stimulate interest by getting experts to disagree. I looked at my watch.

'Shit,' she said, 'I'd clean forgotten. You want to meet this Lennox character at Da Vinci's at seven. It'll be a tie and dress joint, you know?'

I looked down at my Center Parc t-shirt.

'Bugger,' I said. 'The tie I brought is in the missing case.'

'Put your proper shirt back on. You put it in your hold-all. If they like the look of you, they'll lend you a tie. But I have no dress. Anyway, I'm still enjoying all this. I'll stay here.'

She meant the obscene show out on airfield.

'I was hoping you'd come with me. Show me the way.'

'Fucking be your driver, you mean.'

I shrugged.

'OK. I'll get dressed.'

She headed towards the bathroom again. Rather pointedly I looked at my watch.

'Don't worry, I'll be ready in time.'

She tossed her hair and pouted over her shoulder as she closed the door behind her. I turned back to the TV, tried to forget how badly I wanted to have a shower, clean my teeth.

A grizzled Afro-American in a now rumpled greysuit was holding a black egg of a microphone at chest height in front of the Federal Agent who, for most of the afternoon, had been managing the media for the FBI. The linkman sported a thick moustache which conferred on him an air of gravitas that did not preclude occasional exhibitions of warm or horror-struck sentiment. He shifted the microphone to his own chest as I came over from the window.

'Agent Denver, am I understanding you correctly? You have a suspect already identified but not apprehended for this outrage?'

'Joe, it's too early yet to say this man is a suspect. We have a man we are very anxious to interview.'

'OK. Understandable caution there. Please go on.'

The microphone chasséed across again.

'...Afro male, about seventy-five inches, a hundred and sixty pounds, wearing a light-weight combat-style vest, and a straw trilby-type hat, judged to be in his late forties, receding hairline, some grey hair...'

'Do you have positive identification?'

'We think so. The senior purser on flight UA324 said this guy was behaving drunk, but did not smell of drink. However, Wilbur Jefferson, that is his name, or the name he was using, refused to sit down, maintained the window seat he had booked was occupied, and eventually became violent.'

The mike chasséed back again.

'Wilbur Jefferson,' the linkman looked straight at the camera, 'you know a Wilbur Jefferson, and the description fits, phone the police now. Number at the bottom of your screens. Agent Denver, tell us about Jefferson...'

Oh sure, I thought. At the first mention of Jefferson, I had gone bananas. Heart palpitating, cold sweat, knees like jello. But a part of my brain stayed rational and gradually reasserted control. Pardon me while I just phone that number and tell them Jefferson is dead.

'The Flight Controller was called, and after further altercation during which the Flight Controller reminded him of his rights as a ticket holder and their limitations, Mr Jefferson left the plane declaring he'd rather not fly at all than fly in the wrong seat, and that he'd be suing the airline.'

During all this they flashed up a photo-fit, or whatever. He looked just a little like Jefferson, but his face was fatter, with plump cheeks. He was wearing shades.

'Tell me about his baggage.'

'He checked in a large canvas hold-all, kept back a soft leather black holdall and a matching bag as a cabin luggage. The check-in clerk remembers asking him if he wouldn't prefer to put the larger one in the hold, but he said there were papers in it he'd work on during the flight.'

'And what more do you know about Jefferson?'

'It seems he is a private investigator operating out of La Jolla, south California.'

'The township up coast from San Diego?'

This was all crazy. I took a turn round the room, banging my shins on a low drinks table. The voice of the linkman was rising with excitement, as he pressed an ear-plug into his ear.

'I'm sorry Agent Denver, but I've just heard a new development is breaking over at LAPD headquarters in downtown Los Angeles and we are going over there right now where my colleague Gail Ventura has the latest...'

I collapsed into the one large armchair, gripped the arms.

Gail Ventura was a busily cheerful reporter doing her best to repress her cheeriness. Blonde, she wore a red suit with a cutaway jacket that emphasised the seven or eight pounds she really ought to lose. I missed the beginning of what she was saying.

'... will happen again unless one hundred million US dollars are deposited in a Cayman Islands Bank with withdrawal procedures and protected transfers guaranteed on presentation of agreed access codes. The name of the group is Americans for an Independent Chiapas. Chiapas is a region of southern Mexico where left-wing insurgents have taken control of rural areas...'

'What will happen again?' I moaned.

Lola was standing in the bathroom doorway again. I had no idea how long she had been there. She looked fresher, calmer.

'Didn't you hear?'

'No!'

'There'll be another bomb like this one within one week if the money isn't deposited in exactly the way they want it to be deposited. Where are you going?'

I was putting on my jacket.

'Down to the police headquarters. Put them right about Jefferson the way I should have done right at the start.'

'Hang on. Let's think this through.'

I sat on one of the beds, put my head in my hands.

'Look. If things go wrong you could end up on Death Row...' She moved over to the TV and turned down the volume.

'Why should they go wrong? What on earth do you mean?'

She sat down on the edge of the bed again, took my hands in hers.

'A man whose appearance was close enough to Wilbur's got on that plane, got himself thrown off, left a case like the one you brought into the hotel, maybe the same one. We know the real Jefferson has already been murdered. But that's not going to be easy to prove, is it? Without a body. And they'll pretty soon dig up Wilbur's leftie past. And yours too. He told me about that. Whatever doesn't fit they'll alter, ignore, forget...'

'But you'll bear me out!'

'Me! A twenty-year-old drop-out with a criminal record?'

'You have a criminal record?'

'Oh, just a drug-bust. Possession. Community service. But it won't help.'

'No, it fucking won't. Sorry. Forget I said that.'

I stood up, took another turn round the room.

'So what am I going to do?'

'Calm down for a start. Then I think we ought to get out of here. We don't know how long we've got. Already they'll be turning over his apartment in La Jolla and eventually they'll find something connecting you to him. But even before that someone here may remember you. And how you claimed you'd lost a soft-leather black bag. Shit, one way or another, they'll get to you. So. We get out. And stay out. Go up to Da Vinci's. See what happens there.'

'I could just get the first flight back to Blightie.'

'Where?'

'England.'

'Brazil might be a better choice. Or Cuba. No. You, you, you use what time God gives us to find out just what is going on.'

'And how do I do that?'

She looked at me with pity and some scorn. More pity than scorn, I thought.

'Don't ask me. You're the private dick, aren't you? And we might as well start by going to Beverley Hills. But Kit? Have a shower first.'

Chapter 12

Ten minutes later she looked at me appraisingly. Grey, pin stripe jacket, grubby brown shirt, off-white whip cord jeans, Oxfords, still with that Tijuana shine. Thinning black hair plastered sideways across a shiny dome. Apart from the fact she looked clean, neat and beautiful her turn-out wasn't much better for a formal night out — tight white cropped jeans, once again the San Diego Zoo Panda t-shirt, minimal sandals.

'Supposing your case was on that plane and you're not going to get your change of clothes back,' she said. 'You'll have to buy some more. But at least until you do you really do look like a gumshoe.'

The first of several times one person or another suggested I do some shopping. How could I know where it was heading?

'Fuck off,' I muttered.

'Such a charmer!'

She hoisted her backpack. I picked up my small bag which was a mite heavier than it had been because I'd managed to get Jefferson's Beretta into it while Miss was occupying herself in the most recent of her ablutions. I followed her out and down the corridor.

In the elevator I said: 'Won't they challenge us, leaving without checking out?'

'I doubt it. After all we're not carrying much luggage and anyway that's why they took a scan of your Visa card.'

She was right. In all the comings and goings no one cast more than a casual glance at us as we crossed the huge atrium.

'It's all very well,' I said, as we pushed through the doors that opened from the big lounge area into the parking lot, 'saying I'm a private investigator and should know what to do. But it's a business, you know? With routines, procedures. You need an office with communications stuff, back-up, agencies, information resources, access to the Internet and data bases. Without all that I've no idea where to begin.'

'It'll be back to basics then.'

'Basics, as I recall, include an office and a waiting room with a frosted glass door between, a desk with cigarette burns, and a filing cabinet holding a quart of bourbon and a shot-glass. And a hat.'

'A hat we can get you.'

'It's got to be the real thing. Felt, high-crowned, a broad black grosgrain band, snap-brim...'

'Brown?'

'Of course.'

'A brown fedora. We could raid a museum. Or Warner Brothers costume store.'

She unlocked from the driver's side, opened the rear passenger door, slung her backpack into the backseat, and got in behind the wheel. I got in beside her. At that moment the mobile I had not even known she was carrying in her backpack went off with a tinny version of the William Tell gallop. We both struggled to reach it from between the high-backed front seats but in the end I had to get out and get the whole bag for her.

She answered it. 'Yes... No... Are you sure... OK.' She buttoned out, put it away, said nothing to me, but her mouth set into a hard line. Then she fired up the motor.

She took us back down Westchester and on to the San Diego Freeway, heading north, and for ten minutes or so and for the first time the magic hit me. In spite of everything, including the column of black smoke behind us, and the continuing if intermittent yelp and howl of police and utility sirens I couldn't repress the feeling. Over to the right, seven or eight miles away, across that enormous flattened grid, the towers of downtown L A rose like a futuristic space-fortress out of the darkening air with its smog line. Beyond it, the hills climbed to the wooded escarpment and that tatty over-familiar sign, tiny at that distance so you'd miss it if you didn't know where to look, spelling out along a crest the one word HOLLYWOOD. Know where to look? Of course I bloody knew. Wouldn't you?

I read the signs. Cienaga, Venice, Marina. Then up the slipway we swept, over San Diego, down on to Santa Monica Freeway. Gridlock here and there below us, and something of a snarl-up for us to, feeding back down into the river of red lights but we kept moving, and for a lot of the time at the fifty-five mile an hour limit, especially when the pooled car lane operated. As we angled east the names at the intersections, junctions, became yet more spangled with diamond dust, tinsel anyway. Shortly after Wilshire we took a left and presently parked.

Da Vinci's. Looked nice from outside. Small tables, arches, hazed glass in gilded frames separating the booths. Not many customers. Perhaps not the night to dine out with all the local interest on TV. I glanced at the menu stand, also in a gilt frame. Caesar Salad featured at the top. Been there, done that. Lola was in consultation with the maitre d' or whomever.

She came back out.

'I was right. We're not dressed up enough. He's not there anyway.'

'How do you know?'

'I asked.'

I turned. A middle-aged man on his own at a booth near the window, but shielded by a partition from the entrance so she couldn't have seen him, half rose to have a good look at me, then sat down again, went back to his meal. Which looked like a fish risotto. He was a neat looking guy with a well-trimmed moustache and pointed beard.

'Look, it's a quarter after seven. He'd be here by now.' She got back in the car. 'Kit. I've got people to see. You can take me to their house and then I'll tell you a good place to stay. OK?'

Although she'd said I could take her, she drove. We crossed Sunset and climbed into the hills up Coldwater Canyon Drive. Forest and scrub clung to or climbed the slopes and above them small palaces peeped out of sub-tropical gardens, palms, oleanders, jacarandas, the sun behind us dusting everything now with rose, the clear sky above and ahead of us darkening through indigo to the deep blue of space. Then near what I sensed must be the ridge, the spine of the sierra, we took a left down a long narrow windy road. There was a small signpost — Mulholland Drive.

'Hey! This is where David Hockney has his pad!'

'Yeah? Limey movie-star? What was he in?'

A couple of miles of narrow, winding blacktop, climbing and falling, and she pulled in on a bend where the curve of the road made a lay by, and killed the motor. Silence and a sort of peace after the maelstrom of traffic we'd been through and the winding road. A cricket or cicada, there's a difference apparently, chirped of course, and the cooling engine ticked. There was a steep bank to an old stone wall brushed by the boughs of an evergreen oak with a swathe of pinkish white briar roses tumbling over it. Opposite, in a similar wall but without the bank, there was a pair of wrought iron gates. Lola opened her door into the road, swung out knees and legs, leant back to touch my cheek with a cool finger.

'Five minutes. OK?' Then she raised her finger as if talking to a dog. 'Stay!'

She paused at the gate with her back to me for five seconds or so, then the gates swung open and back, and with another half wave she was gone. The gates shut themselves. Firmly. Standing no nonsense.

I'm over fifty. It's just possible I'm developing late onset diabetes, early. I'm just too bored with the idea to be bothered checking it out. Anyway, when I want to pee, *I have to pee*. Did that, under the briars, struggled with the fucking buttons those whipcord jeans had, blast from the past they'd seemed at the time of buying, lit a cigarillo and sauntered across the road.

Number pad on the gate, that's what had let her in, she knew the combination. And some of the wrought-iron was twisted into fancy curlicued letters. In the gathering dusk I couldn't make much sense of them. There was a number, though. 1123. 1123 Mulholland Drive. Easy to remember.

She was back before I'd finished the smoke and I chucked the butt. Made a nice little spatter of red-sparks on the blacktop.

'OK,' she said, and handed me Jefferson's keys, 'I've found a place for you to stay. 'Drive straight on till you come to the San Diego Freeway. Take the San Diego Freeway South sign when you come to it. Keep right on until you get to Wilshire Boulevard West. It brings you onto Ocean Avenue just north of Santa Monica pier. Almost facing the pier, I think it's to the north of it, there's a motel, the Paradiso. You're booked in. Have a nice evening. Don't do anything stupid that might attract the attention of the Highway Patrol. OK?'

No. Not OK. But she'd gone, back through the gates. I made out some of those curly letters. What I took to be a D, a G, an E, and still I didn't get it.

*

The next half-hour was hell. First, I realised, or rather the driver of an oncoming car did, that I'd omitted to turn on the lights and the dusk was already thick enough to make them a good idea. He flashed me, but even so there was a moment of panic before I realised what it was he was trying to tell me. I managed to get on the freeway going the right way, south, God knows what would have happened if I'd gone the other way, probably I'd have ended up in Canada. As it was, as she had predicted, the ocean saved me from going any further than I needed to. On the way, driving on the right with a left-hand drive I kept drifting right, often as far as a quarter of a car width into the right-hand lane and got hooted out. But not by the Highway Patrol.

It was twenty to eight when I got there and just about dark.

The Paradiso was where she said it was. A low complex of terraced cabins round a courtyard with more off to the side and a parking lot at the back. It was seedy, rundown and cheap, surprisingly so considering its situation — almost opposite the pier, with a palm-lined avenue between. But then Los Angeles beaches are where people live or go to for the day. You don't go to them for a holiday. Which meant if, as a single male, a foreigner, I hung around for too long, say more than a couple of nights, I'd become as obvious as a tarantula on...

Anyway I checked in in a small square office, from which the barrier could be raised and lowered making it seem like a guard hut or block-house. There was an electrical insect killer that scored three times during the procedure. The deskman was Afro with a pocked face and grey curly hair. His eyes were bloodshot and the little finger of his right hand had been broken and badly set so it sort of trailed behind the rest.

'Sure,' he said. 'You have a room in your name.'

Paranoia was setting in.

'When was the reservation made?'

'Can't say. Before six o'clock when I came on duty. Let's see your Visa card.'

How much before? Before we left the Golden Gateway Inn? Certainly well before we made it up to 1132 Mulholland.

He took the card. This time it was an old-fashioned metal slide he used. Not an electronic scanner.

'Sign here. I rip it up when you've paid. Or use it if you haven't. Cabin forty-eight on the ground, back of the lot. Parking, follow the black top through and out on to the side street that leads back on to the main road. It's one way so you have to drive through here to get to it. Leave this on the dash.'

He handed me a plastic circle with the number forty-eight and a key that really was a key.

'There's a swimming pool, but it's closed till ten in the morning and a diner on the corner, but it's closed too. There's a burger joint on Main Street down the road towards Venice, coupla hundred yards. Have a good night.'

I parked where he said, under a chain-link fence that closed off a vacant lot, walked back into the compound, got into cabin forty-eight, dumped my small bag. It was not a nice room and I decided to

96

go for a walk, find something to eat.

I crossed Ocean Avenue with its palms and oleanders, which in England we would call the prom, and came to the long concrete ramp that ran down to the pier and provided vehicle access to it. The Ferris wheel, all lit up turned against the gorgeously luminescent Pacific sky, the helter skelter, fairy lights, all the fun of the fair and the music that goes with it — not the hurdy-gurdy stuff you'd get in England, but Rock and Roll classics. Kids and pubescent girls screamed, mums and dads ate hot dogs, muffins and those plate sized chocolate cookies. Smells of vanilla, coffee, and cheap cooking oil.

I hung around about halfway down the ramp and lit a cigarillo, breaking the 'never more than one a day' rule. The last in the tin. Let's make it the last ever. Surfers in black wetsuits tried to make something out of nothing as the swell sank away with the evening calm. The huge swathe of sand arced south towards Venice and the smaller pier, where Robert Duvall and Michael Douglas shot it out in *Falling Down*. Lights there too, strung along the coast, Muscle Beach and rollerblading. Would I ever get to see it? On the other side the Pacific Coast Highway emerged from an underpass and ran north, parallel to but below Ocean Avenue, towards Malibu.

I trod on the butt and no one told me off.

Chapter 13

I walked back across the central reservation where, in the yucca spikes beneath a palm yet again a cricket chirped, a tedious beat but somehow suggesting tropicana and hot nights. Maybe it was a recording on a loop, put there by the tourist office. I found the burger joint. There was a queue, a line, of mostly young people in wetsuits with the tops peeled down or leathers with knee-pads for rollerblading, the girls with wet hair and sarongs tied over bikinis. Lots of beads about, a tang of marijuana in the air, and joshing. A couple came up to join their friends in front of me and jostled past me. I tried to resist.

'Fuck off, Grandad.'

Again I realised I was as conspicuous as a you-know-what, but to back out of the line would draw even more attention so I hung on in and got my quarter pounder.

I ate most of it on the way back. Not wanting to have to chat with the neanderthal in the office, I went in by the back street, past the Pontiac, chucking the end of the burger into the gutter.

Back in my room I sat on the edge of one of a pair of single box-type beds in the tiny hot room, with a can of Diet Coke from a dispenser in the yard. I turned on the TV. The crash, the explosion, the outrage still dominated the airwaves, apart from two channels on which the film of *The Avengers* was showing at different stages. Ralph Fiennes and Uma Thurman sinking their reputations in a muddy fest of pseudo style but with comic moments. Was that really Eddie Izzard? Almost I got hooked. Any port in a storm.

No. Not that port anyway. Back to the news stations. One of them was running a summary update, taking the events in the order they were presumed to have happened. It was known that four days earlier a booking on the flight had been made by a man calling himself Wilbur Jefferson. He had used a credit card and a telephone number that tied him to a Wilbur Jefferson, an Afro-American private investigator with an apartment in La Jolla and an office in downtown San Diego.

He checked in for flight UA324, destination Kyoto, twenty minutes before boarding began. He took a small leather shoulder bag and a larger, but still cabin-size, soft leather bag on the plane and checked in a big canvas holdall which was later found to contain a miscellany of clothes and other stuff bought the day before at the Del Amo

Fashion Centre on Jefferson's card.

Once on board, the man called Jefferson made a fuss. He had booked a window seat, he said, but he had been placed in the centre aisle. He refused to take the seat the cabin crew offered. He wasn't violent, he didn't shout, he wasn't drunk. He was just very, very firm. Eventually he said that if he didn't get the seat he wanted he'd leave the plane. The flight controller, also an Afro-American, was called in by the chief steward and the plane's captain. The flight controller played it by the book.

Interviewed he said: 'Jefferson picked up his hand luggage from under the seat in front, and I took him off the plane. Then I organised getting his big canvas holdall out of the hold.'

'So he didn't take the second piece of hand luggage? The one the check-in clerk said he could take on as cabin luggage. The one he put in the cabin locker.'

The flight controller's dark skin went corpse-coloured.

'Shit man, no one told me he had two pieces of hand luggage.'

That was all the flight controller had to say. The interviewer turned to one of the other airline officials.

'But the larger piece of hand luggage must have been scanned at the security barrier?'

'Yes. And the record shows it held what looked like three large manuals, the sort you get with new software, and a Discman.'

'So the manuals were hollowed out to hold HE and incendiary and the modified Discman doubled as a receiver and explosion initiator?'

'Something like that.'

'But what would have happened if the flight controller had found him a windowseat? He would have had to take it, and he would have been killed with the rest.'

'Not necessarily. There was almost certainly a second person involved, with the means to send the signal which initiated the explosion. No doubt they had a simple line of communication open between them: if Jefferson didn't get off the plane then they'd abort, try again another day, no doubt from a different airport.'

'So. There's probably a second guy involved.'

'Almost certainly.'

'And the authorities, the FBI, the police, are working on that assumption?'

'Of course. But they're up against it.'

'The threat, you mean.'

'That's right.'

'They've got a week in which either they have to find these guys and the guys behind them or pay up a hundred million bucks.'

'That's right.'

'Will they pay?'

'Sure they'll pay. Once they've decided who pays, they'll pay.'

The newscast concluded with reconstructions of what had happened on the plane intercut with actual shots of the wreckage and the emergency workers clearing charred bodies some of which had partially melted into the fabric. Apparently the explosion had triggered the emergency oxygen supplies, a fireball had rolled up the main body of the plane at a hundred miles an hour even before the fuel tanks blevvied, and so on. It was not nice. It was fucking horrible.

I turned the TV off. Sat on the bed and tried to think.

Why was I there? There being the Paradiso Motel. How had I got into this mess? How far back did it go? Right, follow it through. Be a private dick.

I'd been at the Golden Gateway Inn because Lola said Jefferson would be there. A reservation had been made in his name, a reservation that predated his death. He had connections over the border in Mexico, with Guzman and the Farmacia San Cristobal. Admittedly Tijuana is about as far from Chiapas as you can get without leaving Mexico, but, that's hardly relevant. Supposing Guzman was a sympathiser with the peasants, and knew Jefferson was booked into the Golden Gateway.... Supposing Guzman booked him onto UA324 and put a ringer through the check-out and on board in his place... No. This is not behaving like a private eye at all. Start with facts and try to stick with them.

Lola. She'd picked me up. Stayed with me. Made sure I was in room 538, overlooking the runway, when UA324 blew up. She'd manipulated my every movement from the moment she'd flashed her bum at me until the moment a couple of hours or so ago when she sent me down from Mulholland Drive to this crummy motel. Including having a fuck with me when nothing else offered. Right. So. Whoever else is involved she's right at the centre of it. Think, Kit. Fucking think.

Why has she put you here? So the FBI can come storming in and blow you apart? Or arrest you? Show trial. Two commies from way back... but Jefferson? They'd never find Jefferson because he was dead... why was he dead? Because he knew the legal system, he'd beat it, they'd never get away with framing him... But me?

Suddenly I felt frightened. Shatteringly tired as I was I found myself composing a news item: 'Still protesting that he had found his friend Jefferson dead in Jefferson's own apartment, three days earlier, Chris Shovelin entered the gas chamber at 8am, this morning, and was pronounced dead by the LAPD Chief Medical Officer five minutes later... Mrs Tojo Hito who lost her husband in the Flight 324 disaster wept profusely and declared gassing was 'too good for the bastard, he should have fried'.'

Shit! You're supposing again. Facts.

What was it all for? To make a hundred million bucks. What could get in the way of that working out? Lots of things, but my arrest by the FBI could well be one of them. They'd be reluctant to pay up if they knew one of the chief operators was in jug. And maybe unwittingly, through Tijuana, through Lola, I might be able to establish lines to the leaders of the conspiracy. Things I knew might not be significant to me but they could be to the FBI. And anyway, why leave me alive to fight my case through the courts? So. Why had they put me here, in this crummy motel?

I shivered, looked round the tiny room which suddenly seemed bleaker, nastier, more like a prison cell than ever. There was a burn mark on the pseudo parchment of the bedside lampshade, pink anti-termite or roach powder round the line where the rough plaster of the wall didn't quite meet the crumbling composition floor. There was no glass in the picture of white breakers turning into white horses as they tumbled towards the shore. How the fuck did I get here? There was no doubt about that. Lola sent me here. Lola, who claimed to be Jefferson's friend. Lola who'd had sex with me not long before the plane blew up. She'd sent me here, to a motel I had not even known existed, but where there had been a booking in my name since before six o'clock when Neanderthal came on duty. You want to kill someone? Where better than at the dead of night in a cheap groundfloor motel room?

Dead, and my body disappeared, the hunt for me and the non-existent Jefferson could go on, uselessly, while the public and the authorities worked themselves up into a lather waiting for the next plane to drop out of the sky, and... paid up.

I could barricade myself in, sit on the bed with Jefferson's Beretta in my hand, and still be a sitting duck, probably not properly awake, for anyone who broke the flimsy door down. In the end I did the sort of mad thing one only does when nightmareishly exhausted and faced with a situation which is surreally improbable but inescapable. I found two spare blankets and pillows on the floor of the hardboard wardrobe. Closet. Two roaches gave me a fright as they dropped out of the folds and scurried away under one of the beds, but they only served to strengthen my resolve not to stay in that room longer than I needed to. I arranged the bedding as artfully as I could in the corner bed, covered the lump with the blanket and sheet and pushed them about until they took on something of the look of a recumbent figure. I opened the window inwards, leaving a framed mosquito net in place, let the slatted blind drop over the other frame, turned off the light, and went back to the Grand Am.

I moved it backwards so light from the street lamp on the main road no longer fell across it and slipped into the back seat. I put my bag on the sidewalk side for a pillow, checked out the Beretta, pulled back the slide to put a round up the spout, pulled back the hammer and put the safety catch on. Then, still holding it in my right hand, I hoisted my aching legs up, bent my knees, tucked my left hand under my cheek and tried to sleep. All very silly, you might think. But it turned out this was one of the few things I got right.

The car was hot and stuffy. Opening a window was out of the question — far too complicated. Out of the question for five minutes. Then I got out, got into the driver's seat, switched on the ignition, on the second go found the right button to open the rear left-hand window, which would be above my head, just two inches, turned off the ignition, got out again and got another fright as a rat scurried down the gutter with a piece of my burger bun in its mouth. Roaches and rats. I hate the fuckers, both of them. I was having a bad night.

Almost I closed the window again, but told myself not to be a fool. Got back in, listened for a moment to the susurration of breeze in the palms on the main drag, then caught and tuned into the more distant surf. Three cars went by, along Ocean Drive, I supposed. I began to muse on how Grand Am, which I supposed stood for Grand American, would not do in England any better than Nova, *no va*, does in Spain. It evokes, I said to myself, Grannies and Duchesses... I slept. Heavily.

The car shook. Not mightily, just the equivalent of the little jump a person gives on the point of sleep, but it woke me. Just. Someone, something, another vehicle surely had bumped, ever so slightly, into the front fender. My first reaction was to leap up with a 'What the fuck?' on my lips, but my legs had gone stiff and as I moved awkwardly my left hamstring went into spasm. Cramp. I almost yelped but I was up enough now to see through the very narrow gap between the two front seats just what it was had nudged the Duchess.

The one word, in gleaming white raised sanserif capitals on a shiny black tailgate, high above the Duchess's hood or bonnet. Chevrolet. Bile exploded in my throat, my heart began to thump, the cramp tightened its hold like a vice. I couldn't have moved, not quickly anyway, even if I had wanted to.

Voices.

'Room forty-eight.'

'You told me that already.'

'And that's the car. The Pontiac. You have the key?'

'Sure.'

'OK. Don't screw up.'

'I won't.'

By then I was as flat as I could be on that back seat. I was, I told myself, in almost complete darkness, the front seats with their headrests were high, the back of the car was high too to allow for a deep boot, trunk. So long as no one actually peered in I might get away with it.

I slipped the safety catch of the gun to off, my hamstring gave me a jolt, and I put it back on again. Premature ejaculation can be a problem in more circumstances than one. I sensed, rather than heard, one of the men cross the road and walk towards the compound. A car door was closed gently, but that was all. The other man had got back in the Chevy pick-up but he was not yet driving off. He waited. I waited.

Six silenced shots, like burst paperbags, in six seconds. The seventh a second or two behind the others. The first man came back. I stayed very low. These were people I really did not want to meet. I couldn't see him but again I could hear them. No sound of the cardoor so the second man had stayed in the pick-up. I did hear a click or two though, as my would-be killer ejected and replaced the magazine of his weapon. He wouldn't mess about a second time.

'He's dead?'

The voice a quiet, sandpapery whisper.

'As a Ke-entucky fried chicken.'

'Did you check him out? Did you go in?'

'Didn' hev to. He'd left a window open, there was netting but I pushed it in. There was light enough from outside.'

'You can't be sure he's dead.'

'With seven forty-fours in him? He didn't even bleat.'

'You better be right. You remember what to do now?'

'Drive up to 'Frisco, check in the wheels and hang out at the Riviera on sixteenth.'

'Fuck up, you die.'

And now at last the Chevrolet's motor fired and it moved off leaving a trace of fuel fumes on the nightair. Which was quickly subdued by Cacherel for Men as the remaining guy got into the driving seat in front of me. The vehicle dipped under his weight, came up again. The fat Texan who'd said he was Jerry Lennox's bodyguard. Jake Carson. I should have recognised the accent. But the scent was a dead giveaway even I couldn't miss.

Chapter 14

He made his way into the underpass, angled right, came out the other side. Presently the street lights dropped away and the only light came from illuminated signs and the headlamps of oncoming cars. We were now, though I didn't know it yet, on Highway One, The Pacific Coast Highway. The interior settled into a steady half-light as a vehicle fell in behind, a hundred yards or so back, content to cruise at our speed. I felt a sneeze coming, and even the possibility suggested the sooner I made my move the better. I wanted him to discover my presence while he had both hands on the steering wheel, not with what I presumed was the shiny magnum he had carried at Homage in one of them.

I eased off the safety-catch again and began very slowly to manoeuvre myself into a sitting position, keeping the high back of the driver's seat between us with its head rest, then just as I tried to get myself up into the middle the cramp fastened its muscle-crunching claw on to my hamstring again.

'Shit,' I said.

'Fucking Christ,' he said.

Of course my appearance in his rear-view mirror was not simply that of a stranger hidden in the back of the car but that of the ghost of the man he had just pumped seven bullets into. The car lurched across two lanes towards a pier supporting a flyover, signposted Sunset, the vehicle behind, one of those giant trucks with a grill like a Greek temple from outer space, sounded a horn like the Titanic's hooter and lurched into the gap we had vacated to avoid us. I leant across between the seats, twisting my chest to fit the narrow gap and pushed the wheel with my left hand, just in time to miss the concrete, and we were under and through.

Meanwhile Carson, traumatised though he was, with popping eyes and fat face as white in the lights as the moon's, was groping with his right hand for his waist band. But the lurch back to the left had thrown my body, the top half now in the front, to the right and away from him with my right hand, holding the Beretta, swinging wildly.

It went off, of course, with a bang in that space that was truly deafening. For a second we waited to see where the bullet had gone. But neither of us screamed with pain or keeled over dying, no glass shattered, and the Grand Am rolled on on a more or less straight course.

Still with my legs and lower half in the back, with my left arm round the back of the driver's headrest holding me up, I brought my right arm and hand round and let him feel the muzzle on his right temple, which was now streaked with sweat.

'As you see,' I said, 'I'm as likely to shoot you by accident as on purpose.'

'I shat myself,' he said.

'Can't smell it.'

'Not much. Got a grip almost straightaway.'

'All I can smell is that after-shave.'

'I have to use it. He says I have B O.'

'Was that Mr Lennox in the pick-up?'

He compressed his lips, narrowed his piggy eyes. I pulled back the hammer again, clickety-click, just like in the movies.

'You shoot me, we crash,' he said, dead cool. I had to admire him for it. 'You're not belted up, you go through the windscreen. Bad scene.'

He eased his foot down, took us up to seventy-five.

'You break the speed limit, we get worse than a ticket.'

He eased off a little.

'Seems like a Mexican stand-off,' he grunted.

'Till we stop. Then I shoot you. How long before we hit traffic lights? Run out of petrol, gas? I don't care if it's the Canadian border. I can wait. Keep both hands on the wheel. All the time.'

Great these automatic clutches. Shifting gear was no excuse for taking a hand off the wheel.

He drove on.

'Where are we?'

'Highway One, the Pacific Coast Highway, heading north. Malibu just down there to the left.'

Another place I would have liked a look at. All those beach houses. *Sleeping with the Enemy*, the first twenty minutes or so. Loved him, hated her. Hockney again has a beachhouse he escapes to when the Mulholland Drive pad gets too crowded.

I had a think. Then...

'You're up shit-creek, really, aren't you? I mean you're not going to be flavour of the month with your bosses. As I recall, your boss told you — 'Fuck up, you die'. You fucked up.'

He thought about that. I don't think it had yet occurred to him that he had fucked up. He glanced at me sideways, mean look in those piggy eyes.

'Maybe I'll get a chance yet to do it. The business. Ain't that what you limeys say?'

'I don't think so. I don't think I'll let you take a second bite at the apple. What I was thinking was this. You tell me everything you know about what's going on and I'll let you out of the car and you can just melt away, disappear, be out of it.'

'Go fuck yourself.' Then he shrugged. 'Anyway, what do I know?' Pause.

'I'm just a gofer. A "hey-you".'

Was this true? You only had to look at him to suppose it was. I realised he was becoming as much a problem for me as I was for him. Moreover the cramp was back. It was tolerable if I kept my leg motionless, agony if I moved. I knew that if I was going to shift it I would have to walk on it sooner rather than later.

A sign flashed by. Rest area, half a mile. Well, I knew what that meant.

'Take the next exit.'

He did.

'Park under those pines as far as possible from any other vehicle.'

There were about ten vehicles, four of them trucks. In all of them their drivers were sleeping. There was lighting, but very dim, from globes on plinths set in the shrubberies. He pulled in, stopped, left the engine murmuring but not so I couldn't hear the crickets again, and not far off but further than at Santa Monica, the surf.

'If you want the parking brake on I'm going to have to take ma hand off the wheel.'

'Hang on. Wait. Keep your foot on the brakepedal. Open your window.'

He knew now we were in a situation where I could shoot without risking death on the highway. I eased myself out of the rear passenger door in such a way that there was only a second when I didn't have the Beretta trained on his head. Nevertheless, it was a hairy moment, especially with that fucking hamstring.

'Right now. Cut the engine. Now, the hand brake. Out you come.'

He came out, legs first, then hands on the stanchions on either side of his head, the way overweight men do. Then he hauled himself up, his cotton jacket swinging away from his huge stomach, revealing the enormous butt of the Magnum stuck in his belt.

'Don't worry,' he said. 'The thought didn't even crawss ma mind.'

I thought then he was going to go for it, maybe he did too, but the moment passed, and he shrugged again.

And then I saw it. The black stalk, only an inch long, with a bobble on top, sticking out of his top pocket.

'First,' I said, 'the gun. Finger and thumb only, hooked in the trigger guard. Put it on the ground between us. Easy now. Remember how easily this goes off. Goo—ood. Now the mobile from your top pocket, down there by the gun. Better and better. Back off, but stay in the light. Turn round. Head for that tree. Hands on your head, face the tree, press yourself against the tree.'

Californian scrub-oak, not big, but big enough.

Hands on his head lifted the back hem of his jacket and under his huge spreading bum I could see the dampness. Or maybe it was just shadow.

He was fifteen yards off and I raised my voice.

'I'm going to get back in the car now. But the window will be open and I'll have a bead on you as long as I can see you. Just stay there till I'm gone. Behave.'

I picked up the Magnum which weighed a ton and put it in my jacket pocket. It made me feel lopsided as I stooped for the mobile. I picked that up too. The cramp bit again and at last I felt able to take a short hike, ten yards this way and then that. It eased at last. As I got in the car the Magnum clanged against the side-panelling.

He behaved. He turned into the light as I drove past and gave me the finger. The middle one, short and fat. I could live with that.

Chapter 15

I drove on through the darkness. There was less traffic now. Presently there was some mist, but not thick enough to be a nuisance. There were short stretches when the highway upgraded to freeway and then became highway again. A sign read Santa Barbara 33 miles. Santa Barbara — another name. This time I wouldn't miss it. I looked at my watch and my head swam at the thought of the maths involved. I caught the digital on the dash. Four thirty-seven. I must have slept in the back-seat longer than I'd thought. Trees, oaks and palms, loomed through the mist in their natural colours, though still muted. In the central reservations there were oleanders in bloom, white and mauve. Half an hour, then another sign: Santa Barbara next four exits. I took the second.

Again I found myself on a prom, low-rise homes in their own gardens on the right, on my left grey ocean, heaving in a long gentle but powerful swell, merging into grey mist beneath a mother of pearl sky. A big bird, dark grey but black against the sky, flapping on huge untidy wings behind a long beak, slightly pouched, cruised beyond a line of widely spaced palms, in the same direction as I was going. Wow! A pelican! Has to be! I held to its pace for three hundred yards or so before turning right, away from the sea, into a carpark. Even as I pulled on the parking brake, the exhaustion returned, rolling over me like a wave. I just made it into the back seat, and fell asleep, this time with my knees in the air and my head back.

I doubt I slept more than an hour, but it helped, it helped a lot. I woke up hot and sticky, with a mouth like a badger's armpit, stiff in every joint, but no cramp. The sun was streaming in through the back window but had only just cleared the low roofs on the other side of the feeder road. Half-six. I needed a piss, a wash, a change of underwear, breakfast.

On the oceanside of the prom, behind a screen of palms, oleanders and a low box-like hedge, (huckleberry perhaps?) there was a single story, pavilion-like café and restaurant, both closed. Then there was a step down to sand, and, a hundred yards away the ocean, opalescent, heaved as if it were still in a dream-filled sleep. All I needed was a towel. Surely someone, the afternoon or evening before, had left a towel? No. Fuck that, I'm going anyway. I walked across the sand which was as unmarked as moondust had been for Armstrong, came to a shelf, dropped below it and stripped to my boxer shorts.

The water was cold. Much colder than La Jolla, almost as cold as Bournemouth in August. Which isn't bad at all if you're not on the latitude of Majorca and expecting temperatures to match. I waded through the surf, which wasn't high, duckdived into the first that would have swept over me and swam out beyond the break point. I peed while I swam. Strictly breaststroke; the school I went to, a minor private school with pretensions, thought the crawl was working-class, something gents didn't do. I turned on my back, let the ocean lift and drop me, gazed into the sky above, blue now but brushed with a wash of burnt-off mist still pink then yellow with the rising sun.

Elemental. Surrendering to the push and pull, the buoyancy of the sea, gravity, the turning earth, the moon, all the things that make the waves roll in and the tides turn. And the joints in your fingers hurt, and your testicles burrow up into your groin.

I waded back, a big one crept up behind and gave me a playful push, I staggered out and found I should have left my clothes on the step of sand, not below it. They were swirling, tugged by the tails, in about an inch of water. Cursing like... like a mafioso in a Scorsese movie, I gathered them up and lurched on to the higher ground. A couple, early thirties, smart casuals, inside arms linked, outer ones holding leashes at the end of which were two huge, straining, grey short-haired hunting dogs, surged past.

'Hi,' they cried, 'have a nice swim.'

No, I won't. I've had a nice swim and now everything's horrid because my clothes got wet, and you did fucking nothing to save them. But I grinned, and with a casual wave sat down on the gritty sand as if everything was as splendid as it could be in this best possible of all worlds.

Shivering, I gathered up my clothes, stood up, and the Colt. 44 nearly dropped out of my jacket pocket. So I reversed my grip, aiming for the collar, and of course this time it was the mobile that went. I stooped to catch it before it hit the wet sand, and the gun landed on my toe and hurt like hell, that hurt that comes a second or so after the impact, long enough for you to know it's on the way, hurdling the synapses between toe and brain.

I counted to ten while the next wave gurgled girlishly round my ankles and tugged at my trousers which had slipped down the shelf again. I got a grip, both psychologically and practically, and limped back across the sand, over the concrete paving and the blacktop to the carpark, and no, I hadn't lost Jefferson's keys, though I gave myself a fright for a moment thinking I had.

Sitting in the driver's seat, I got out the driver's manual again and checked out how the heating worked. Yes, I had the sense to turn on the engine and leave it running. And no, it didn't overheat because running the heating was taking the heat away from the engine. And yes, the windows did steam up and it soon felt like a wet-heat room. Then I had the sense to spread my trousers, the whipcord jeans, on the bonnet, hood.

I dug out the mobile. Nice one. Chrome-cased Nokia. I turned it over in my palm and thought about it. Whatever else, I thought, it's time again to act like a pro. I keyed in star-six-nine. Got the voice: You were called yesterday at sixteen forty-three hours. Caller's number was withheld. Then I tried redial and after listening to fifteen rings gave up. So much for Kit Shovelin, the Great Detective.

By eight o'clock the damp patches had just about disappeared from shirt, pants and jacket, though they had left interesting salt contour lines. The shorts were still damp, so what the hell, I did without them. Luckily, I was decent when the knock on the window came.

I stretched across and wiped off the condensation and looked up into the face of a cop.

I thought. But he turned out to be a hotel security guard. Fumbling about for a moment, I turned the ignition off and then on again so I could get the window down.

'Buster, you're on private property here.'

'I thought I was in a car-park.'

'A what?'

'A parking lot.'

He hitched his belt. Now one thing I had already noticed but have not yet had occasion to remark on, is the current American craze for nostalgia. This guy, pale Afro-American, big, big stomach, hands like hams, was dressed like a Keystone cop. Neat shaped hat with shiny peak, a row of silver buttons. He was losing his cool.

'Yeah, this is a fucking parking lot. But it's a hotel parking lot. Radisson. Clients only.'

'Great,' I said. 'They do breakfasts?'

'They sure do.'

Better and better.

I let myself out, the cramp took my hamstring in a vice but I rode

111

the pain, locked up, gave him a 'there you are my good man,' look rather than an actual tip, hobbled across the feeder road. I glanced back. Keystone had his hat tilted back and was scratching his head, the way they always did. In silent movies.

A small courtyard, a low marquee, took me into the foyer. The reception clerk looked up. 'Good morning, sir.'

'Good morning to you too.'

I followed the signs to the restaurant. Eggs benedict, fluffy pancakes with whipped cream, sour-dough toast, a bowl of three different sorts of thinly sliced melon garnished with strawberries, fresh orange juice of course, and all the coffee I could drink. There were healthy-type cereals too, but I passed on them.

That was better, much better. I sat at a table by a window, the sun streamed in, there was a swimming-pool with a spa, while beyond the road and the prom the ocean twinkled. An English family sat down at a table nearby; mum, dad, lad of about eighteen, girl of fourteen. They seemed cheerful. The lad ate an enormous amount from the all-in buffet, the dad said he'd stick with a salad at lunchtime and ate almost as much. Mum and daughter said they'd have a swim in the pool, dad and lad would try the ocean. Then they'd go down the prom and have a mooch around the pier and marina.

'The guide-book says the pier's still a working pier,' said Mum.

'Clockwork?' asked Dad facetiously.

'No, stupid. Fishing boats still use it.'

By now I was almost in tears with nostalgia for normality. And England. And my own kids.

The waitress put the usual leather folder with the bill inside at my elbow. I could have signed, invented a room-number, but I put my Visa in instead after adding two dollars fifty to the total for a tip. She took it away, and at that moment the mobile went off. Three bars of a Country and Western classic, don't ask me which, I'm not a fan.

'Jake?' I heard. 'You're a fuck. You are a dumb dumb fuck.'

I closed the call.

Was it the guy Carson had talked to behind the Paradiso motel? Could be. That could mean Jerry Lennox himself. The guy I'd been paid quite a lot of money to find. Nothing to suggest it wasn't him, so, could be. It jingle-jangled again.

'Don't you hang up on me, you dumb fuck.'

'Don't you call me a dumb fuck. It's you and Carson are the dumb fucks.'

A moment of silence. Shocked silence, I supposed. Then, 'Fuck.'

And the phone went silent.

I took a crap in the hotel rest-room, made my way back to the car, drove it along the prom to the harbour the English lady had described. Everything was sunny, bright, clean, which in America, I was learning, means money. This was La Jolla again, not Santa Monica. There were two piers with a big calm bay between them. The furthest, which I had passed on the way, now seen across the flat glaucous water, was clearly the 'working' one, big and brown with big sheds on the end, though even at that distance I could see the café and shop signs. It was long enough and wide enough to take cars and vans. Perhaps the fishing boats tied up on the other side.

The pier I was on was smaller, stone, and on the inside of it a grid of marina berths filled several acres. It was packed with small yachts and motor cruisers. Beyond the marina there was a mole protecting it all from the ocean. There were birds as well as boats. More pelicans sailed across the satin surface between the piers or cruised on huge wings to land on buoys or mooring posts. There were two sorts of heron, the smaller maybe some sort of bittern, white egrets, lots of cormorants. A couple of harbour seals cruised about occasionally flashing their sleek fat arched backs or tummies. And best of all a pair of skimmers, flying in perfect tandem, black on top, white underneath, long red bills that scoop the surface for small fry, swooped out of nowhere, scarred the water and soared away. There were people too. Nice, normal people. California girls in shorts messing about on boats. I was getting to like Santa Barbara.

The mobile went off.

'Mr Shovelin?'

'Speaking.'

'Carson here. Jake Carson.' Street noises in the background. Public phone box.

'Oh yeah?'

'Yeah. Mr Shovelin, I really need you to do something for me.'

'The guy who put seven shots into my bedding?'

'Yeah, well. Doin' like I was told. Mr Shovelin? Could I ask a favour?'

'A favour?'

'That mobile. It's giving me a loada grief? *Loada* grief.'

'So?'

'Bin it. Chuck it in the ocean. Whatever?'

'Carson? Go fuck yourself.'

I walked the quarter mile back south and east to the 'working' pier and along its quite considerable length to the clapboard buildings at the end which might once have been where fishing boats tied up but now seemed to be mostly cafés and the sort of gift shops that sell knick-knacks made of shells. One café had an upper deck. I bought a latte at the counter and sat out there in the morning sun looking across the bay, up into the sierra and out into the ocean. Heaven.

Jingle-jangle.

'Mr Shovelin?'

'Speaking.'

'The "Kit Shovelin met Wilbur Jefferson in Cuba in sixty-eigh".'

Christ, it must be the fuzz. The feds?

'I never met Jefferson in Cuba.'

'Just testing.' A laugh. 'Where did you meet him?'

'Paris. Boul' Saint Mich'. Listen. Who am I talking to?'

'Jerry Lennox.'

That took my breath away. Lennox or not though, one thing I felt sure of, this wasn't the guy had sent Carson into the Paradiso to fire seven shots into me, back in the Pleistocene or last night, whichever was the more recent. This guy had a soft, drawling sort of voice. The other's had been raspy, a smoker's. Which, considering the stink in his den at Homage, had not surprised me.

'I understand you've been employed by my father and half-sister to find me.'

'That's correct.'

'They know perfectly well how to get in touch with me if they want to.'

'They do?'

A pause. Coupla beats.

'Mr Shovelin,' the voice went on, 'do you know where Jefferson is?'

He waited. There was something about that voice got to me. Hard to describe in a convincing way, but it said: level with me. I'm on your side. Useful asset if you're selling something.

'Mr Lennox? Jefferson is dead.'

Long pause then a sigh like a cloud full of rain.

'How?'

'Bullet in the brain. I found him in his flat. Home. Apartment.

Then his body vanished, was... taken away. It's a long story. I think we should meet.'

'Maybe.'

He rang off.

Star-six-nine.

It began four-one-five. The waitress was sponging down the table next door to mine with a spongette and antibacterial spray. I asked her.

'Four-one-five? That's San Francisco. You're welcome.'

I fingered in the first number Mrs Heart had given me, got no answer, tried the second. It too was four-one-five and again no reply. Then, after a count of ten, jingle-jangle.

'Shovelin?' Her ladyship. Mrs China Heart. 'Mr Shovelin? Hi. How's Santa Barbara?'

I covered the mouth-piece with my palm, looked around, almost guiltily I suppose. But then I thought: Nice try.

'Santa where?'

'Cut the crap. Listen, Kit. I think we ought to talk. Properly. Not on a phone. Where can we meet?'

'Somewhere very public, with crowds around.'

'Universal Studios? Anaheim? Disneyland?'

'No.'

'You're not back in La-La-land then. How far up the coast are you, Kit? Thing is, we're all a bit worried about you. Did you know the feds have tied you and Jefferson in with UA324? Listen. Can you get to Monterey by this afternoon?'

I had no idea.

'Maybe.'

'I'll meet you in the aquarium at one. The main attraction is a huge tank, two storeys high, with a gallery as well as a first floor viewing area. I'll be on the gallery at one o'clock.'

'Mrs Heart?'

'Yes.'

'Carson told you I had this phone?'

'No. I looked in my magic mirror and saw you with it.'

Snow White. One of the first films I ever saw. Not the first time round, of course, but when they brought it back, shortly after the war. The Queen/Witch gave me nightmares for a decade. China knew that, as well as the mobile's number?

'Dumbo, I star-six-nined you.'

115

Back in the car I looked at the fold-out map of California Jefferson had left inside the handbook. Monterey was all of two hundred miles, the dash clock said half ten. Again, I tapped the number she'd given me two days before.

'Make it half two,' I said. 'No. Three o'clock. Be on the safe side.'

'You are in Santa Barbara.' She added: 'Take the interstate, 101, not the highway. It's quicker, an easier drive.'

Bugger that, I thought. I'm not turning down what might be my only chance to drive up one of the most famously scenic routes in the world. Anyway, if she, they? knew what road I was on they could arrange an interception or worse.

Then of course it hit me. You and Jefferson tied in with UA324.

I was the objective of a manhunt. Did the police, the FBI know what car I was driving? I tried to think back. The reservation at the Golden Gateway had come with complementary car-parking facility. Had reception asked for a car registration number? Had the police in La Jolla discovered Jefferson's car was missing?

I looked very briefly at the alternatives and concluded there was nothing for it: for the time being I'd have to chance it. At least as far as Monterey. And it all added up to even better reasons for taking Highway One rather than the interstate.

Chapter 16

I had to give the Randolph Hearst Castle a miss, drive across Big Sur without stopping, leave out Carmel. But it was a good drive, especially from San Simeon, corniche style, very high above the sea, those great rocky high promontories, tree-crowned with pines dropping almost sheer several hundred feet to boiling surf below, and guano coated islands covered with birds. For much of the way, the Monterey Chapter of the Hell's Angels were never far off. They overtook me, I passed them congregated outside a burger joint, back they came, a raucous ribbon of black leather, flowing beards, silver studs, gleaming chrome, Harleys. I didn't see a single police car the whole way. Maybe they knew the lads were out for the day. But before that, and not long after San Simeon, I did stop on some dunes to watch, along with a hundred or so tourists, a colony of elephant seals, basking like so much dead meat in the sun and sand, or rearing up their huge bull-necks in roaring standoffs.

'The females are hundreds of miles away in the fishing grounds towards Alaska, feeding their young,' a lady with a badge shouted at us through an amplified microphone, over the thunder of the surf. 'All these are males.'

No wonder all they did was bicker and sleep.

The highway left Carmel on the left, going inland of the bay it sits on, climbing a wooded hill and bringing a wider bay into view with Monterey in the near corner. Carmel. Triggered a memory and not just of its erstwhile mayor, Clint Eastwood. Lola. Daughter of Mrs Paz y Winters who played bridge and drank Beefeaters in Carmel.

Two forty-five. No problem at Monterey. The sign-posting was transparent. The Aquarium turned out to be at the end of Cannery Row, a street of converted sardine canning factories that had never been called that when Steinbeck was writing about it: he made the name up. It was still bridged with closed walkways, walled-in galvanised corrugated iron, connecting the fish processing buildings with the actual canneries, but it was now all boutiques, gift shops, most of them as tacky as any I've ever seen. Apparently one day the sardines just didn't show and the whole business closed down. Even sardines have some sense. But it was fun too, big crowd of trippers, working-class families out for a good time from San José and the Bay Area. I parked on the roof of a multi-story. There was a notice. No

Solicitors. I'll drink to that. But I think it meant beggars.

The Aquarium was something else.

I didn't see all of it, anything like, but it was clearly a hell of a place, beautifully laid out, modern, though much of it was a converted cannery. I had no difficulty finding the tank China had mentioned. One of the star attractions, it was huge, thirty feet high, a wall, a well of glass. I climbed a wide flight of cantilevered stairs to a gallery, leaned on a rail overlooking a viewing area below, with the big windows of the tank in front of me. It was filled with hundreds of fish of all sizes and colours from a big slaty blue pythonesque eel to a shoal of anchovies who span in a globe like a swarm of bees, but silver not black, shifting and flashing as they changed direction when something big enough to scare them came near. There were, too, brilliant blue fish, vermilion fish, purple fish, spotted and striped fish, cruising between huge columns of pale olive-coloured, green and orange kelp that climbed from the shingly bottom, past rocks to the quicksilver surface above our heads. These columns swayed and if you fixed your eyes on them, it seemed you and the tank swayed and they stayed still.

Three o'clock. Feeding time. A lady in scuba gear pranced and danced weightlessly while feeding the fish from a large string bag. Her hair streamed behind her like a mermaid's. She was weird, a strange combination of natural, graceful beauty contrasting with the almost ugly contraptions that masked and clothed her, but allowed her to breath and move, pumping out quicksilver balloons and streaming bubbles of air.

Out in the viewing area a second lady, this one fat with scraped back blonde hair and a microphone, talked inanely to her through a radio link and with the kids in the large audience.

'Here's a WHOLE calamari!' One of the larger fishes took it in one gulp. 'Wow!'

She went on: 'Kelp is a very inneressing plant. It's a algae. Out in the bay on a sunny day it can grow fifteen inches. Fifteen inches in a day. Would you like the algae in your swimming pool to grow fifteen inches a day? I don't think so...'

I couldn't believe all those kids had swimming pools in their yards. Not even in California.

'Mr Shovelin.'

China Heart's elbow touched mine. She was wearing a formal pale blue two-piece linen suit. Her hair was neat, still with the lock that fell towards one eye. A necklace of big white beads, faintly nacrous, rested on the shelf of her collarbone above the cleavage of the jacket. It drew attention to the leanness of her breastbone, its faintly freckled look. You don't get that on youngsters. The lipstick and nail lacquer were the same ever so slightly blueish red she had put on at Homage. I wondered again about the pearl in her navel, but also recognised that for the first time I'd seen her she was dressing her age and station. Tucha the Hillary Clintons. She looked out across the audience below and at the tank.

'Good, isn't it? We're sponsors. Not the biggest by any means. But substantial. There's a restaurant downstairs.'

She turned away. Falling into my usual role of unquestioning obedience I followed.

The restaurant, self service, but quality, was close to the foot of the stairs. She took a tray, an Earl Grey, a couple of small chocolate-chip cookies. I went for the larger cookie and another latte. I paid. We took a table close to a tank, open above us to the sky, that held three sea-otters — two shy and female, one of whom kept in a corner and spun itself round and round in the water, like an obsessive mental patient; the third a male who cruised round them, but was not a nuisance as far as I could tell. China ignored them.

'You look awful,' she began. 'What happened? I take it Jerry didn't show at Da Vinci's? What makes you think he's in San Francisco?'

'He called me.'

'He knew the number? How come he knew the number of your phone?'

'It's Jake Carson's. My guess is your brother gave it to him.'

'So why have you got it?'

Either this was no performance, or she should have been in films. I crumbled my cookie, ate a nugget. They don't make them like that back in Blighty. Really, they don't.

'It's a long story.'

'Skip it for now.' She glanced at her Rolex, loose on her thin wrist, she had to swivel the dial up. 'Did he tell you he was in San Francisco?'

'No. Like you, I did star-six-nine. The number began 415.'

'The rest of the number?'

I reeled it off, but some devil got into me and I deliberately gave the last three digits as 900.

'Eight. Eight, zero, zero. It's useless. It's the Handlery Hotel, just off Union Square. It's the one we use as a pied à terre. Not as chic as some of the others, but they know us. He doesn't live there.'

'He said you know how to get in touch with him.'

'Sure. At the Handlery. He won't tell us where his pad is in the city but he picks up mail, email, and messages there.'

'You could have told me that. You could have told me he was in San Francisco.'

'Shit, Shovelin. You're coming on a bit, aren't you? I'm the client, remember?'

Ice in her eyes, but I waited. The eyes lowered.

'He moves around. We had no reason to suppose he was in the Bay Area,' she finished, a touch lamely. Then she powered up the I'm-the-boss routine again. 'Listen. I have a meeting at half-past, which is why I could be here. Since you have come this far and you have possibly had a call from Jerry you might as well go on to San Francisco and check-in at the Handlery. I'll organise a reservation for you. At least I'll know where to find you.'

'So will the police.'

A tiny puzzled frown, then: 'Oh you mean because of the airliner? You've not been named. They don't know your name. Just that the man they call Wilbur Jefferson had an accomplice. Who, like him, was some sort of commie. Did you know Jefferson was a commie? Are you a commie? Never mind. It's not important.'

Did this contradict what she had said on the phone? Not quite. But it put a different spin on it. What were they up to? Clearly she, at least, wanted me in San Francisco. That was fine. That's where I was going anyway — after all that's where Jerry Lennox was.

She very briefly dabbed her mouth with a paper serviette, and stood up, looking at the Rolex again as she did so.

'Please,' she added, 'please spend some of the money we gave you on some decent clothes? All right?'

The second attempt to get me into a shop. But the first had been Lola's.

No kiss this time. But she offered a hand for me to shake, or hold for a second. With her glove on. She was reminding me that I was the hired help, and hired helps don't argue. They don't get kissed either.

She walked off, unchallenged, towards a private area marked for members and sponsors only. A woman at a desk actually dipped her head when she paused to ask her a question. What had she achieved? With hindsight, two things. One, that I should head for 'Frisco.

Two, buy some clothes. Did those make it worth the trip? Well, yes. Actually, they did.

Clothes. The gift shop. Not for me. But I bought a nice sweatshirt with sea otters on it for Richard. Rosa? No. Rosa was cool and I reckoned clothes decorated with sea otters, dolphins, whales and even giant jelly-fish were probably uncool.

I wandered back out into Cannery Row and on my way to the car-park bought the *San Francisco Examiner* which had just arrived. Settled again in the driving seat, I began to read it. Most of the reporting was garbage and I mean no disrespect. The authorities were simply not giving anything away and the reporters were having to fill it out with eye-witness reports, interviews with 'experts', reactions, and comments from public figures.

But what was really at the centre of it all was the threat. The media had got this wrong too when it was first reported. This is how it went now: the bombers, still claiming to be supporters of the Chiapas Peasants' revolt, wanted one hundred million dollars deposited in the Cayman Islands-based Banco de Corpus Cristi Internacional not within a week but within forty-eight hours. If that didn't happen another plane would be blown out of the sky before the week was up. No hint of where or how or when, just that it would belong to an American airline and most of the passengers would be American. Could be anywhere in the world, internal flight, external, or between foreign airports.

Ground all planes? You're joking. Various estimates were made on how many American airline flights take off in a week, and none of them came in under five thousand. The plain, straightforward fact of it was that the cost to all the airlines, not to mention the inconvenience to all their users, which included freight, of closing down for a week, outweighed the loss of one plane and its crew and passengers. Even a Jumbo? Yes, even a Boeing 747. Even if all the relatives of the victims sue? Even then.

Polls had already been taken. If you are planning to fly in the next few days will you now make other arrangements? Twenty-three per cent only were giving a definite 'yes' — bus, train or automobile would do at a pinch instead. Or postponement. The rest were up for that five thousand to one chance. Anyway, most expected the airlines to pay the blood money. If the cost were shared between them it would be peanuts.

But here the government agencies were making different noises.

Give in to this, there'll be another demand within a week. Not even necessarily from the same gangsters who made this one. Floodgates being opened were spoken of. There'll be one a week until the airlines stop paying. And no: the government itself had no intention at all of bowing to these demands and putting up taxpayers' dough. In short, the blood money would not be paid. An FBI spokesperson summed it all up with direct brutalness: 'It's their move,' she said. 'To make this work they've got to blow up another plane. And we're making sure thay can't do that without exposing themselves more than they already have.'

A separate column dealt with the accomplice. Since Wilbur Jefferson, the San Diego private investigator, was on FBI and CIA files as a one-time holder of extreme left-wing views it was likely his accomplice was similarly motivated. Moreover, during most of the time Jefferson had been active in left-wing circles he had been living in Paris, France and London, England, it was possible the accomplice was English or French. The Deuxième Bureau of La Sûreté and the Special Branch in New Scotland Yard, were actively helping the FBI with their enquiries.

Not as much as I could, I said to myself.

Again I thought, really it is now high time I went to the authorities and told them Jefferson died of a gunshot wound to the head a minimum of forty-eight hours before UA324 made its unscheduled return to earth.

They weren't going to believe me. They were going to check me out, find I had known Jefferson in the seventies and had for a time been a member of the Workers' International. They would discover that I had been in a room at the Golden Gateway Inn overlooking the take-off runway at LAX when the explosion happened, and they'd find I was carrying a mobile phone capable of calling up whatever gadget the man who called himself Jefferson had left in his bag. Back to the scenario that had kept me awake, the one that ended with me behind glass doors in a gas chamber.

Anyway, if I did go to the police, China and the general would want their money back.

What was I to do? Clearly I was in deep shit. I folded up the paper, looked for my tin of cigarillos, remembered I'd had the last, damn near went back to the Row to see if I could find a salespoint. The thing was, if I wasn't going to go to the police it was clearly time to start being a detective again.

How about Lola? OK, how she had picked me up on the beach was explained by her story, how she had a message for me from Jefferson. But there were two Lolas, were there not? The voice on Jefferson's answer phone tape, ahead of his message to me, that claimed to be Lola. But that one spoke with a broad southern accent and way of speaking. The Lola I knew had an educated West Coast accent. But there again, some people, especially intimates if not, in this case, lovers, adopt comedy accents as a joke.

There was a lot wrong about my Lola but where it really went bad began with the hike up to Mulholland, the way she ditched me there and sent me down to a motel where a few hours later connections (as they say in racing) of China came to murder me. Connections, indeed. But was Carson, in his capacity as failed murderer, a connection? The Lennoxes, father and daughter, knew him, tolerated him about the place, about Homage, but he was employed by Jerry Lennox, not by them. So he, and the man who had been with him in the Chevrolet pick-up could be involved with the missing Jerry Lennox I was being paid to find, and Lola too, without China or the General being involved at all. But that made Lennox seem like one of the bad guys and my instinct told me this wasn't the case. Not if he was the guy had phoned me from the Handlery. But when had my instincts ever been right enough for me to trust them?

And how did UA324 fit into all this? Clearly it was no coincidence Lola and I were in a room overlooking the airfield when it crashed. But how could they frame Jefferson for it when they had already killed him? What was Lola's connection with the Lennoxes? Clearly there was one — she'd sent me to the Santa Monica Motel — Carson had been driven there with the sole purpose of killing me. But may be Carson was a player for two different groups at once? My head swam. Sometimes I was almost ready to say, even admit, that I had hallucinated his dead body, the .44 hole in his head. But that way madness lies.

And through all this hard thinking I missed the one point that needed to be addressed. Twelve hours earlier, or a little more, Carson and person unknown had made a pretty determined effort to kill me. And now I was being sent to San Francisco instead with another hotel room pre-booked for me. Why? The answer was in the newspaper I had just read, but I hadn't the wit to ask the question, let alone answer it. It was all there, and I couldn't see it. Can you?

One modus operandi I have developed over the years is to check out everything I'm told, both by clients and by anyone a case brings me into contact with. Find a lie and you have a loose end sticking out of the ball that can lead to the whole thing unravelling. But, like I'd already said to Lola (was it Lola?) this wasn't easy without the services normally available to a properly capitalised business. However, there might be one statement I could have a go at. Lola had said her mother, Paz y Winters, drank gin and played Bridge in Carmel. If I could find her I might be able to check out just how real Lola was. And Carmel was just fifteen miles away, back down Highway One.

Chapter 17

I took Highway One back south and the first exit for Carmel, followed the signs. Right from the start it struck me as a weird place.
Small houses, some little bigger than cabins, in tiny neat fenced
yards. A lot of trees, mostly pine, but none very big. And yet somehow it all smelled of money. It was to get weirder. But first I needed
a room. On the main drag, just above what I was to learn was the
town centre, the Dolphin Inn had a vacancies notice. A tiny courtyard
surrounded by two storeys of verandahed and balconied rooms, a
tiny pool, and an older house that had the office. All fairly normal,
and I got a first, or do I mean second, floor room. Pricey, but, I was
told, a basket containing a continental breakfast would be left outside my door in the morning. I paid a night in advance, taking the
money from the Wells Fargo bag which I still kept locked in the
Duchess's glove compartment.

The clerk, could have been owner or family from his general atti-
tude, a burly man in check-shirt and jeans, took down the vacancy
sign once I'd done the formalities.

'You're plum lucky,' he told me, 'we're booked out, the whole
town is, but I had that one cancellation.'

I squeezed the Pontiac into a space too small by six inches and
took my small bag up a flight of outside stairs. The room was OK.
The usual. And along with the Gideon there was the local phone
directory.

Just as I hoped there was a Paz y Winters, and just the one. I took
a breath and dialled. Yes, dialled. Lot more dialling phones in the US
than you'd think and carrying letters on the finger holes as well as
numbers. This allows them to buy a number that spells out a word,
clever commercial ploy... I'm digressing.

'Residence of Mrs Winters.'

'Could I speak to Mrs Paz y Winters please?'

'Who is this calling?'

Hispanic accent, female, probably the help.

'My name is Christopher Shovelin, I am a British enquiry agent
and I would like to see Mrs Winters regarding beneficiaries of a will
I am trying to trace. That is, I am trying to trace the beneficiaries.'

'Mrs Winters no buy nothing over the phone...'

'Please... I assure you I am not selling anything—' Quick as a flash, this, before she could put the phone down. Fortunately I heard a voice in the background: 'Elena, who is it?' then a conversation muffled by a hand over the mouth-piece. I crossed my fingers and held on, then...

'You had better tell me who you are and the nature of your business. Something about a will, I understand. I'm afraid Elena's English is not all that good.'

'You have a daughter, I believe.'

'I do. Dolly. She's sitting right here beside me. If this concerns her, you should speak to her.'

I began to feel that prickly excitement a gumshoe gets when he plays a hunch and finds it's adding up to twenty-one.

'Really, Mrs Winter, I should see her, establish identity and so forth. There are documents to sign, affidavits, that sort of thing, perhaps I could come round?'

'That will not be possible, not this evening. I am about to go out. I have a bridge engagement.'

'Tomorrow morning?'

There was a pause. Again muffled voices. Her daughter? Perhaps.

'Ten o'clock, Mr Shovelin.'

And she rang off. No more questions. Odd. Nevertheless I felt pleased, very pleased. She had a daughter called Dolly, as good, in its Anglo-Saxon way, as a short version for Dolores as Lola was hispanically. And she was there. And she wasn't the Lola I knew, because she would have reacted to my name if she had been. We were getting somewhere. At last.

I had a bath and a short nap, made myself a coffee. Six o'clock, time to have a look around, maybe even buy those clothes everyone wanted me to buy, then a meal.

I said Carmel was weird. I now discovered just how weird. Main Street was shops but shops like you've never seen before or not so many in one place. They were all boutiques. Some selling designer clothes, many by, I should guess, local designers — they featured arty textures, and arty splodges and geometric shapes or stylised dolphins, whales and sea otters, the denizens of the deep just down the road. Buy a new wardrobe in one of these, I thought, and I'll look like a fairy and I don't mean the one on top of the christmas tree. Others specialised in high kitsch: bronze, ivory and alabaster statues and groups featuring yet more friendly mammals, or, more frequently, groups of humans with no clothes on also being friendly, but not too friendly, to each other. They had no style, not even stylisation. They were not lively enough to be erotic nor specific enough to be porn. Then there were faux antiques, mostly imitation Second Empire — marble table tops, ormulu attachments, and so on...

The place was dead. Later I was told streetlighting had only recently been installed and then in the face of organised opposition who kept the lamps dim and widely spaced. There were very few eateries and only one bar I could find. I turned down a pizza joint decked out like it was a trattoria in Spoleto, checked out the bar served food, and had one of the worst burgers I've ever had. For the hell of it I tried a non-alcoholic lite root-beer. Never had one before. It tasted of eucalyptus.

*

Ten past ten the following morning, and still in my disreputable clothes, I was standing outside an art deco villa with rounded wings, mostly glass, on the hill near Carmel called Seventeen Mile Drive. Most of it is wooded with pads like this one hidden in the trees, but lower down there is a patch of coastline where sea otters breed and there's a golf-course. The mean bastards actually make you pay to do this drive which seems a bit steep when the whole Sierra Nevada and even Big Sur are mostly free. What's more, it was raining. Not heavily, just a thin drizzle, little more than a precipitating sea-mist, dropping out of a featureless grey sky. So much for the California climate. The ocean was too cold to swim in and it was raining rain, not the orange juice the song promises.

So. Ten minutes late, there I was at the top of a short half-moon pea-shingle drive, beneath substantial cedars, looking up at the huge geometrical multi-coloured fan in the fanlight. I pushed a bell-button by the big bronze door.

'Residence of Mrs Paz y Winters.' Not the hispanic help this time, but her ladyship herself.

'Mr Christopher Shovelin,' said I.

'Ah. The private investigator. You are late. Elena will show you up presently.'

It was all in keeping. The beige, taupe, and mushroom marble triangles arranged in starshapes, the orange and black key pattern round the dado, the fan palms in polished copper buckets, the chan-

127

delier, the sunburst clock. I was beginning to get the sense that Mr Paz had driven a hard bargain with Mr Gallo or whomever he had sold his patch of vineyard to. Nor could I sense the possibility of the Lola I knew moving easily in these surroundings, though I did remind myself that she was a drop-out. So she said.

Elena turned out to be older, more severe, more accomplished at her job or the part she played than I had expected. I followed her tight grey bun and her loose tweed suit up the sweeping stairs with their chrome zigzag rail, down a short corridor. She stopped and opened a door for me on to a large, airy bright room, the feature of which was the big semi-circular window making a focal point at what seemed like a hundred yards away. The two walls that led up to it, at right-angles if they had been allowed to get that far, were also largely filled with glass. Through them the view, framed in cedars, was first of a rolling dropping lawn, then a steeper drop of wilderness covered with huckleberry down to the ocean a mile or so away. To the left rocky headlands and to the right the smaller islands where seals, sea-otters and sea-birds multiplied.

There was an acre of deep-pile snow-grey carpet between me and Mrs Paz y Winters who was standing in the semi-circle of glass in a grey silk morning gown inspired by Yorry, built by Chanel I guessed. She was big, a stone or so overweight, pounds which lent presence rather than stole it away, her hair groomed to a tight but curly bob and coloured a very, very pale strawberry blonde, almost white. She must have been a beauty at twenty, a goddess at thirty. Now, at fifty? impossible to be sure, she could have been sixty-five, she was let's face it, a dragon.

And like all the best dragons she guarded a princess. Sitting, very upright, in a large armchair upholstered in dove grey satin with tiny embroidered pink roses (nothing as vulgar as leather) sat a thin, pale girl with Rita Hayworth red hair groomed by a hairdresser better than any Rita ever had. She was wearing a white T-shirt, white shorts, white socks, pro-tennis shoes, only a moron would have called them sneakers or trainers, and she held what I took to be a state of the art graphite racket between her knees.

'This,' said la Señora, 'is Maria Dolores. My daughter.'

Oh no it isn't, Oh yes it is... the temptation to slip into the pantomime versicle and response was, after a moment of doubt, deeply resistible.

'I believe you wish to speak with her regarding a will. My husband had remote cousins whose chief residence was near Granada, Spain. I am surprised though that they should think of us after all these years. I take it though that you are English? Or French?'

'My name is of Huguenot origin. I am English. Mrs Paz y Winters —'

'Winters will suffice.'

'Mrs Winters. There is no will. But I have come to assure myself that the young lady who is with you is not only called Maria Dolores but is your daughter. You see, I believe there is another young woman around who has been impersonating her.'

Mrs Winters and her daughter exchanged a brief but serious glance at each other, then the real Dolly or Lola, looked at her watch, which was so small it would be impossible to read the name of the maker even supposing something in as bad taste as a brand-name appeared on it.

'I really must go, Mama. They'll start without me if I don't.'

'You're going to play in this rain?'

'It's almost stopped. And anyway they've got one of those wind-over roofs.'

A private tennis court? No surprise at all. But a roof you could wind over it if it rained?

The princess rose, floated past me on the perfumes of Arabia, at least six inches off the ground, and with the merest nod went out of my life for ever.

'Mr Shovelin, am I then to take it you have practised a deception on me?'

A plea of guilty would clearly cop a severe sentence. I temporised.

'You could say that, ma'am.'

'Yes or no, sir!'

'Yes.'

'Explain why.'

I sighed. I hoped to be asked to sit down, but I clearly didn't have the class for that and to avoid any misunderstanding in that area Mrs Winters remained standing too.

'It's a long story.' I chewed my lip, pushed my sweaty hands down the thighs of my more-than-ever grubby whipcord jeans. 'But it goes something like this. I am involved in an affair... No, I'll start again. I have been employed by a Mrs Heart of Homage, near San Diego, in South California, and her father General Lennox, to find Jerry Lennox, the general's son. During the course of my investigations I was approached by a woman, a young woman, who called herself Maria Dolores Paz y Winters. She told me a little of her history: that she was your daughter, that you lived here in Carmel. For reasons I won't go into now I began to feel certain that her appearance in the case I am working on was not a coincidence and that she might not be the person she said she was. I am here now to check out my suspicion.'

Mrs Winters waited before answering, giving the ocean the once-over, checking the help had dusted it properly. Then she turned back to me.

'I should have preferred it, Mr Shovelin, if you had come to me without subterfuge and without this cock and bull story regarding a will. Indications, and not merely those you have brought with you, point to the likelihood that the young woman you refer to is in fact Nicola Heart, the daughter of my cousin, China Heart.'

Vertigo. Without asking I sat on the arm of the nearest chair.

'She is an unstable woman, as indeed is her mother, lives beyond her means, as, I daresay most of her family do, and has committed and been prosecuted for at least two indictable offences, one of which was a driving offence some six months ago. She lost her licence for a year.'

A glimmer of understanding came through the darkness like the promise of moonrise.

'She has been welcome here, and indeed has been, at times, a close friend of my daughter, a friendship I have not encouraged but which, taking into consideration the family connection, I could scarcely forbid. On this, the last occasion she stayed here, she left with several documents of my daughter's in her possession including credit cards and her driving licence. To be blunt, she stole them. So. Yes. You were right to suspect she was posing as my daughter. Now... If that is all.'

She cleared her throat, and rang a little tinkly porcelain bell.

'Elena will show you out. Good day, sir.'

She did not offer me her hand. Possibly because she was not wearing gloves. Elena, who must have had sharp hearing to have heard that bell, came in.

'Mr Shovelin is leaving.'

Back down those stairs. The steps were so shallow, yet wide too, they made me feel awkward. Shows what a peasant I am.

At the door Elena placed a hand on my forearm, looked back and up over her shoulder.

'They are all liars, Señor,' she whispered. '*La doña, las señoritas, todas.*'

'The rich usually are,' I murmured. 'But thanks for warning me.' *El pueblo unido jamás será vencido.*

*

Back in the Duchess the vertigo returned. Lola, the Lola I knew, really China Heart's daughter? My mouth went dry. A sick sort of feeling grew in my stomach. Had she been planted by Mom to keep an eye on me? But there again, was she on her mother's side? Was she the final link tying in the Lennoxes, Uncle Jerry he'd be, with the bombing of UA324? Perhaps instead of going on a spree killing with Koreans as his target, Jerry Lennox had gone for a plane load of Japanese instead? And what about Elena's comradely warning? They are all liars...

Since I'd paid the entrance fee, I parked by the sea opposite the islets where the sea-otters and the rest were. Tell the truth, I was still in shock, and needed a break. That Lola was not who she said she was had not been a great surprise. That she was the daughter of China Heart was. The questions chased themselves round my head like a pack of uncontrollable puppies. Were she and her mother in cahoots? How did it all relate to UA324? Was she the same Lola who had left a message on Jefferson's phone? The same Lola who could help me? But then she wasn't Lola at all, was she? What had Mrs Winters called her? Nicola? Yes. Nicola. And so on. There were at least a dozen more.

There was quite a crowd of us, between the car-park and the low rocks that stepped down to the grey sea. In plastic macs for the most part, some with umbrellas, almost all with seeing aids of one sort or another, binoculars, telescopes, camcorders with zoom lenses. Not a lot to see without help, just darker grey dots in the grey bay amongst the floating grey kelp, and then suddenly a lot of those nearest me began to get very excited about one of those dots.

'Isn't that something?'

'No but really, isn't that something?'

'That really is something.'

That just about summed it up.

So I asked a pleasant looking woman with a couple of kids if I could borrow her fieldglasses for a second, since I didn't have anything like that with me, and her two kids, about ten years old, were squabbling over what looked to me like a very expensive camcorder.

'Sure you can, but two minutes max, OK? This is a first for me too.'

It took me most of the alotted time to get a fix on the right dot, and adjust the focus, but then I got it. A mummy sea otter floating on her back suckling a babe. Silly how things like that get to you — but remember this was the wild, not a zoo. I sensed the woman's impatience and handed the glasses back.

'Thanks a lot, that's made my day.'

'Not at all.' But she was looking at me curiously, and maybe with a hint of hostility too.

'Say, you look an awful lot like that English guy they want to interview over the air-bomb thing. Older of course.'

I pulled myself together, not too visibly I hoped.

'No! Really? On TV was it? Boy, am I going to have one helluva day if folks reckon I'm that guy's lookalike.'

And I walked off through the drizzle as nonchalantly as I could, forcing myself to pause and read some of the stuff off a laminate information board.

Parking the Pontiac in the tiny lot at the Dolphin Inn, I found the landlord, if that is what he was, squeezed up against the car I'd managed not to scratch. Oh Jesus, I thought, here we go again. But it was worse than I thought. I turned the ignition back on and pressed the button that dropped the driver's window. He almost got his head in. Coffee and something fruity on his breath — blueberry?

'Say, mister, I don't know what you've done, but I like to give a guy an even break. There's three bozos waiting for you in your room. You can skedaddle if you've a mind to, and I'll send your things on if you get back to me with an address.'

'You let them in?'

Of course that riled him.

'They said they'd kick the door in if I didn't. I don't need grief like that.'

'I'll go up and see them.' And I closed the window and began to hoist myself out.

'Shit,' he growled. 'Some people.'

'OK. Thanks. You meant well. But I can handle it.'

I headed for the stairs. He called after me.

'If they want to pull your head off, tell them to pay your bill first. It's gone eleven and then some. You're into day two.'

All three were wearing dark lounge suits and the ties of the two men were sober enough for a funeral.

The older of the two men was sitting in the one armchair by the window behind the coffee-table. His hair was as white as the muslin curtain behind him; his hands, which had the over-clean look of someone who has never even picked up a screwdriver, were clasped together on his knees. His eyebrows were bushy and dark which gave him a look you often find in the Irish, and his dark eyes glittered with bonhomie. However, he had the bad complexion, the purple eye-sockets and premature wrinkles of an addicted heavy smoker. He also had a heavy jaw, the sort that says don't mess with me. Instinctively and at once I hated him. Was there something familiar about him? Yes. Did I work out what? No.

Actually, I also hated the other two on sight. The second was taller, part Afro, say an eighth, athletic build. He was standing behind the first. The third I did recognise, in spite of her formal clothes. She was the obese woman who had ticked me off for smoking in the park at La Jolla. She was sitting on one of the two upright chairs, placed slightly back of the bossman and to the side. They looked posed, for a portrait or a photograph. There was a gravity in their postures, a sense of awareness of their authority and importance.

'Do come in, Mr Shovelin, and take a seat. My name is Fowler. My colleagues are,' he indicated each in turn, the man first, 'Davidson and Cooper. Perhaps you would like to look at these.'

His two-pack-a-day voice rasped and occasionally rattled. All three of them, with the slight flourish conjurors use, passed me small leather holders which opened out to show photographs on one side and a brief document on the other. They were overprinted in thick, blue sanserif with the letters FBI, just like on the X-files. But the names and signatures were the ones he'd given me, not Scully and Moulder or whatever.

What's better than introducing into a story a person with a gun? Make it three persons. With three guns.

Chapter 18

I handed back the IDs. They looked authentic to me, but what would I know? Fowler, who was clearly the ranker, pitched first.

'Mr Shovelin, we'd like to ask you a few questions. Agent Davidson, give the man a chair.'

The Afro athlete swung the last chair in for me, placing it carefully opposite and in front of Agent Fowler . I sat on it. The questions went on for two and a half hours.

When did you last see your father?

'Just a few questions. But first I must make it clear that you have been driving an automobile rented to a third party, and that this is a serious offence since it invalidates the insurance the rental company provided. It is up to the rental company to decide whether or not to lay a complaint though I should warn you they usually view such matters very seriously. Driving without insurance is a federal offence carrying a maximum penalty of five years... I mention these facts in the hope they will encourage you to be truthful and complete in your answers to our questions...'

'I didn't know the car was rented.'

But I might have guessed. Back at the Paradiso motel Carson had been told to drive to 'Frisco and check in the wheels.

'Jefferson always rented. It is more difficult to identify the driver of a rented car since a good rental firm will maintain confidentiality. The hirer in this case is on of the most reputable companies in the business, a firm called Alamo. I am surprised the documentation is not with the handbook in its folder.'

'It may be. I never looked.'

But I recalled the map of California had the word Alamo printed on it, and showed where, over the state, their car-rental offices were. I had assumed Jeffersone had picked it up at a filling station or wherever.

I thought it through.

'You mean if I don't answer your questions, you have the means to bang me up.'

'Right. Let's move on.'

At this point Davidson, the part Afro, grinned broadly, came from behind Fowler, scooped up the four-legged stool from in front of the dressing-table and sat beside me, hardly angled at all, almost as if he were on my side, the lawyer I should have asked for.

Agent Fowler continued:

'I do not think it will come as a surprise to you Christopher...? Do you mind if I call you Christopher?'

'I prefer Kit.' Actually I would have preferred Mr Shovelin.

'Kit, then. Kit. You will not be surprised to learn that we are part of the federal team investigating the UA 324 bomb and the threat that followed.' He put his elbows on his arm-rests, made a church with his fingers, the way we used to as kids, interlacing three, four and pinkie, with forefingers pointing up like a spire under his chin and his thumbs crossed beneath them. 'So let's start at the beginning.'

He looked at me, friendly, quizzical.

I shrugged.

'Fine by me,' I said.

He frowned, then sharply, pointing at me with the steeple he'd made:

'How long have you known Wilbur Jefferson?'

'Thirty... thirty-one years.'

'You can be sure of that? The date? The exact date?'

'Not sure of the exact date, no. But May, 1968. Paris.' I gave it five seconds. Then: 'France.'

'Don't fuck with me Kit. I know where Paris is.'

Agent Davidson leant towards him.

'Chief. There's a Paris in Texas.'

'Davidson, shut the fuck up, why don't you?'

Davidson shrugged, sat back, looked at his pale finger nails. Fowler, keeping his fingers intertwined, spread his palms. Open the door and see the people.

'Coupla pinko motherfuckers, weren't you?'

He pulled out a pack of Marlboro and began to fidget with them. Agent Cooper frowned.

'Light up, Chief, and I leave.'

Fowler put the pack away and grinned at me.

'Agent Cooper's pa died of lung cancer. She's obsessive as a result.'

'Passive smoking kills eight thousand people a year in California alone.'

'The fuck it does...'

I was just beginning to relax and enjoy all this, it was probably their intention that I should, but at that point Agent Davidson suddenly stood up, faced me and smashed me openhanded, very hard, across the left cheek. The first pain I felt was actually in my neck which was badly jarred, then the sharper burn came across my face. I'd bitten my tongue and was spitting blood.

I was very, very frightened.

'Chief asked you a question, motherfucker.'

Of course by then I couldn't remember what the question had been.

Had we, Jefferson and I, been lefties.

He might as well have asked the HCUA standard question: 'Are you now or have you ever...?'

So, they took me through all that, the year I'd spent with Jefferson in Paris, France, the affiliations we had belonged to, were we ever arrested? Charged? Committed? It soon became apparent that they knew most of it already. Eventually, I said so.

'Look. You clearly know all this. Obviously you have been given access to security files on both of us. I'm not going to deny a thing you might already know.'

'What about the things we don't know?'

And Davidson hit me again.

'How should I know what you know and what you don't know?'

I was bloody near weeping.

Fowler seemed pleased about that. Cooper opened her purse and gave me a tissue.

'OK. Just so long as you understand where we're at. You're a fucking leftie, so's Jefferson, right from back in the sixties to the day before yesterday when Jefferson went to Cuba for his vacation, and you sent a check for fifty English pounds to the Nicaraguan Solidarity Fund. So. Now tell us why you came to San Diego.'

I took them through all that, then right up to the point where I left Jefferson's body in his apartment and went down to the park above the cove at La Jolla. I turned on Agent Cooper.

'And that's where you ticked me off for smoking in a public place,' I said.

She went white, then red. The other two looked at her. Agent Fowler especially looked as if he might get out of his chair and batter her to death. But they were good. Control was back in five seconds, and Fowler was back on course without any overt comment on what I had said.

'So then you went back?'

'Yes.'

'And Jefferson's body had gone.'

'Yes.'

'Got up and walked. No sign of breaking and entering?'

'None I could see.'

'You're trained to notice even clandestine signs of that sort of thing.'

'Over the years I've trained myself to be observant.'

'So then you rang 911 and asked for the police.'

'No.'

'Now, Kit this is where it gets interesting. This is the point where you are telling lies about that body or it is the point where you committed your first felony by failing to report it. Either way I smell shit. Chicken shit. Tell me why you didn't phone the police.'

And so it went on. Mostly I told the truth. I didn't leave out a lot, but I said nothing about the chinoiserie cabinet, the Beretta, or the Microcassette. Nor, for the matter of that, did I mention Carson's .44 in the glove locker in the Pontiac. Perhaps I should have done. For at one point Fowler, who had stood up and was standing behind me, almost put her chin on my shoulder. She smelled of L'Aimant by Coty which was the perfume my mother used to use.

'Kit. We found a gun,' she said, 'a Beretta in the bedside drawer, right here. Where did that come from?'

I hesitated. Inspiration came.

'Lola. The girl who called herself Lola. The girl I now know was really Nicola Heart, Mrs Heart's daughter.. It was hers. She left it behind when I dropped her off. That was later...'

They looked at each other. Icy, expressionless, but I felt a question hung in the air that they weren't prepared to discuss in front of me. Anyway, this time they didn't knock me about for telling a porky.

'We'll come to all that later. Let's get back to where we were.'

I told them I'd been hired by General Lennox to take over where Jefferson had left off, to find his son Jerry, how I'd got a lead out of his waste-paper basket. I said nothing about my trip to Tijuana. I'd almost forgotten about it myself, so irrelevant had it become. They then took me through Lola/Nicola's appearance on the beach at La Jolla through to room 538 in the Golden Gateway Inn and how I and Lola/Nicola had seen UA324 blow up from the window. And at that point they more or less stopped asking where I'd been, what I had done.

Fowler did the church bit again with his hands, leaned forward over them and smiled, like he was the pope or something.

'You see, Kit. We have a problem. There is a substantial body of evidence that indicates it was your bag that a man called Jefferson left on flight UA324.'

'And we're pretty sure,' Agent Cooper intervened, back now in her chair on my left, 'We're pretty damn sure a competent prosecution team could make that stick. You see, the only person who can vouch that you did not pass your bag to Jefferson in the foyer of the Golden Gateway, and indeed can swear you didn't initiate the explosion by activating a a mobile adapted to do the job, is Nicola Heart. Now, she has a criminal record, and proven associations with Mexican terrorist organisations. You didn't know that? So. If she was with you at the Golden Gateway Inn she was there under an assumed name... You can imagine what a meal a competent DA could cook up out of all this, and believe me the LA DA's department is competent...'

'There again,' Agent Fowler resumed, 'there is your own association with the left. I repeat. Your record says that you have supported Sandanistas in Nicaragua and that you still subscribe to the Nicaraguan Solidarity Fund; even that for a year or so in the late sixties you were a member of of an obscure Trotskyite sect...'

'And of course,' Davidson added from the other side, 'there is the whole question of Jefferson. Is he really dead? Or is he out there waiting to help you, his old buddy, to put a bomb on the second plane...?'

I thought for a moment, felt a sort of commitment surge back. To Jefferson? To the truth.

'He's dead. Believe me.'

'We read your lips.' Still Davidson. 'But difficult to prove without a body.'

'So,' Fowler revealed the people in his church. Again. 'We really do have enough to pull you in. We could make it stick. We could get it past a Grand Jury. Eventually we could get a conviction. Kit. Mr Shovelin. You could get gassed.'

There was silence at last. They waited. Suddenly I realised that. That they were waiting. The ball was, as they say at my feet. I pulled myself together. Kicked for touch.

'Except that,' I said, 'you, the three of you, you don't actually believe I had anything to do with UA324.'

They all leant back and smiled, hands clasped loosely on their knees.

'It's such a privilege to work with someone as intelligent as you, Kit. Let's just say,' he went on, 'we are still keeping a very open mind on it, a very open mind.'

He looked at us all, a quick glance at each.

'I don't know about you, but I could use some lunch.'

The pack of Marlboro appeared again.

'Don't.' snapped Agent Cooper. 'Or go out on the balcony.'

*

Agent Davidson went out for sandwiches, came back with a choice of corned beef with three mustards, salad on the side, or smoked salmon ditto, and the sodas we had ordered. I had my usual Diet Coke. Agents Fowler and Cooper had 7-Up, Cooper's lite. Davidson, the tough guy, had a Jolt — all the sugar and twice the caffeine. When we had finished eating we put two round sachets of Starbuck in the motel coffee-maker. Fowler and I added Half-and-Half, Davidson took his black. When Agent Cooper realised she wasn't going to be allowed to go through the whole process again with a sachet of decaff she did without. Fowler asked me inane questions about the Royal Family, Davidson wanted to know the rules of cricket. Apparently, because it is played with a harder ball than baseball and less protective clothing, it was becoming the game of choice in the wastelands of Compton, Los Angeles, where the local youth like to appear both cool and tough. A Jamaican ex-pro was giving lessons to the gangs. Fowler went out on the balcony for a smoke. I said I wanted a pee, and Davidson came with me. Clearly a mite of suspicion still hung in the air that I might make a break for it.

When it was all cleared away we got cosy again, Fowler especially pulling his armchair in closer, almost knee to knee.

'For the moment,' he said, 'we'll leave Jefferson out of it. He may have been an active member of the plot, he may, like you, have been merely a tool, a dupe. Your version is that he was the latter, but that he rumbled the bombers and got wasted. You think, that for all the Lennoxes are a degree or two right of Hitler they are somehow involved in unspecified ways. Nicola Heart, anyway, who is not on the right... Well, that has yet to be proved. Let's all remember though that children, often indeed especially those of rich parents, often react very negatively against them. One thinks of the Heart woman. So Ms Heart's affiliations with disaffected Mexican peasants does not implicate her parents in similar leanings. I feel sure if we went for them they'd come up with perfectly legitimately sounding explanations, and let's remember that family is highly respected, wealthy, and about as likely to offer comfort and support to a peasant revolution as sprout wings and fly. So, let's sideline all those aspects for the moment and concentrate on what is really germane.'

He shifted in his chair, leant back in it a little, crossed his legs, put his left forearm across his knees, his right elbow on his left forearm, and cupped his cheek in his right hand. His smile was solicitous, understanding, a confessor's or a kindly boss's rather than a friend's. It looked as genuine as the proverbial three dollar note.

'So, the picture looks like this. This may not be how it is, but it is how we see it as of now. Jefferson was employed to find the missing Jerry Lennox. Nicola Heart, a left-wing revolutionary saw a way of making him the fall-guy in the bombing of a plane flying out of LAX. He rumbled this and was glocked, and you were manoeuvred into taking his place—'

'Hang on a minute.' The word 'glocked' had filtered through the gates of my brain. 'How do you know the gun that killed Jefferson was a Glock.'

'Manner of speaking,' he pushed on, not hastily, but not allowing me space to develop my intervention. 'Now, we can assert with absolute confidence that the blood money will not in fact be paid. Neither the US government, nor the airlines will contribute a cent. So the terrorists will have to use a second bomb and it is our contention that the terrorists will attempt to use you to get it in place.'

'Why? Why me?'

'Kit, come o-on. You or somebody like you are already a prime suspect. Once you're back in circulation they'll manipulate you, through the Lennox connection probably and your assignment to find Jerry Lennox, to be at the next airport, even booked on the plane on which the next bomb will be placed. A bag you have handled, or even own, will be or will appear to be the one holding the explosive and initiator. You may be blown up with it, more probably you will be gunned down, or otherwise dealt with in the aftermath. Maybe, even, you'll apparently get free. Case against you, watertight. They just wait until we pick you up and put you in the slammer for life. Or death. But before all this happens the next threat is put in place. This time, after two airliners have dropped out of the sky, the agencies or the airlines pay up. Public opinion and the shareholders in airlines

140

insist. End of story.'

Hands sweating again I rubbed them on my knees. Although I knew the answer, I had to ask the question.

'So what do you want me to do?'

'It's obvious, isn't it Kit? We, Uncle Sam, the people of this great country if you like, but anyway, the FBI want you to go along with them. Do everything they say, appear to co-operate. Of course they'll conceal from you their real intentions, it'll probably all look as if it's part of finding Jerry Lennox. And, through a cell phone we'll give you, you just tell us what they're asking you to do. Until it gets close to the *momento de veritá...*'

'*Veridad*. It's a Spanish word, not Italian.'

'Steady, Kit. No one likes a smart ass. Where was I? Yes. Until it gets close, we'll probably just tell you fine, carry on, do as they say. As it gets critical we'll give you more specific instructions. One thing you can be sure of, we'll get you out of it unscathed.'

'Oh yeah?'

'You bet. Apart from the fact we love you, we'll need you to testify in the aftermath. There we are. That's the proposition.'

I drew in breath, gave my bottom lip a nibble. Tried not to think of the moment of truth when persons unknown might ask me to board a plane that might, or might not blow up. I found I couldn't. Not think of it, that is.

'And if I say no?'

'Kit. I thought we'd explained. We can lock you up right now for infringements of automobile insurance law, carrying a concealed gun in the auto you had no right to be driving in the first place, a gun you have no licence for, all that pending putting you away for ever, or worse, for UA324.'

'And meanwhile they go on knocking planes out of the sky until they get the money they're after?'

Fowler leant forward.

'Let's be thoroughly cynical about this. We could keep you in storage some place secret. Wait until the authorities pay up, as they will do after the second or third aluminum shower, then bring you out and prosecute. That way everyone's happy. The Agency has solved a case, the Chiapas peasants have their dough and airplanes can fly safe again.'

Bastards. Could they ever sink that low? Well, yes. I've read books about the FBI, factual books, seen the films. But if cynicism was to be the name of the game I could play too. Deal me in.

'As of now I'm on a thousand a day plus expenses for looking for Jerry Lennox. I could lose out on that.'

'Lot of dough.'

I shrugged.

'Five hundred if the general fails to pay.' Fowler put his head on one side. 'It's more than any of us get.'

'Plus my airfare back to Heathrow, when it's all over. First class.'

'You drive a hard bargain, Mr Shovelin.'

'Got to make a living.'

Silence spread over the room, then they all three sighed, relaxed, grinned. Venality they understood, they even trusted. I did my best to relax too.

'Did I not say this guy's intelligent?' Fowler shifted to one side to get at an inside pocket.

'Here's the phone,' he went on. 'Now listen. It's locked. Don't fiddle with it at all, Don't press any buttons. But when you want to call me just press the blue one that unlocks it, then the redial. If I ring you just unlock, see it says lock and unlock on the display, but lock it when we close the call. That's all. Fuck about with it any other way and we've lost contact and we're all fucked. OK?'

'Right.' It was racing green. The other one I'd taken off Jake Carson was black with a chrome outer casing. Shouldn't be a problem unless I needed to use one or other in the dark. Suddenly, and my heart lurched at the thought, I realised I was going along with them. For real.

'Tell me, Kit, what was your next move to be?'

'I met Mrs Heart yesterday. We, she and I, believe Jerry Lennox is in San Francisco. He uses the Handlery Hotel as a mail drop and pick-up. I was to go there yesterday evening. I should be there now.'

'So, all you have to do is drive to San Francisco and check into the Handlery. We'll have your reservation confirmed just in case they didn't hold the one Mrs Heart made for you. And while you're on the way try to think of an excuse for being a day late.' He looked at his watch. 'I guess you'll make it by six o'clock tonight. San José to San Francisco will be gridlocked. Take my advice. Take 101 inland to San José. If it turns you on, take a small detour to San Juan Bautista and see where *Vertigo* ended. But don't expect a tower, Hitch matted it in. 101 gives you like a beltway round the east of San José but leave it on 88. Go up the east side of the Bay on 88, follow the signs for the

Bay Bridge. Cross the bridge, at that time of day all the traffic's going the other way, shouldn't be a problem, it's a great experience, some say better than the Golden Gate Bridge itself, and after about ten blocks take a left filter which is actually a right since it goes under the freeway, onto Harrison, up Fifth, cross Market, up Powell, two, three blocks and you're on Union Square, take a left along the south side, you're already on Geary, the Handlery is half a block off the square. Can't go wrong.'

'Hang on. If he goes up Powell as far as Bush he can drop off the Grand Am at Alamo. He won't need a vehicle in San Francisco, parking is a bitch...'

Cooper, who'd been pretty quiet ever since I'd dropped her in it, took the chance to reassert herself in a male world.

'Bush is one way the wrong way,' she began. 'To get to the Alamo he'd be better taking a left down Market out of Fifth, driving down to Taylor, take a right up Taylor, seven, eight blocks brings him on to Bush going the right way for the Alamo.' She turned to me. 'Then just a short walk down Powell, through Union Square, take a right into Geary and the Handlery's in front of you on the left. Can't miss it.'

They all stood up. I did too.

'You know your San Francisco,' I said.

'Oh, are we?' said Agent Davidson, and they all broke up. Then, in turn, they offered their hands. After a moment's hesitation I took them.

'Nice meeting you, Kit. Now you are clear about when you should use that phone, aren't you?'

'I think so. As soon as I think someone is manipulating me to get a case that could be identified as mine onto a plane.'

'Also, if or when you actually get in touch with Jerry Lennox.'

'Oh. Right.'

At the door Davidson turned to me.

'Sorry I had to rough you up Kit. No hard feelings?'

I shrugged.

'We'll be in touch.' And his white teeth flashed in a smile full of the sincerest bonhomie.

As they went out Fowler said quietly but audibly: 'What a swell guy! What do they say about the limeys? Hearts of Oak!'

No doubt I was meant to hear it.

Chapter 19

Almost immediately Agent Cooper was back, ducking her head round the door.

'I guess you're wondering about La Jolla.'

'It's not the only thing.'

'No, Kit, I don't suppose it is. But I want you to know this. The Bureau have been monitoring this particular situation which has been up and running for several weeks. We knew Jefferson was being suckered into it, but we couldn't quite see how or why. We knew you were coming in and I followed you from Lindbergh Field to his apartment, and then when you came out, down to the ocean. Fowler's right. I'm obsessive about smoking in public. My obsession let me down. I'm in therapy for it and it won't happen again. That's it.'

She held her hand out.

I ignored it.

'If you were so clued up about it all why didn't you stop them from blowing up that plane?'

'Clued up? Not at all. We knew they were up to something but at that stage we had no idea what. Not until the plane blew.'

She looked at her podgy hand which was still stuck out in front of her, and pulled it in, smoothed her already very smooth, pulled-back hair.

'Good luck, Kit. You won't see us. But we'll be close. You've got the cell phone. We'll look after you. Alive you're more use to us than dead. Take care. Oh yes. Agent Fowler wants you to know we've left you the Beretta, but we've taken the Colt .44. OK? See you around.'

She went and as I finished my meagre packing I thought: if that Magnum was the gun that killed Jefferson, then maybe it's in the right hands. But it's not a Glock. And Glock makes nine millimetre automatics, with a lot of plastic in them, so taken to pieces and with the metal parts carefully distributed or disguised, it's possible to get through most airport security. Was that relevant? How should I know.

And then I thought: if Agent Cooper was following me in La Jolla, where were the other two? Shifting Jefferson's body? This was all too confusing. I gave up on it and wondered instead if I'd get to San Francisco in time to buy some more clothes. I looked at my watch.

Did the sums. Not likely. Then I checked out or tried to and found they'd done it for me, paying, according to the clerk, a young woman now, for the second night since it was well into the afternoon.

*

I took the road east out to Salinas, where Steinbeck was born and where I joined the 101. The self-scanning radio found a local rock station celebrating Mick Jagger's fiftieth birthday so I sang along to all those early numbers Jefferson and I had bopped and even jived to. Ruby Tuesday, Little Red Rooster, Satisfaction. Don't go much on the later ones, but that's middle age for you, I suppose. Then there was a news bulletin. A nutter in Atlanta Georgia, who played the stockmarket on the net and got fed up losing, took three pistols into the office he used, killed a dozen or so and then offed himself. By now Kennedy Junior, as a news item, was well over the horizon, UA324 was heading that way. An axeman who beheaded girls in the Yosemite National Park hardly rated a mention.

What a country! But it put me in mind of the fact that I was still meant to be hunting a likely psychopath with a lot more artillery than an axe, or a couple of pistols. How would Jefferson's Beretta stand-up against an M 60 in the hands of a crazed killer? I gritted teeth and drove on, though I have to say right then I'd have given a lot to be back in Bournemouth, tracking down a couple of Irish cowboys who'd charged a pensioner five hundred quid for black-topping a ten yard driveway.

I crossed the Bay Bridge about an hour before sunset under a perfect sky spoilt only by vapour trails. Ahead the skyscrapers of downtown San Francisco were a cluster of light pillars climbing towards Nob Hill; as I crossed Yerba Buena Island, the bay stretched like a polished flat plate of pale turquoise right past Alcatraz to the orangy-red of the Golden Gate Bridge. Then the piers of Fisherman's Wharf and the Embarcadero together with the World Trade Centre closed the view down.

Thanks rather to the map than their instructions it all worked out for once as it should. I dropped the Grand Am off at the Alamo on Bush and Powell, more Bush than Powell actually, and walked down the two blocks to Union Square. Then I walked back up them and retrieved the Wells Fargo bag from the glove-locker just before a mechanic got there first. I was lucky — Jefferson's Soul Compilation

145

had gone from the tape deck.

Already I was liking San Francisco very, very much. Apart from occasional shafts high up on the skyscrapers the sun had gone but the clear sky was still bright, the big buildings were lit up and glitzy, and by a happy chance I was on one of the three cable car routes still left. A couple rumbled by, one up, one down, packed to the gunwales with waving youngsters standing on the running boards, the bells clanging like musical fire engines. The hill dropped as steeply as all the films one has seen said it should past the ornate frontage of the Sir Francis Drake Hotel. That reminded me that he, we, actually got here two hundred years before the Spaniards founded their Mission. He called it New Albion and claimed it for Queen Elizabeth I.

On I went, carrying my old holdall, past a Borders bookshop which announced it stayed open late and which I promised myself I would visit, into Union Square with its own delicate, almost rococo statue of Liberty, so much prettier than the monster on the other side of the continent. There was even a permanently parked red London double-decker bus now used as an information centre. With Macy's facing me I took the right into Geary. By now I was humming the Gilbert and Sullivan standard 'He is an Englishman' and nearly gave a beggar a heart attack with the five dollar note I gave him.

I wasn't sure why I felt so elevated: partly perhaps because I'd got shot of the Pontiac, the Duchess, the Grande Dame which, though in every respect a fine car, had always made me feel a touch uncomfortable, we just weren't made for each other; perhaps I had a sense that here was where everything would be worked out and this whole wretched, not to say tragic episode would burn itself out; but mainly I suppose, well, San Francisco.

I didn't actually have flowers in my hair, but I felt as if I might have had.

The euphoria lasted as far as the Handlery. First the bag-boy, a small Oriental, clearly thought I was a solicitor not a potential guest. When I said I had a reservation he looked at me, at my jacket, my bag, my once-white jeans and shoes too, and told me this was the Handlery Union Square Hotel. That is, not a rooming house on the wrong side of Market or in Tenderloin.

My passport and so forth, plus the reservation for a room that had been held for me on Mrs Heart's insistence, though I had failed to turn up the day before, eventually got me into 362. But first the reception clerk gave me a city map.

'Your first visit to San Francisco, Mr Shovelin?'

I agreed it was.

With a conjuror's presdigitation she put a line through each of Sixth, Seventh, and Eighth Streets south of Market, Tenderloin, and one or two other areas.

'Avoid these,' she said. 'The rest of the city is safe.'

The room was standard... but the bathroom poky with a sliding door, and the window opened on to the patio de luz, the air-well. I felt China had let me down.

Then, of course, she rang.

'You've got a fucking nerve,' she began. 'You're a day late. Where have you been?'

I made up some cock about the automatic clutch on the car playing up.

'Oh really?' And she meant it to hurt. 'Anyway. I take it you're back on the job now. That is, looking for my brother. Jerry? Remember him?'

'OK. But I'd like a lead on him.' I picked up the phone and walked to the window. Across the well, and on the floor below, a not unattractive middle-aged woman in a flesh-coloured slip was sitting at the dressing table pushing a brush through her hair. The net-curtains were drawn giving her a soft-focus edge. Then a grey haired man with a pot-belly, wearing boxers, came into view, kissed her neck, and pulled the drapes. Very Hitchcock.

'I mean you must have some reason for thinking he's still here,' I finished.

'Jake Carson phoned from a hotel called the Riviera on Sixth. When he got there he found a note waiting for him from Jerry. The note said he'd be around for a few days and he'd be in touch.'

I thought of the weapons Jerry Lennox had in the back of his pick-up. I thought of axemen and disappointed market-players who turn into spree-killers. Then I wondered. Maybe he was planning to ask Jake to check a holdall filled with Semtex on to a flight out of the international airport.

'You could go and see him yourself. Jake, I mean.'

'Hey. I'm paying you. Remember?'

'Mrs Heart. China. I think you should go to the police.'

'If you don't find Jerry in forty-eight hours, I will.'

'Why not now?'

'No. Think about it. If the police move in on him he'll end up in

147

the morgue. Do you really think that that Atlanta man killed himself?'

She had a point. Anyway, as she had just intimated, she was the client. She and her dad, the general.

'OK, I'll get right on with it. If I want to get in touch with you I use the numbers you gave me before?'

A moment's pause.

'Yes. Oh yes. And one more thing. You're practically next door to Macy's, Sachs is the other side of the square. If you want the casual look there's a Gap either on Geary or Post, I forget which, east of Union. But anyway get some decent clothes. Please?'

'I'll put them on your bill.'

'Be my guest.'

'I lost a case too. My bag.'

'So you did.' A pause, then: 'I've got a spare one you can have.'

She said it so casually, and I was so tired, it didn't register the way it should have.

I looked at the map the reception clerk had given me and checked out what I had already remembered. If the Riviera was on Sixth south of Market then Carson was rooming in the badlands. Bugger that, I thought. I'll wait for daylight. I went out though, back up Powell to Borders, after looking in the windows of the big stores which were closed for the night. Outside the Handlery I noticed a poster attached to a lamp-post thanking Michael Tilson-Thomas for becoming chief conductor of the San Francisco Symphony. Cultured place. Good manners too.

In Borders I bought a couple of Burroughs I hadn't already got, one of them the cat book Jefferson had had by his bedside, the other his film script, *The Last Words of Dutch Schultz*, an Elmore Leonard, *Split Image*, and a Jim Thomson, *The Golden Gizmo*. None of them easy to find in the UK. Then, almost next door, I found a diner called Lori's which, the nostalgia again, was filled with fifties memorabilia including a two-tone cream and pink Cadillac with chrome tail-fins, posters for Elvis films, real juke boxes. Yet it wasn't in the least tacky, but bright, clean, fun, as if it had opened yesterday. I had steak, fries, a Caesar on the side and a knickerbocker glory. I drank diet Coke, but wished, just for the hell of it, I could have had an Anchor Steam. I read most of *The Cat Inside* and sang along, to myself of course, to Eddie Cochrane and Three Steps to Heaven.

Où sont les neiges...?

Chapter 20

Next morning I thought: which shall I do first? Shop or find Jake Carson? I decided, shop first. If I'm going to get mugged, rolled, or shot I might as well go down looking smart. I skipped breakfast, counted out a couple of grand from the Wells Fargo bag, stuffed the bills in my inside pocket and set out. I crossed Powell, had a mooch round Maceys, bought a couple of button down shirts in pastel colours, orange and blue, and a couple of quietish silk ties, three pairs of socks and a pair of very dark brown loafers with gun metal buckles, didn't see a suit I liked nor the hat I wanted. Next stop GAP, not for me, but for the kids: when I told them I was going to California Richard rabbited on about how everything like trainers and jeans were so much cheaper while Rosa, in spite of being only ten, said I was to be sure to go to a GAP since the nearest to Bournemouth was in Bath, and their mother wouldn't take them that far just to shop. They then wrote out all their sizes in American as well as English.

I bought jeans for both, bustier tops for Rosa but refused what were called trainee bras, and T-shirts that said GAP all over them which was, so Rosa had told me, the whole point. The oriental serf actually held the door for me as I went through. Clearly the bunch of logoed glossy bags I was carrying had done wonders for my street-cred.

I put on one of the shirts, a tie and the loafers and set out again, asking the reception clerk if she knew of a decent, old-fashioned gents outfitters in the area.

'Try Cable Car Clothiers on Sutter,' she said, 'go up Powell a block past Union Square, take a right, and you're there.'

Just the place. A wide deep shop run by a lady of fifty and her mother who must have been eighty, and who were delighted to have an Englishman who spoke real English in their shop. Much of what they sold was English, they said, or anyway European. I left with a dark, light-weight suit, with what I took to be an Italian label, Canali, basically brown but with a simple blue check, a short rain-coat whose blue matched the blue in the suit and, yes, a deep brown, high-crowned, snap-brimmed, felt fedora with a wide black grosgrain band, made by Stetson, and bugger all change out of the second grand. At last, I thought, I'll look the way a private eye should.

Back in my room I decided on second thoughts that if I was going into the badlands I'd be better staying in my old clothes, and anyway it was getting late, almost eleven o'clock, so I left it all there and set out on foot.

I took a hike down Powell, crossed Market into Fifth, took a right past the Old Mint on to Sixth, passed a gun shop, and headed towards the freeway flyovers, the ones I'd driven in on, that come off the Bay Bridge and head to San Francisco International. In contrast to the evening before the cloud cover was low enough to sit amongst the tops of the higher skyscrapers and the air was chill. Let's repeat the old saw just once and say it's true. Mark Twain said the worst winter he'd ever spent was summer in San Francisco.

The clerk at the Handlery had been right. Each block was seedier than the one before, the menace grew. Beggars in doorways, one of them shooting up. A ten year old Lincoln Continental cruised by with heavily tinted windows and four Afro-Americans in sharp suits just discernible. Then a guy in fringed leather, space age black helmet, on a 1500 cc BMW bike pursued by a city police car, with a barrage of flashing spinning lights on its roof and sirens yelping like the guinea-pig from hell. No way was it going to catch the bike, but at least they were making a statement — a gesture anyway.

The Riviera was almost up against the flyovers and the traffic noise was a steady roar. Brick-built, it had four storeys with a fire escape on the end wall and it looked as if the latest earthquake had knocked it about a bit. Or may be the one before. The foyer smelled of cheap booze, disinfectant and vomit, was panelled in nicotine and had flower-corolla shaped lampshades covering four of five bulbs above the middle, the ones on the side walls were bare. A leather sofa leaked wiry bristles that were nothing like horsehair. There was a desk with a corpse behind it.

Well no, not really. But he looked like Dustin Hoffman in the centenarian make-up Hoffman wore at the beginning of *Little Big Man*. He was reading *Hustler*. No. He was looking at *Hustler*. Upside down. He seemed to need only one hand to hold it.

'Jake Carson?' I asked.

'If he ain't in 406, try the Breakfast Muffin three doors down.'

I headed towards the elevator.

'Elevator don't work.'

I headed back to the street.

The Breakfast Muffin was about as different from Lori's as you

150

could imagine. Wide and deep it was scuffed, grubby, cracked, damaged. Not a lot but enough to give it an aura. The floor was some sort of corky stuff the colour of dry blood with shallow holes to bare concrete here and there, the tables were red laminate with aluminum edgings that harboured a dull orange line of grease. There were framed colour prints of sunflowers and they weren't signed Vincent. As well as Carson there were four or five other customers scattered about, none of whom looked as if they bought their clothes in Union Square.

Carson was sitting near the self-service counter, at a small table against the wall, facing the street entrance. He was wearing a jacket even nastier than mine, a grubby blue shirt with open collar, mother-of pearl press-button studs for buttons, jeans and a tooled belt with a Harley Davidson buckle. His pink and yellow colouring glowed in the pink fluorescent lighting. He was doing at least three things at once: reading a paper, smoking, drinking coffee, eating his second doughnut. His small fat fingers were powdered with sugar and there was more round his mouth. A mobile, the twin of the one I'd taken off him, was in the top pocket of his jacket, just the way he'd carried the first one.

He looked up as I came down the narrow gangway between the tables.

'Shit,' he said. 'You again.'

I went to the counter. The system seemed to be self-service for prepared food, but order anything you wanted cooked special. I ordered a coffee and French toast. The Asian waitress said she'd bring it to the table. The kitchen area, dark and greasy apart from matt stainless steel plant, was exposed behind her. I took my coffee and pulled out the chair opposite Carson. He shifted — to keep the street in view.

'Hi,' I said. 'Mrs Heart says you've heard from Jerry Lennox. She'd like to know more about that.'

'The fuck she would.' He went back to his paper. Last night's *Chronicle*. Looked as if it had spent the night in a trash can. Then he looked over the top of it. 'Listen, buster. I break your nose. I fucking try to shoot you. What more do I have to do to keep you off my back?'

'Can't we be friends?' I asked.

He shrugged.

'You told Mrs Heart that Mr Lennox said he'd be in touch with you,' I repeated. 'Has he?'

He folded up the newspaper and put it on the edge of the small table, to the side of us. It fell off. He left it where it fell. He leant back and his beady blue almost lashless eyes found mine.

'What you done with the Pontiac?'

'Took it to Alamo, the hirers.'

'Where?'

'Here. The return office up on Bush. Near the corner with Powell.'

Slowly the sun rose in his big fat slob's face.

'Mrs Heart. I done told her you took the mobile off of me. No way I couldn't. But I never told her I'd lost the automobile too. I was meant to check it in here after I'd done the business on you. So what you done's fine. Just fine.'

It dawned on me I'd made a friend after all. Scored a brownie point anyway.

Then something else dawned and brought with it yet another attack of mental vertigo.

'Are you saying it was Mrs Heart told you to go to Santa Monica?'

'Yip.'

'To kill me?'

'Yeah. After that airplane dropped out of the sky taking off from LAX she said that motherfucker's done his bit, off him. Was her hubby, Mr Heart came with me.'

'Oh shit,' I said, and looked around. Suddenly I felt very frightened, suspicious of everyone in sight and especially of the noise that had just erupted behind me.

'But she told me her husband was killed by the General...'

It was no use. He wasn't listening.

Four student types, backpackers without their back-packs, check shirts, jeans, walking boots, two boys two girls, had come in. They walked past me, close enough to brush the back of my chair or stick a knife in my neck, and stood at the counter. They were Australian. They could not make up their minds what they wanted. Nor could they decide how to spend their day. They were trying to make up their minds about both at once.

Meanwhile, I was still trying to come to terms with what Carson had told me. It was like trying to get your breath back after you've taken a blow in the diaphragm. Carson finished his second doughnut, wiped his fingers on his lapels, lit another Marlboro with his Zippo. I looked around. Neither he, nor the Aussies, nor anyone else in sight seemed on the point of offing me.

'Can you tell me,' I said, leaning across towards Carson, 'where I can find Jerry Lennox?'

'Yip.'

'How come you know where Jerry Lennox is, but no one else does?'

One of the Australian lads wanted chocolate chip muffins because they seemed to be the speciality of the house, no he didn't, he wanted one chocolate chip, one blueberry. One of the girls wanted fresh pancakes with corn syrup and whipped cream. No cream said the Asian girl, anyway we stopped serving breakfast. The other boy wanted to go to the Museum of Modern Art, just up the road, the other girl wanted to go to Haight Ashbury and see the Beatniks, like they were specimens in a zoo. I waited.

'I guess he just likes to have me around,' Carson said. 'Know where I'm at so he can call me when he wants me.'

A man came in. He was small, not more than five six, but round and fat, two hundred pounds. He had a wide-rimmed cotton hat, the padded sort with seams, a shit-coloured soft leather jacket over a checked shirt, pale grey trousers, polyester and wool mix, grey tasselled loafers. He wore rimless spectacles, his face was ruddy, not open-air ruddy but hypertension ruddy. He stood with his hands deep in the slanted side pockets of his jacket, pushing the bottom forward so it covered his belly.

He stood behind the Australians and fidgeted, shifting from one foot to the other, grunting, whistling. He cleared his throat.

'What the fuck does one have to do here to get served?' he asked.

One of the Australian boys was now in a deep argument with one of the girls, the fattest, she more than filled her jeans. She wanted just orange juice, nothing more. He wanted her to have more than that, they had a long day ahead of them. She said he was contradicting himself. He'd told her she was too fat, now he wouldn't let her have a slimming breakfast.

'Can I see the manager, please?' The man behind them called. No. Shouted. The word 'please' sounded like a threat.

'Do you know how many calories there are in a glass of orange juice?' the Australian lad demanded of his fat girl friend.

Carson stirred uneasily, glanced over his shoulder. The newcomer was only three yards from him, and slightly behind him.

'What's the matter?' I asked.

'Fucker's packing.'

'How do you know?'

'It's something you learn.'

'Manager is cook too. He cooking,' said the Asian girl. And indeed at that moment a small guy who could have been her brother, came out from the back and handed her a plate. She took it, came round from behind the counter, picked up a knife and fork wrapped in a paper serviette, put the plate which had two triangles of eggy bread on it in front of me, and said: 'Would you like more coffee?'

I said I would. She brought over the Cona flask, topped up my cup and Carson's, checked we had tubs of milk and cream on the table, headed back. As she passed the guy in the hat caught her elbow.

'Take my order. *Now.*'

The Australians agreed to split, they'd meet on Fisherman's Wharf at three o'clock, entrance to Pier Thirty-Nine.

'Please, these people were here first,' said the Asian girl, and tried to break free.

The guy with the hat held on, dug his fingertips into her biceps, made it hurt.

'Fucking chinks, you fucking do what I tell you and take my order. I want two eggs, sunny-side up, grits, bacon...'

'Hey, cobber, pack it in,' said the Australian who had just finished saying breakfast is the most important meal of the day. 'We're next in line. And let the girl go.'

'Make me, fucker,' said the man with the hat, who, quite suddenly, and without letting go of the Asian girl, had become the man with a gun. A big gun. A big black automatic. 'Make me and make my day.'

Carson shifted sideways in his chair, shifted his weight on to one hip, pulled out an even bigger gun from his waistband, a chrome Colt .44, the twin of the one I'd taken off him, and laid it carefully on the table but left his palm resting across the butt.

'Jack!' he called. 'Jack? You don't want to hurt no one, put that piece away. OK?'

The man he called Jack turned, dragged the Asian girl across his body, making a shield of her, she dropped the coffee flask, it caught a concrete patch on the floor and exploded, Carson levelled his gun, but didn't fire. The man he called Jack did and blew the top of Jake's head off.

I got blood and worse all over my left shoulder and some on my plate too.

By now I had the Beretta cocked and ready to fire on my lap.

Without really thinking about it, which was the way they taught me was best at the pistol club I belonged to for a time, and without bringing the Beretta out into the open, I shot the man whose name was Jack in the knee. He dropped his gun, let go of the Asian girl, and rolled back into a chair and table before ending up in a heap on the floor in a pool of coffee and broken glass. Seems, like all bullies, he could hand it out, but couldn't take it. He screamed.

Still using the table for cover I got the Beretta back into my jacket pocket, got up, set out for the door. The diner was oddly silent now, all I could hear was the blood rushing in my ears. No one tried to stop me. Why should they?

I put a five spot on the last table. I hadn't eaten any of my eggy toast and I didn't think anyone else would either. But it didn't seem right not to pay for it.

Chapter 21

Holding the serviette over most of the blood patch I walked the two short blocks up to Howard, which is almost back in civilisation, and caught a cab. The driver wasn't happy that I was going no further than the Handlery, but I promised him a twenty and kept the promise. One happy cabbie.

I got back to my room, chased out the Filippino maid who was cleaning it, had a shower. Then, as I came out of the tiny bathroom with its sliding door I caught sight of my bloodstained jacket in a heap on the end of the bed, and knew I had to vomit. But it was all bile and spew, a hell of a lot of effort and a teaspoon of blood. Sweating and shivering I got back on the bed. I felt very lonely indeed. Apart from anything else, if that blood meant I'd blown an oesophageal varicose vein I could be bleeding to death. But no. When that happens it'll come by the cupful. But I'd had enough. I wanted out.

There was a phone book. I found the number for Virgin Atlantic, used the hotel phone. Yes, there's a daily flight to Heathrow at 16.30, check in three o'clock. No, today's flight is fully booked. We could put you on standby...? No. No thanks. Try another airline? But the panic attack was fading. It was being next to Carson when that maniac shot him set it off. That, and knowing that at one point in it all, China Heart had been ready to have me killed.

What made her change her mind?

I looked at my watch. Oh shit, here we go again. Take away eight hours plus one made it twelve minutes past eleven. Still so early? I ran it through again. In the state I was, though I'd already done it a hundred times since I arrived, I nearly gave myself a brainstorm, but came to the same answer. Ring Mrs Heart? Tell her Jake Carson was dead and our line to Jerry gone? No, I still felt too shaken. I lay on the bed, picked up the Burroughs film script I'd bought, *The Last Words of Dutch Schultz*, found the frontispiece newspaper photograph of a dead man disturbing, put it down.

For fuck's sake, I said to myself, think, act like a private eye.

And although it was a day or two since he'd been around, 'Yeah, time you did,' said the voice in my ear. 'What you think I called you out here for?'

And that did it, that was the moment I got a finger and a thumb on the loose end and pulled.

Private eyes, as I've already said, need to develop certain skills. They need to be able to observe, see, hear, pick out details others wouldn't notice. When I want to I can cast an eye over a whole room for about twenty seconds and lock away in my data bases every detail. Some PIs rely on hi-tech microrecorders even micro cameras, or they stick with lo-tech and write it all down in a notebook. The ex-Plods go for the note book. Basically though, I rely on the hi-est tech I've got, my brain.

Another useful ability is to take the content of what any voices in your head say to you with a pinch of salt.

'What do you think I called you out here for,' was what the voice in my head had asked. But the last thing Jefferson the real had said to me was 'They told me this morning you are on your way...' Memory skills I may have but putting them to good use, making the right connections comes slower. I hadn't questioned that 'They told me...'

'You are on your way...' I'd taken this to mean, and I bet you did too, that I had left England, or left home, I had set out with the money and a Virgin Atlantic ticket. It could have meant, yes, he knew then I was coming, but it was the first he'd known of it. Maybe he had just seen the messages to me that someone had put on his computer and my answers to them. But the question I had not asked, and I bet you hadn't either, was...

Who the fuck are 'they'?

The two messages that had brought me over were emailed. They had been sent from Jefferson's home PC. The people who had murdered him had had easy access to his flat, and his office, either because they had keys or because he trusted them and let them in or because they threatened him, had some hold over him. Certainly they had keys to get in, move the body, search his flat and take from it anything that might point me in the right direction.

I'd been brought over, shit, let's be careful about this, it was possible that I had been brought over not by him at all but by someone else.

Who? WHY?

Why looked easy. Up to a point I'd worked it out already. With a little help from Agent Fowler.

Jefferson and I had been set up to look like the bombers of UA324. Why us? Lefties. Commies. Comrades. Just the types who'd want to lend the Chiapas peasants a helping hand. A guy impersonating

Jefferson had put my bag on the plane, I'd been within radio signal range when the bag blew a hole in the side of the plane. When UA324 dropped out of the sky it looked like I'd done my bit. So I could be offed in the Santa Monica motel. But then, by the time I'd made it to Santa Barbara I was worth keeping alive. Why? The authorities, the airlines had called the bombers' bluff: no blood money was to be paid. So. A second bomb, a second aluminum shower had to be arranged, a fall guy would be needed, so why not use me again?

Who? Well, China Heart I already knew was a part of it, and her errant daughter too, Lola/Nicola who stole a driving license and ID from her cousin and was ready to shag me in order to keep me in the hotel room where they wanted me to be. But careful here. Jefferson and I had been manipulated. In his case maybe by threats and intimidation, in mine by, well, let's face it by venality, venery, and vacillation. Or boneheadedness. But who else? This was a big operation, others must be in it too. The ladies had to be part of a team and a team with considerable resource, resources as well. For instance, how had they known Jefferson and I were lefties thirty years ago? It wasn't something either of us shouted our heads off about in the normal run of things, though of course it wasn't either something we'd deny, or were in any way ashamed of. Nevertheless. Did they have access to secret files? FBI or CIA files?

Yet in spite of being so well resourced things had gone wrong for them. Between sending for me and my arrival Jefferson had had to be murdered. Maybe there had been crossed lines, broken chains of command, cock-ups. A failure of nerve perhaps. Above all Lola/Nicola's assumed identity had been blown and the FBI were on to them, had been on to them well before I arrived. And I was still in the middle, the tethered goat the Feds were going to use to bring them all in.

By now my head was spinning, the mental vertigo again. Maybe yours too. But I'd started the whole line of thought by retrieving the one message from Jefferson I could be sure was genuine. But there had been a second on that microcassette. Lola/Nicola need not be the only Lola involved.

How did it go? The tip of the tongue taking a trip of three steps down the palate to tap, at three, on the teeth. *Lo. Lee. Ta.* There was another Lolita. She worked at Crabwise, La Jolla. She was not Lola/Nicola. Why had Nicola assumed her name, even a personna, an occupation that echoed hers, as a waitress? Perhaps because she thought I might stumble on Lola's existence, a reference to her in the apartment, something of that sort, and she wanted me to assume that she, Nicola, was the Lola in question. And she already had a cousin called Lola, or anyway Dolores, who lived in Carmel, and whose ID she'd already nicked. Coincidence? Not really. We always stand contingency on its head, call it coincidence with hindsight, after the event. The point is if that situation with the license and the credit cards hadn't already been in place, she'd have thought of something else — and that something else would then have looked like the coincidence.

This, I admitted to myself, was not wholly satisfactory, but it did all point to one thing. On that microcassette Jefferson had told me to get in touch with the real Lola, the owner of the sassy voice that had been on the answerphone. And I hadn't.

I attacked the phonebook again, found how to get enquiries, got the number of Crabwise, La Jolla.

'Hi there. This is Crabwise. My name's Dolores. How can I help you?'

Bingo again. I took a deep breath.

'Dolores. Is that the Dolores is a friend of Wilbur Jefferson?'

Silence. Then...

'Who is this?'

'My name's Kit Shovelin. I'm a friend of Jefferson's.'

Again the silence.

'I'll ring you back. Give me a number and five minutes.'

I gave her the Handlery number, extension 362. She was less than five minutes.

'Mr Shovelin? OK, I'm out of the public area now. What is this?'

The voice was southern, had a black throatiness, almost certainly the one I'd heard on Jefferson's answer phone. And certainly not Lola-Nicola's.

'Lola. Do they call you Lola?'

'Sure they do. You called Dolores, you Lola. Or Lolita.'

'And you know Wilbur Jefferson.'

'Sure I knew him. Say, are you Kit Shovelin, the limey?'

'Yes.'

'Got a message for you.'

'Hang on a minute. You said you knew Jefferson.'

'Wilbur Jefferson, he dead.'

I waited.

'They found his corpse on the shoulder of Interstate 5 yesterday morning. Run over. First they said it was a road accident but the local fruits say he was beaten up first and it's a gay killing. Head beaten in then runned over after he was dead. You a friend of his? You a fruit too? Sorry if I upset you. Tell the truth I'm upset too.'

She gave a big sniff.

I got a grip.

'Lola,' I managed to say. 'The message?'

'Yeah. Hang on a minute. I got it somewhere. Just a phone number for you to ring. That's all.'

Again a pause, then...

'You still there? Funny thing. You just gave me a four-one-five number and this is too. That's San Francisco, aint it? Jefferson he say if he ain't around to see you, call him on this number...' and she read it out.

The irony was I'd hunted out Carson on China Heart's instructions in order to find where Jerry Lennox was hiding himself. For some reason, it was surely no contingency, he'd been shot before he could tell me. But as a result my memory and thought processes had been given the boot they needed, and now I had my route to him in front of me, but for myself and Jefferson, not for China Heart.

I tried not to think of Jefferson with his head rearranged so an autopsy wouldn't show he'd been shot first. I pressed the right buttons. It rang. The repeated single ring. A man's voice.

'Yes?'

'Whom am I speaking to?'

'Who do you want to speak to?'

I took a breath. The voice was right, as far as I could tell.

'I'll start again. I'm Kit Shovelin. You rang me day before yesterday. Apparently from the Handlery Hotel.'

'That's right. How did you know this number?'

'It's a long story. But basically Jefferson left it with a girl, Lola, who works at Crabwise in La Jolla, asking her to give it to me.'

'Ooh-kay,' said slowly. Another guy who liked to think before speaking, he let about twenty seconds go by. 'Just tell me where it was you didn't, I repeat, *did not* meet Jefferson for the first time?'

What the fuck, I thought, then I remembered the last time I had spoken to him.

'Cuba.'

'OK, Kit. I guess you want to talk to me.'

'Person to person, if that's possible.'

'I don't see why not. You're here in San Francisco?'

'Yes.'

'Listen. Er, let me think this through. I'm going to be tied up until one o'clock. Do you know Washington Square?'

'I've got a map.'

'Be there then at, oh, let's say half one, on the Columbus Avenue side. Er... Know what I look like? Anyway, by then I'll probably be carrying a City Lights shopping bag. And come alone.'

And he rang off.

Jerry Lennox, the fascist nut, shopping at City Lights? Pardon me.

Was this the point where I should contact the Feds? Agent Fowler had said: 'You just tell us what they're asking you to do. Until it gets close to the *momento de verità...*', but had later added that they wanted to know if or when I made contact with Jerry Lennox. They had been quite clear about it. I had no option. Agent Cooper had added: 'You won't see us. But we'll be close. We'll look after you.' So they probably had a tail on me, or were tapping the Handlery extension. Either way they'd find out if I hadn't told them if I didn't. If you see what I mean. I really believe, that at that point, knowing what I thought I knew, I had no option.

I hunted out the green mobile Agent Fowler had given me, pressed the unlock button, then redial.

A female voice said: 'Federal Bureau of Investigation, how can I help you?'

'Get me Agent Fowler, please.'

A different ring. Then:

'Mr Fowler is tied up right now, his line is busy. Will you hold?'

'I'll hold.'

They played a Rossini overture. It took me most of the five minute wait to place it. The Thieving Magpie, of course. Then:

'Fowler here.'

'Shovelin.'

'Kit! Great, wonderful to speak to you. So what's new?'

I told him China Heart had sent me down to the Riviera to meet Carson, how Carson got killed, how, nevertheless, I'd made contact with Lennox through a different route and now had an appointment to see Jerry Lennox in Washington Square at half one.

'Carson gave you Lennox's number?'

I hesitated. Before I could answer...

'Course he did. So why does Lennox want to see you? Only one way to find out. You be there. We'll be there too. Don't worry. I've not forgotten this is the guy had Carson fill a load of motel bedding with bullet holes thinking it was you. We'll pull out all the stops. Marksmen on the roofs, Davidson and I will be right there, there'll be paramedics and a blood-waggon round the corner. Like the movies. How will you get there?'

'Take a cab?'

'No, I want you out in the open all the time, in a crowd. Much safer. Take the cable-car. Buy a day ticket at the bottom of Powell. Hang on, where are you?'

'The Handlery.'

'Fine, fine. Ticket at the bottom of Powell, then make sure you get the car that's got Powell-Mason on it, not Powell-Hyde, and get off at Union. That's Union Street, not the Square. The stop has a sign says Union for Washington Square, it's a block away. But listen. Kit?'

'Still here.'

'Allow half an hour, no, forty minutes. There's always a long line in the tourist season. But that's what we want. You in a crowd so we can keep near you without being obvious.'

He rang off and that was that.

It had sounded as if Lennox might be on the way to City Lights. One of the first left-wing bookshops to be opened in the western world. The place where Ginsberg's *Howl* was first read and published. Owned by Lawrence Ferlinghetti, another of the major Beat poets, was he still alive? I didn't want to leave San Francisco without visiting it. The Beats? You don't know who the Beats were? Visit them on the Web. There must be a hundred sites.

I checked the address in the phone book, looked it up on the map. Three blocks up the diagonal Columbus from Washington Square. Right, I thought, I'll go there first. Maybe I'll get a sight of him before we meet. I took a glance at the photo China had given me, the young WASP face with the lock of fair hair, the preppy clothes that looked out of date. Shit, I thought, I've seen that face somewhere recently. But where? Who? Well, I reckoned, I was about to see it again.

162

Chapter 21

Oh no, I wasn't. At least not straightaway.

First the cable-car. Shame I wasn't in the right mood to enjoy it. Joined the line at the bottom of Powell, got my ticket in the kiosk, watched the old man who turns up to give a hand pushing the cars round on the turn table. Told myself I was too old to stand on the footplate, sat on a slatted seat inside. Wimp.

Got off at Union, walked a block up Columbus to the square, paused to watch a coupla middle-aged guys doing feng-shui or whatever it's called, that slow, magic dance, on the grass, like birds they were, balancing on one bent leg, arms like slowly outstretched wings. It was the way they were so together made it great to watch. And so San Francisco.

Columbus, like Market, runs across the grid, but north-west — south-east, which means it makes an angle of forty-five degrees not ninety where it crosses Broadway and it's on that triangle City Lights is sited. At that time it was a mess. Although most if not all the stock was new it had the grubby, higgledy-piggledy look of a used book store, with black painted shelving, wooden floor-boards, low doorways, a badly-lit cellar. There were notices apologising, blaming earthquake damage and consequent structural repairs. Worst of all the upstairs which was advertised as the Beat section with a coffee area was closed off.

However, the old-fashioned layout with most stacks protruding into the rooms, made it possible to scout round, suss out the people there without too overtly peering at them. The books were interesting too. Not least because I hit upon several titles that wereon Jefferson's shelves at La Jolla, especially ones actually published by City Lights. Had he bought them here, or had he used mail order?

I got there about a quarter after midday. There were no more than seven or eight other customers. Of course I wasn't sure at all Jerry Lennox would be there. He might be down his local One-Stop with his City Lights bag, shopping for lunch. None of the people in the book store looked like the photograph. They seemed to be all of a type — the young side of middle-aged, cheaply dressed with understated style, neatly turned out. No kaftans, no beads, no weird hairstyles, not weird by Brit standards anyway, though a couple of the men wore it longer than most American males I'd seen. But there was just the one old-timer, huge grey beard, long straggly grey hair, none too clean, granny specs, long coat over strange, baggy trousers that looked as if they had been cut from cheap curtain material. Middle-aged Hippies are one thing but this was the generation before — a very senior citizen Beat. Then I felt someone closer behind me than personal space conventions permit in such places and a voice, quiet, low, not quite a whisper, the voice of the man who called himself Jerry Lennox on the phone.

'Kit? Kit Shovelin?'

I turned. Our faces were no more than a couple of feet apart. Short beard trimmed to a point, moleskin donkey jacket dark navy, T-shirt black and plain, black 501s, clean dark sneakers. His hands were strong, reddish, freckled, like his face, the sort of skin that doesn't like sun and protests if it sees too much. Pale blue eyes that looked serious or sad, large bony nose, late forties, moustache and pointed beard trimmed short and neat, yes I'd seen him before. Sitting on his own at a table in the Da Vinci restaurant, Beverley Hills, waiting for someone. Waiting for Jefferson. He did not look in the least like the guy in the photograph China Heart had given me.

'Even on the phone I guessed it had to be you, as soon as I heard the limey accent,' he continued, satisfaction showing in his voice. 'And now I've seen you, well, of course Jefferson showed me pictures of you. You were younger in them, but much the same.'

He took my hand, and then very naturally put his cheek against mine. My response was neutral to negative. A hint of a smile touched those sad eyes as he pulled back. Not wanting to offend, and to negate any suggestion I might have left that I found the intimacy offensive, I gave his hand a squeeze.

'Buy you a coffee?' he murmured.

He took my elbow.

'Shame they're closed up here. But there's a coupla good wop caffs down towards Vallejo.'

'Good wop caffs' in an English accent. Bastard was sending me up. I realised I was in danger of liking him.

'You really are Jerry Lennox?' I asked, as we got out on to the sidewalk. The sky was still grey, the chill of sea mist still hung in the air and the mist itself round the needle-top of the Transatlantic Pyramid at the far end of Columbus.

'Not what you expected?'

'Not what I was told to expect.'

'I am Jerry Lennox. The real Jerry Lennox.'

A right took us into Vallejo. There were a couple of Italian café-restaurants with the usual chrome framed chairs with red plastic strip seats and backs, round tables with black laminate tops, out on the pavement. Lennox found one at the end of its café's territory, back to the wall, and we sat down with the two empty chairs in front of us.

'Tell me about it then,' he said.

I started. The emails, that probably weren't from Jefferson, asking me to come out. How, when I replied that I couldn't make it, keys and the fare had been brought by courier.

I went on to tell him how I'd found Jefferson's body, how I'd gone out, how it had disappeared by the time I got back.

'His apartment had been searched, gone over?'

'By an expert.'

'Things missing?'

'Probably. Hard to be sure.'

'Nothing of mine there? No photos, letters, anything like that?'

'No.' A touch more light... 'But you think there should have been?'

'Oh yes.'

Said slowly, with feeling and meaning.

A waiter arrived. Lennox ordered a double espresso for himself, I asked for a capuccino and something to eat. Breakfast, I'd missed, remember? The waiter wanted us to eat properly, off the lunch menu and was sour when we refused.

'Danish OK?'

'I'd rather have a croissant or toast. Listen,' I said, when the waiter had gone, 'this is a hell of a long and complicated story, but one thing I should tell you now is this. This morning I met Jake Carson in a diner on Sixth. I think he was going to tell me where I could find you. He got into an argument with a red-neck lout who shot and killed him. This may have nothing to do with everything else, but you ought to know.'

Lennox had gone pale. Clutching the circumference of the table, his knuckles whitened.

'Never as single spies, eh? But always in fucking battalions.' Then he let breath out in a long sigh. 'How does Jake fit into it all?'

Fucked if I know, I thought, my head swimming again. But I tried.

'When I first met him, out at Homage, he said he was your bodyguard. Later he tried to kill me, apparently under your instructions...'

'*My* instructions?' The shock and surprise in his voice just had to be genuine.

'But I'm beginning to realise the man I thought was you wasn't you at all. I never saw him. I just heard him tell Carson to go to the room they thought I was sleeping in and shoot me. Was Carson really your bodyguard?'

'No. He liked to think so though. He reckoned he owed me. Fifteen years ago I got him out of a correction centre where he was being heavily abused. He's... he was... a bit touched, simple, nothing serious, I made the family take him on as a general gofer. But, the way emotionally retarded people often are, he had one or two very finely honed skills. Electronics and IT particularly, in a very practical, hands-on way. Why did this lout take him out?'

'He was threatening the staff and customers in the diner with a gun. The red neck, I mean. Carson, Jake, intervened. The killer used the waitress as a shield and shot him from behind her... Oh shit. I've just thought of something...'

It was Carson's gun, the Colt .44 Magnum. If it was the same gun, and not its twin, then the FBI had taken it, they said, from the Duchess. And given it back to Carson? Hardly. Either that or we were talking coincidences. Again the mental vertigo.

'He was going to tell you how to find me?'

'Yes.'

'It was no accident or coincidence he got killed. In fact I can guess who did it. Fat guy, red face, odd hat...?'

But at that moment the waiter returned. Once we were through with the little jingling ritual that goes with serving coffees and so forth, it was Jerry who went on asking the questions, though it was me who wanted to.

'So just what was the job Jefferson apparently wanted you to help him with?'

'Well, of course he never told me himself. But Mrs Heart, your half-sister? said she'd employed him to look for you. Find you. The story was you'd disappeared in a new Chevrolet pick-up, on the night of fourth July, with a load of weapons, and that you were on your way to a spree killing, possibly ethnically cleansing a public school in L. A. There was also an attempt to show you up as some sort of neo-nazi, fascist thug. They had memorabilia in your rooms at Homage...'

'They had WHAT?'

I described the rooms and the shrine to National Socialism. Jerry shook his head through most of it.

'But I don't even have rooms there any more. I cleared everything of mine out when I broke with them finally and moved up here permanently five, nearly six years ago.'

I spooned foam and chocolate powder between my lips; he tore off the corner of a sugar sachet. I crumbled the croissant.

'This is weird,' I said. 'They seem to have created a whole fictional character who doesn't exist, and called it you.'

'Tell me more about that.'

'Oh, that you were the son of General Lennox's second, or was it third? wife, that you were more or less brought up by China, your older half-sister because your mother was a lush, that when he married again she was shipped off to Costa Rica without you, that China, although your surrogate mother, seduced you when you were fourteen and she was twenty or so...'

'She really ought to take up fiction writing.' He laughed minutely. 'Screenplays rather than novels, I think, don't you? Mind you the first part is true, but not the seduction bit. One thing though. If they were employing you to find me, they must have given you a photograph.'

I pulled it out of my inside pocket. He took one quick glance at it.

'That's her husband. Lyle Heart. It's an old photo. At least twenty years old. Reproduced on modern paper or reprinted from the original negative.'

'It must have been taken quite shortly before her father, the general, ran him over, killed him.'

He laughed again. 'Oh no! This is another of her fictions. Lyle is alive and well, though not in as good shape as he was then. He's always been a heavy smoker.'

'Oh shit.'

He put his hand briefly over mine.

'Don't blame yourself. Even a PI has to believe quite a lot of what he gets told.'

I finished the croissant, not a big one, brushed flakes of pastry from my mouth.

'You knew Jefferson,' I asked, 'for how long?'

'Five years. I'm a lawyer. I work for a charity, against discrimination, for equal opportunities, that sort of thing. Back then our chair was being prosecuted on faked evidence for corruption, we got Jefferson through a gay register... well, you can fill in the rest.'

At that moment something quite unimportant happened. I felt jealous. Not, I think, of sexual favours exchanged between them, but that this guy had known Jefferson far more intensely than I had, and that somewhere, twenty, thirty years ago I had lost an opportunity. Anyway... let go of something I should have held on to. Lennox's eyes met mine for a second, both of us keeping our faces dead. He knew. He knew too I knew he knew. I finished my cappucino. He looked over my shoulder down Vallejo towards the quays. A ship's siren sounded, gulls mewed. The mist was beginning to lift. A patch of hazy but hot sunshine reached the floor of the street.

He turned back.

'So,' he said. 'What's behind all this?'

Doubt trickled back into my head like an injection of poison.

'Don't you read the papers? Watch TV?'

'Not if I can help it. And usually I can.'

'You know there was a crash at LAX.'

'I saw the headlines on other people's papers. Wasn't Kennedy Junior on board?'

Was he having me on? I looked at him. He shrugged, gave a half-smile, the sort a small boy at school produces to mitigate what he knows was a guess, and suspects was a wrong one.

'OK, tell me about it,' he added.

I told him. The plane had blown up, a hundred million had been demanded to forestall the same thing happening again, the authorities and the media believed Jefferson had been involved — I knew that couldn't be so, I'd seen him dead forty-eight hours earlier.

'Jesus Christ. This is heavy stuff. Serious. Worse than I expected.' He bit his lip, ran the point of his tongue across it beneath the moustache. 'It must have been what he wanted to talk to me about. We had an appointment to meet at a restaurant in Beverley Hills, actually on that night. He didn't turn up. Sorry. Go on. The FBI.'

'Somehow or other the FBI connected me with Jefferson, I suppose it wasn't difficult. They tracked me down, got into a motel room I was staying in in Carmel...'

'What were you doing there? It's a horrible place.'

'Yes.'

I tried to explain how I'd gone looking for a Dolores Paz y Winters in Carmel how it seemed Nicola Heart had been impersonating Dolores, how her mother seemed to look down on the Lennoxes as unreliable people who had spent all their money...

'A lot of this is yet more bullshit, you know. But not all of it. The family are bust, badly in debt, but not Aunt Agatha... That's what we call Mrs Winters. Anyway, go on. You were telling me about the feds.'

'They were waiting for me when I got back from the Winters' place. That's when they first contacted me.'

'Whoever these guys are, they are not the FBI.'

'Who are they then?'

'I shan't know for certain until I've seen them.' He signalled for the waiter.

'But you think you know.'

'Yeah, I think so. One is tall, sort of squared off face like a coffin, white hair, yes? The second is Afro, good-looking, ingratiating manner...'

'Not entirely. He hit me twice.'

'Well, there's more than one way of getting under a guy's guard. And the third I'd guess was an overweight woman with a redface, probably the cleverest of the three. Has BO which she masks with perfumed talc. I'm right, aren't I? I can see from your face I am.'

He took a bill-fold from his hip pocket, peeled off a couple of fives, waived the change.

'Come on. I've got a guy coming to see me, a client, but you and I have got a lot more to talk about so you may as well come with me.'

He stood, paused for a moment.

'You know,' he said, 'Jake Carson could have made the device that brought down that plane. Maybe they killed him because they didn't need him any more.'

I stood, he took my elbow again, hung a right down Montgomery, then took Green Street back on to Columbus, a block above Washington Square. I could see the small trees, the patch of grass, the tiny playground for children. Those good old guys had packed in their Feng-shui. If that's the right word. Secretaries were sitting on the benches finishing lunches bought from sandwich bars. The traffic was heavier now. Only ahead of us was there still a bank of iron grey mist hung like a bolster over the Bay. From behind us the high sun now shone from a clear blue sky, flashing off the chrome and glass of cars and buildings alike, warming my back. The area lacked the glitz and the glamour of downtown or Union Square, but was pleasant, not squalid like Sixth. Restaurants advertised pizza marinera, pasta with clams, though here on the border between the two communities there were Chinese outlets too. A gusty breeze made an invisible soup out of the odours. There were a lot of people about.

We crossed Stockton.

'Lantern-jaw is Lyle Heart, China's husband, he's the fascist...'

'Oh shit.' OK, the photo was twenty years old, twenty years of the weed can age you a hell of a lot. But the eyebrows and the jaw-line should still have been a giveaway.

'They were his rooms you were given to look through as if they were mine. The Afro is called Davidson, he's actually the cook at Homage...'

I remembered the beef sandwich with relish made from freshly grated horse-radish.

'... quite a good one. Cooper does the estate accounts, not the whole family business you understand, but just what's at Homage. She's a transexual and actually used to be in the FBI but they asked her to leave when she told them she was having the cut. So she has all the expertise and an insider's knowledge of how the Feds work. Incidentally she got the run up to the cut wrong, the hormone mix, which maybe is why she ended up fat and smelly. All three are crooks, each in his or her own way, and very loyal to General Lennox. They generate some income for the family and themselves from smuggling branded medicines, antibiotics, Viagra, the latest in AIDS suppressants, over the border from Tijuana, Mexico. They then sell them below the price the drug corporations set in the US but way above what they paid for them and of course without scrips. But the medical insurance companies are using clout to bring the prices down and I guess the racket's run into trouble or maybe just isn't generating the cashflow they're used to... The profit margins were never that huge.'

'Was that through the Farmacia San Cristobal?'

'Yeah. How did you know that?'

'I found the telephone number pencilled on Jefferson's office table.'

'Oh yes? You see, I'd worked out who their supplier was. Jefferson and I did a deal with Guzman, who's an old style Zapatista. We emptied one of the rooms in the old *finca*, the one with all the AKs in it and sold them to Guzman for a truck load of the new anti-HIV drugs. There are a lot of guys up here who need them and can't afford them. I guess they rumbled we were behind it and shot Jefferson. They then hired you to find me so they could off me too. I think. But maybe there's more to hiring you than just that.'

'I met Guzman,' I said. He told me to tell you to cool it, lay off until you'd heard from him.'

He nodded.

'That figures,' he said.

We'd reached Union Street, on the corner opposite the square. He turned back for a moment.

'Incidentally the General, I just can't call him Pop, although he is my dad, would have known you and Jefferson were extreme lefties: he still knows the passwords that open the NSA files at Georgetown. Or he knows guys who do. He finished his army career at a desk in intelligence in the Pentagon. He already knew of Jefferson through keeping an eye on me and through him the files led to you'

Then he crossed the street. As he stepped on to the sidewalk on the other side, the man he had said was Lyle Heart, but I knew as Agent Fowler, came up to him. Heart was wearing a full, off-white raincoat, unbuttoned, the sort with lots of flaps and straps, much like the one I had bought that morning in Macys. They shook hands briefly.

'Lyle. Hi!'

'Jerry. How y' doin?'

Then Heart fired five rapid shots into Jerry's thorax. Two of the bullets smashed out through his back with a spatter of blood and one hit the ancient Beat who'd just come out of the bookshop but by then it was about spent, so all the Beat suffered was a shock and a nasty bruise. The gun, and I was made sure about this later, was an Austrian Model 18 Glock.

Hands grasped my arms, yanked them outwards and I was slammed against a large silver Buick, an old one, like cars in the States used to be, rounded bodywork, vestigial tail-fins. Somebody kicked my shins to get my legs apart. I was quickly frisked, relieved of the Beretta, and then, with a hand pushing my head down, I was bundled into the back seat. Meanwhile, outside, Heart was still waving the Glock at the crowd, which kept a respectable distance, and with his fake ID, with the three blue letters stencilled over it, in his left hand..

'FBI,' he shouted. 'FBI.'

Davidson flashed teeth at me in a bonhomous grin, went round to the driver's seat. My nostrils twitched at the scent of Coty L'Aimant breathed at me from the other side. In spite of everything, I sneezed, and sneezed again, like a kid. Then I started crying. Cooper asked me why.

'You just fucking killed Jerry Lennox,' I blubbed. 'He was one of the good guys.'

The thing was — as he died his eyes, solemn with death, had met mine. He couldn't say it. He didn't have to. He knew I'd told them where he would be and when.

Cooper gave me a hanky. Like everything else about her it smelled of L'Aimant. I wiped my eyes, got some control though I went on shaking, tried to give it back to her.

'Keep it,' she said.

Chapter 23

Davidson span the wheel and took us in a fast U-turn across Columbus. For a moment the sun seered our eyes and he pulled down the visor. 'Good guy? That was one poisonous cocksucking ass-fucker gone where he can't do no more harm.'

I guessed they were still playing cops and robbers. I made an effort to go along with the charade.

'Christ,' I cried, 'I thought the most you'd do would be arrest him.'

'Hey, Kit. Didn't you see it? Didn't you see the piece Lennox was pulling on Agent Fowler? Could have been a Beretta, what do you reckon, Cooper?'

'Or a Tokarev. Those Mexican guerrilleros could have gotten him a Tokarev.'

'No, frankly. I didn't.'

'It was there, he had it. It was self-defence, man. Self-defence. Back to the Handlery is it?'

'I reckon,' said Cooper. She smoothed her tweedy skirt and smiled at me. Davidson took the Buick straight up Powell, through China Town, over Nob Hill across California with its Notre Dame lookalike cathedral, down the other side, following the cable-car line on Powell for the last stretch. He made a lot of use of the gear stick, a stalk attached to the steering column, the Buick was that old.

'Great views,' said Davidson, at the top, 'especially if you know where to stand. Hope you get a chance to see some of this great city before you have to leave.'

At the bottom of Union Square he took the right and pulled in in front of the Handlery's marquee.

'Meanwhile I guess you'd just better go up to your room and wait there.'

Bemused, I just sat there.

'Yeah, man. Be cool. Just do it.' His voice fluking up half an octave, a hint of exasperation — or desperation? — in it. 'We'll be in touch. Tell you the next move.'

'It's been quite a morning,' I said, feigning, no exaggerating the shock I was in. 'I've seen two people shot dead, and I myself shot another in the leg.'

'Heavy, man. So take some quality time. Put your feet up. Relax.'

I shrugged, took another grin from Cooper but didn't pay for it, stepped out. The Buick cruised away, was out of sight before I could get to the glass doors the Oriental serf who despised me was already holding open.

By the time the lift had reached floor 3, I was thinking they were right — a period of calm, consideration, introspection even, was not a bad idea. A chance would have been a fine thing. I swiped the keycard through the scanner and opened the door. Lola-Nicola was sitting in the one armchair, in all her California Girl glory. She was wearing cut down denims which exposed her copper thighs and an embroidered denim waistcoat, short, fastened with pearl buttons tight enough to give her a cleavage and short enough to leave her navel exposed. It was not the sort of garment you pick up off a street market stall, though the sort of chic it had archly pretended you might. She reached across to the glass-topped bedside locker table and stubbed out her cigarette. The lingering acrid smoke was an instant headache.

'Hi,' she said, and crossed her legs.

*

I had to sit down. There was the end of the bed. It dipped beneath me. I put my elbows on my knees, my face in my hands and I think I actually moaned.

'Surprised?' she asked.

All I could do was nod.

'Yeah, well. You see what those cocksucking morons didn't do, was keep an eye on you between the time you rang them and the time you got to Washington Square. I did. And I know you had a long cosy chat with Uncle Jerry. Too fucking cosy by half. I wonder how much he told you.'

She waited. I pulled myself together.

'From what I told him he was able to guess who Fowler, Davidson and Cooper are. That Fowler is really Lyle Heart, your father. I already knew you were really Nicola Heart and your mother is China Heart. Mrs Winters told me that. In Carmel.'

She nodded.

'Well, that's enough, really, isn't it?'

I didn't ask what it was enough for. The probable answer was — enough to get my body in the Bay with a block of cement on my feet instead of my nice new shoes.

She looked at her watch.

'He'll be here shortly,' she said.

'Who?'

'Dad.'

'Lyle Heart. Not squashed between a car-fender and a cottonwood, then?'

'That's what Mummy told you? No. But it made a nice story, don't you think?'

I watched her for a moment. Her rich full hair was pushed back with studied untidiness into a banana clip with a bit of glitter in it. Her nails and lips were lacquered with the sort of perfection and care a Dutch seventeenth century artist would put into painting a peony petal. There was a small press-button denim purse, matched the shorts, on the locker by the ashtray.

She snaked out a long copper arm, lifted my new hat off the dressing table where I'd dropped it, put it on, tilted it, hand on hip, made a moue in the mirror.

'You got the one you wanted. Good.'

She took it off.

'Can I have it if they kill you?'

I bit my lip. Be cool, I said. But not out loud.

'You're not sorry about Uncle Jerry then?' I suggested.

'It's not your fucking business, but actually no. We were never close. He and Mummy hated each other. And generally speaking Lennoxes are not pleased to have queer commies in the family.' The white of an incisor peeped over her full bottom lip. 'It does seem a bit of a waste though, when part of the point was to stop him telling you the stuff he did tell you.'

She fished out another Lambert and Butler.

'Want one?'

Hell, why not? I reached forward, let her light it. Her hand was steady. And then I'll tell you why not. The strong Virginian was too much for me, sand paper on my throat, and I had to stub it out straight away.

'Wimp,' she said. And smoked some more.

A dripping tap in the tiny bathroom measured out time like it was in short supply.

The phone buzzed. We both made a move. On the way she gave me that look, the one could stop cable cars in their tracks.

'Dad? Hi. Yes, he's here. Yes, he does. No, he's not. *Ciao*, Dad.' She replaced the handset, looked at me.

'You won't, will you?'

'What?'

'Run away.'

I shrugged.

'He's on his way up. If he meets you on the way he'll shoot you.'

I didn't doubt it at all.

Dad. Agent Fowler. Lyle Heart. Son-in-law of General Lennox. Killer of Jerry Lennox? Yes. Jefferson? Maybe. Me? We'll see.

He let himself in. After all, they booked the room for me, they could have as many key-cards as they asked for.

He was still wearing the loose, buckled and flapped raincoat. He pulled the Glock from the pocket his hand had been in and slung it on to the bed beside me. It bounced an inch.

'There you go,' he said, and looked at me, pulling off a soft leather glove as he did so. 'The shells have your or Jefferson's prints on them, we took them from the Beretta. So, old boy, if it comes to it, you shot poor Jerry.'

He pulled out his Marlboros, lit up. The ache grew like a turnip inside my head. I promised myself and the world I'd never smoke even a cigar ever again.

'The Beretta, of course, is licensed to Jefferson. The bullet you fired from it has already been taken by the City Police from the knee of a retired longshoreman, and the casing too from the floor of the diner. Nice shooting. Finally, do I have to remind you that the charges I told you could be brought against you last time we met, from automobile offences to blowing up UA324, can still be made to stick?'

He waited.

'Oh sure,' I said. 'But why don't you just bump me off and drop me in the Bay?'

'Bump you off. What a charmingly... traditional way of putting it. It's an option, I won't deny that, and one we might take. But we still haven't got our hundred million, and you still have a part to play. Problem is we hoped to get you to play it unwittingly. But you're not going to do that, are you? You're not going to put fifteen pounds of semtex on a plane for us just because we ask you to. Not even if we offer you... what? Two million?'

He looked at me, quizzical, his prematurely lined face tinged with ochre the way it gets some heavy smokers.

'No. I don't think so. So a judicious mixture of coercion and threat is called for.' He stubbed out the Marlboro and went on. 'There may come a moment when you might feel you have a chance to make a break for it. What I am trying to make clear to you is that if you go to the police you are more likely to end up on death row than we are. Meanwhile we have to keep you under cover for twenty-four hours or so.'

He looked round the room.

'But not here.'

He sat on the bed next to me, carefully pulling the tails of his coat out so they'd hang neatly rather than be bunched up under him. He was close. From over his shoulder grey eyes, the colour of year-old ice, sought mine and found them. Mine were the ones that flinched away.

'Kit,' he said, and his voice took on a slightly solemn note, 'we are about to make the first of two or three moves through public areas. I have said you still can be very useful to us but as you must by now be aware we are masters of improvisation and your demise will be no serious problem if it is forced upon us. So. If I may use another traditional form of speech, don't try anything on, buster.'

He stood up.

'You will walk beside Nicky. I shall be behind. When it is appropriate you will take her arm in a conventional gesture of familiar intimacy. If you let it go, I'll shoot you. Right?'

He looked around.

'His bag packed, Nicky?'

'All packed, Dad.'

Something I hadn't even noticed. All the stuff I'd bought apart from what I was wearing, and the new suit, plus my old clothes had gone into a large leather holdall with wheels at the back. Nicola/Lola must have brought it with her, and packed it, before I got back.

Meanwhile Dad pulled a mobile from somewhere under his coat, flipped it open, pressed a single preset.

'Luther. Plan B. On the hotel stoup in three minutes, please.' He closed the mobile and smiled at me. 'Plan A was to hang you from the light fitting.'

I didn't ask him why he'd gone for B. I didn't want him to change his mind.

'Pick up the small bag in your right hand, use your left to hold Nicola's right. No. Loosely. You're not arresting her. You're being affectionate, protective.'

He took the new bigger bag himself. Since my hands were going to be fully occupied, I put my new hat on.

In the elevator I asked who Luther was.

'Davidson, of course,' was her answer. Silly me.

At the desk Heart took over.

'Mr Shovelin,' he said, 'is checking out. But he's not leaving the city until tomorrow so he'd like to check the larger of his bags into the luggage room. OK?'

The luggage room routine again. But how was it being worked this time?

At the front door the oriental serf had his tuppence worth.

'Goodbye Mr Shovelin. We do hope you had a nice stay and that you'll use the Handlery Union Square Hotel on your next trip to San Francisco.'

Bag in one hand, Nicky on the other arm, I couldn't tip him. Shame.

*

The big silver Buick was waiting for us. Lyle Heart took the front passenger seat. As soon as we were all in, he let out a low whistle, and dabbed his brow with a silk handkerchief. He broke a couple of small pills out of silver foil and popped them in.

'Halcion,' he said. 'Calming effect. Takes the edge off the speed, now the difficult part's over.'

Davidson drove us down Geary and then began to weave his way up the hill and over the top. Considering it was a grid it wasn't that easy. As he himself kept mutttering:

'Fucking one way streets.'

We ended up just over the crest of Russian Hill, at the west end, probably on Union or Filbert, a block or two above the Crookedest Street.

Just before we stopped, Nicola said: 'Mrs Doubtfire lived just down there. The family that is. Robin Williams, you know?'

Oddly enough I did. Three (four?) years ago took my kids to see it in the Bournemouth Odeon on one of the Saturdays I'm allowed with them. Daughter was upset. Course she was, my ex said afterwards, it's about divorced parents, isn't it? But it's a story, I said. And a silly one. Would you believe it if I turned up dressed as a Scottish nanny? You can't do Scottish, she said. Nor can Robin Williams, I riposted...

The Lennoxes' house had four storeys, an attic and a basement too. The top two storeys had been converted into a duplex with big bay windows that overlooked the Golden Gate which is not a bridge but a strait, and Alcatraz. The top lights of the windows had the original art-nouveau post 1906 earthquake stained glass. Inside the ceilings were high, the fireplaces original, but the furniture and furnishings modern. Some would say postmodern. I won't go into detail except to say one big wall was half filled with a Lichtenstein Interior with Mirror Wall, almost a twin of the one in the Guggenheim in Bilbao, the shades on the track lighting in the split level kitchen were made from titanium, and, well, you get the picture. Five or six million and that was just on the walls or hanging from the ceiling. Did I mention the Calder mobile?

Jerry had been right. These were people who could well be living beyond their means. And yes, the Golden Gate is a patch of water, but it does have a bridge and you could see that too.

China was just about to leave when we arrived. She was wearing a silver fur that looked as light as chiffon, and a scarlet day-dress beneath, could have been Westwood.

'Kit. Such a shame. I'm just off. But Nicky will look after you, I'm sure. Lyle? I'll be back on Tuesday.' She pecked his cheek, embraced her daughter more warmly, touched Davidson's arm. 'You'll be there to meet me, won't you Luther, and you're taking me now, yes? My luggage is by the door.'

She gave us all another wave, grey gloved hand making that vertical circular movement royalty uses, then she was gone, with the louche Luther in tow. Which was a shame. I could have gone on looking at her for at least five more minutes in spite of everything. Killer Queen.

'Dear Mum,' said Nicola. 'Poor thing has a crush on Domingo and he's doing Pinkerton tomorrow at...'

Her voice faded.

'Sydney Opera House,' I supplied.

I had no idea then why, but I sensed from her face and her father's that Plan A was suddenly back on the agenda. I could become a truly postmodern feature, hanging up there next to the Calder. In my raincoat and hat. They could say I was by Beuys. Then she smiled.

'The Met actually, he cancelled Sydney.'

Heart yawned, stretched, looked at his watch.

'I knew something was wrong,' he drawled, his voice heavy with the benzodiazepine. 'I've missed my martini. Darling, I'm sure Luther's left a jug in the Frigidaire. Kit, you'll join me?'

'Just a tomato juice.'

'Bloody Mary for Kit, then.'

'No. Tomato juice. Just tomato juice.'

'Oh yes, of course. You don't drink do you? Case of burst oesophageal varices. Occupational hazard for PIs, I imagine. Virgin Mary, then.'

He flicked on the TV. The screen was enormous, and the sound came from all directions, Dolby Surround, no doubt.

'Responding to the second killing in San Francisco streets in as many hours, the SFPD are right now treating them as unconnected events. Jerry Lennox, gunned down close to Washington Square was a well-known lawyer who worked for gay rights. As of now the police are acting on information that he was killed by a jealous lover....»

Lyle killed the picture, shrugged at me.

'What can you do?' he said. 'They always get it wrong.'

Nicola came back with a conventional martini glass for him, an inverted cone, frosted, the liquor almost colourless, an olive on a stick, and a tumbler of tomato juice with a black swirl of Worcestershire sauce for me. The tumbler was a cube with rounded corners, and weighty with it.

'You know what we can do Nicky, if we want to dispose of our friend in a way that will look like an accident? We'll tie him up, put a tube down his mouth and pour a bottle of vodka in. Those veins pop, and he's a goner. But what a way to go!'

I got a grip, sipped, looked out of the window. The towers of the Golden Gate Bridge, as orangey red as my drink, still trailed a scarf of mist.

'Chancy,' I said. 'Could make my liver shrink rather than swell.'

But I felt dizzy at the thought all the same. No I didn't. It was whatever she'd put in the drink with the Worcestershire was making me dizzy.

'I think you'd better lie down,' she said. 'The last few days have been very rough.'

She took the tumbler, set it on a table, then took my hand. Hers was cool, steady, dry. Mine was all three opposites: hot, shaking, sweaty. I was in a bedroom. I was on the bed.

'What the fuck was that?' I asked.

'Midazolam. Probably what they give you for an endoscopy. It doesn't knock you right out, just heavy sedation. And after it's worn off you can't remember what happened while you were under it. Popular with date-rapists.'

'Thash it.' I heard the words slur. 'But youshally it worksh ishtan-tane...'

'That's because when you've had it before you've had it intrave-nously. Orally it takes a bit longer. Let's get your clothes off before you pass right out.' She pulled off my shoes, undid my belt, yanked at my pants.

'Why?'

'Men with no clothes on don't go running down the street holle-ring kidnap.'

'I shouldn't bet on it,' I murmured, and drifted into oblivion. Later I slept.

Chapter 24

I was mother naked with my right wrist handcuffed to the corner pillar of a black and gilded wrought iron bedstead. The lightfitting above my head was Venetian Murano glass. An oval Madonna, wistful but sexy, framed in gold-leafed gesso with strawberry flowers painted round it, hung on the wall facing me. If it wasn't by Fra Lippo Lippi, it was a damn good copy. Out on the staircase outside a chamber orchestra, conducted by Michael Tilson-Thomas, played Wagner's Siegfried Idyll. Nicola came in, handcuffed my left wrist to the other corner pillar, pulled the muslin gown she was wearing over her head, and fucked me.

I woke up to grey light from the usual morning grey sky, the squawk of gulls, and the rhythmic slaps, not hard, but stinging, that Luther was administering to my cheeks. There was no Wagner, the Madonna was a print, there was no gilding on the bedstead. And I doubt the fucking was real either. But I was naked and the one handcuff was still in place.

'OK, OK, I'm awake.'

He undid the handcuff. His breath smelled of bacon, the best of course.

'I'm hungry,' I said, 'thirsty, I have a headache and I want a pee.'

'The door in the corner has an en suite behind it. Your clothes are on the chair over there. Man, they good quality, especially the suit. English?'

'Italian, I think. But I bought them here.' I thought about it. 'Your bosses paid.'

He leant against the doorjamb, picking his teeth, while I went through the motions, shaved, showered, got dressed in my nice new clothes. There was a full length mirror. I looked more respectable than I had since my wedding. No, better than that even. My wedding suit, even though it wasn't formal, had still been hired and had not fitted anything like as well as this lot. People will see me coming, I thought. Touch haggard though.

He took me downstairs to the also ensuite kitchen which was clean and bright enough for brain surgery. There he put the finishing touches to pancakes and eggs florentine while I got through a bowl of sliced kiwi fruit, watermelon and mango. The coffee was a medium Columbian with cream, perfect in its way but I should have preferred a darker roast. I didn't say so though.

He got to looking at his watch a touch impatiently before I'd finished.

'No toast then?' I asked.

'Go fuck yourself.'

On the way out he picked up my shabby small holdall and handed it to me. It wasn't heavy, only half full. Without opening it I guessed it had my toiletries in it, and the books I'd bought at Borders. He also gave me my new hat and new coat.

'Miss Nicola said you should have these. Put them on.'

The coat was the Burberry mac I'd bought for myself, not unlike the one her Dad wore, but taupe. I pulled the hat so the brim came down towards my eyes and ran a finger round it like Alain Delon does in *Samuräi*.

The basement was a car-bay. He opened the front passenger door of the Buick. I got in. He went round the other side. Set the engine going.

'OK. Be a good boy and you won't get hurt. The Glock I'm packing carries a fragmentation projectile and I'll shoot you in the stomach with it if you cause even an itsy-bitsy bit of trouble. If they don't get you morphine within ten minutes the pain alone will kill you. Right?'

'Right on.'

But he'd jogged a memory. Glocked.

'Did you kill Jefferson?'

He turned down Powell.

'More than one Glock in our armoury.'

And pulled in by the Handlery yet again, taking the space in front of a white mini bus. Along the side the name of a firm, a telephone number, and, in bigger letters: Airport Shuttle. It edged out into the traffic, on a tight wheel-lock, straightened and was gone. Lois Cooper was waiting a yard or so away, in front of the window of a very upmarket antique shop. She opened the passenger door, took my elbow as I got out, handed me a ticket with a number on it.

'You left a bag in the left luggage facility. Go and collect it.'

I did that. She stood behind me while I waited.

'Tip him, when he brings it out. There should be a bill-fold in your hip pocket. Twenty dollar bill.'

'Twenty?'

'We want him to remember you.'

Was it the same black leather bag? Or its twin? It was heavy, loc-ked, with wheels at the back. But not the same, not exactly. Or was it? The trouble is given two bags built in the same way, made out of the same materials, how do you tell the difference? Not the Oriental this time but a small Filipino with a face like a walnut hoisted it into the trunk. I never touched it. He was pleased with the tip. He'd remember me. And the suit, and the hat, and the coat.

State 101 down the inside of the Bay to San Francisco International. Low flyovers over mean streets, housing crowded on hillsides to the right, to the left reclaimed mudflats littered with industries already dying and dead, marshalling yards, quays with hoists like praying mantises. Or should that be preying. The water when we saw it the colour of pewter and only a shade or two darker than the sky. Los Angeles 380 said the white letters on green as we sped under them.

San Bruno and the slipway that would take us up over the free-way and down to the departure terminal. Usual stuff, planes going too slow coming in over the Bay from the north-east, climbing too steeply up, up and away to the south-east and below them girders and glass, bad-tempered drivers dropping anxious travellers, squab-bles over trolleys, where the fuck's the check-in.

But that wasn't quite the way it was for us. First of all Luther tried out a comic routine.

'See the thing, is, Lois, we have to both park the wheels and look after Kit here, make sure he don't do a runner, like these two jobs are in two different places at once, and really both these are jobs for a man, and man, since you had your pecker off I'm the only man here.'

'You're full of shit, Luther. Pull over and let us out.'

And as he put the car by the curb she snapped a hand cuff on my right wrist. The other was already on her left. She slung a purse on a shoulder strap over her right shoulder and then kicked my shin to show it was time to get out.

'You carry your holdall. Luther will take the big case. Shit's sake your hat's crooked.'

She tutted and on the sidewalk in front of the automatic doors straightened it, pulled the brim back over my eyes, tweaked up the collar of my coat. Then she grinned.

'You look like Inspector Gadget,' she said. 'You know they've made a real movie?'

'I've seen the ads.'

During all this the minibus airport shuttle arrived. I could see it reflected in the glass doors. We must have overtaken it on the way. There were six or eight passengers, one of them at least a young girl. As Lois pushed me towards the doors the luggage piled up around them. Then we were through, walking briskly across the concourse, just the two of us. Luther and the Buick, with the big bag still in it, had gone, off to the carparks I assumed.

'Right. In this purse I have two things of interest to you. An FBI ID which I'll show if anyone challenges me why I have you cuffed to me. And a .38 special which I'll shoot you with if you fuck me about. Have I made myself clear?'

I sighed.

'Crystal,' I said.

'Now we're just going into the pre-departure lounge for forty minutes or so and sit in the seats there.'

'What do I do if I want the loo?'

'You pee yourself.'

Well, you know how it is under that sort of threat. After twenty minutes I had my left hand in the pocket of the Burberry and was clutching my dick through the lining and my nice new suit trousers. But I, um, held on. Then, after twenty-two minutes more Luther returned. They had a quick confab and decided my apparent agony was genuine and he took me to the rest-room, but still insisted on holding on to his end of the cuff while I performed. One handed. Left-handed. With a full cut Burberry flopping about me. If you're a feller reading this, try it.

Then they took me into the long hall with the check-in counters and we joined the Virgin Atlantic queue. It was long. No one had been flying American for nearly a week, not if they could get on a foreign plane. I guess it showed their usual forward planning and attention to detail that the Lennox clan had made the reservations at least a week earlier. When we got so there was only one Brit family between us and the desk, Luther handed me a long envelope.

'Ticket and your passport,' he murmured.

The clock on the fascia above the check-in showed ten before four in the afternoon. I was surprised it was so late, but remembered that my sleep had been drugged and long and it hadn't occurred to me to check out the time until then. Basically it was that grey sky Mark Twain learnt to hate so much, had made me think it was still morning. That day it didn't want to shift. I looked at the ticket. Economy. Bastards.

I told the check-in clerk that my holdall was cabin luggage. He asked me if I'd packed it myself. If I had left it untended since I'd packed it, all that stuff. Davidson put the larger one we'd taken from the Handlery on the belt. The clerk wrapped the baggage claim label round the handle, stapled the tag to my ticket, slipped in a boarding card. As we got away we passed another Brit family. I'm almost sure they were the same ones I'd seen having breakfast in the Radisson at Santa Barbara. The girl, and I now realised I had seen her getting out of the Handlery shuttle bus, said to her mum: 'At the end of this flight we'll be halfway, won't we? Halfway round the world.'

'Halfway when we cross the International Date Line,' said Mum. 'We don't get to Sydney till several hours after that.'

The eighteen-year-old lad was telling his dad off, because like everyone else they'd told the clerk that their bags hadn't been left untended since they were packed.

'You fibbed, Dad. We left the bags in the hotel luggage room all morning...'

Nevertheless his dad hoisted a soft leather bag, black, on to the belt. It had wheels at the back.

We headed towards the departure gates and security. With handcuffs and at least one gun? No problem. Lois flashed her badge, her FBI ID. Suddenly Luther Davidson was no longer with us. He'd slipped away somewhere else. She chatted up the guards or whatever, dipped into her purse, came up with a much bigger envelope stuffed with official looking papers. They took us to one side. They went through the papers. They looked at me curiously, then with extreme dislike. The one who frisked me, big red face, big stomach struggling to break the buttons of the shirt that held it in, deliberately squeezed my balls as if he wanted them off. They went through the small bag — it held just what I expected, my clothes and my books. They handled the books as if they were radioactive shit.

'This Burroughs guy,' this one had the lean, thin look of a professional book-burner, 'That the guy was a junkie and a pederast?'

'He liked cats too,' I said.

They let us through.

'What was all that?' I asked, resisting the temptation to stroke my scrotum.

Lois stuffed the papers back into her purse.

186

'Deportation order. You are an academic. You've been on a sabbatical at UC Berkeley, but you were caught getting in the knickers of a twelve-year-old, the daughter of the Prof you were renting a room from. Because of your academic status both here and in Oxford University, England, it was felt OK to deport you rather than have you face a mandatory rape charge. After all you hadn't got further than finger fucking. Don't worry. I'm only coming with you until I've seen you on to the plane. Once on board you're a tourist again. Oh yes, Mr Heart said, if we're asked, you're a lepidopterist. What's a lepidopterist?'

'Butterfly expert.'

'They have experts in butterflies?'

We went up an escalator and got on a travelator for what seemed like a mile into a big circular satellite rotunda, a glassed-in doughnut of a space with a fountain in the hole and pods to planes all round the outer rim. Inside there were numbered sitting areas. The one by our gate, my gate, was nearly full but we still got two places together on a low padded bench for four. We could see the Virgin Atlantic 747 outside with its mock beefcake girl on the nose. They were still unloading in the middle of a quick turn-round. Men in hard hats and red dungarees were even using a lift to take a small car out of its belly. I'd never seen that done before. I said so. Lois looked bored.

I said to her: 'Mr Heart is a whimsical sort of chap, isn't he? Nabokov, who wrote *Lolita*, was a lepidopterist.'

She yawned.

Serendipitously, I speculated. Lois Cooper could hardly have been further from the immortal nymphet. Butch, middle-aged, an ex-man, fat, corseted and smelling of mother. Why had she had it done if she was going to end up like this? I nearly asked her but just in time we were told to get ready for boarding. Then, as we stood up, amongst the general stir all round us, me gathering bag, hat and coat, Nicola Heart suddenly appeared, sweeping round the carpeted corridor between the seating, duster-coat billowing behind her. I wondered what had happened to my Tijuana shades. Left them in the Duchess, I reckon.

'Change of plan, Lois. He's coming with us after all.'

She turned to me. She was wearing Ray Ban shades, real ones, natch, and customised denims under the long cotton duster coat. It had padded shoulders. Her makeup was quieter than usual: she looked like a minor executive for a PR firm, or perhaps a film studio.

Largeish shoulder bag.

'Come on.'

She took my elbow.

'The hat looks nice,' she said.

Lois, her voice fluking for once, bleated: 'What's the matter, what's gone wrong?'

We were already trotting round the rotunda towards the moving walkway. Beneath us fuelling trucks, dumpers, those little tractors they have on tarmacs, the ones that tow the baggage and the meal containers, twisted and turned in their endless measured ballet.

'Gone pear-shaped. AFT and the real Feds are on the way to Homage. They've even called out the National Guard.'

'Why do we need him?'

She meant me.

'Dad thinks he might have hostage value.'

'Him? No chance.'

Thanks a bundle, I thought.

We reached the escalator. Lois went first. Nicola gave me a push.

'Down you go.'

But at the bottom, instead of going back into the security check and passport control areas they headed towards a door marked Private Departures and at this moment Nicola, behind me, seemed to trip and stumble against me, her hand in my back, throwing me forward into Lois. I think it was on purpose. Prevented me from taking in an announcement about a United American flight, probably saying boarding was under way.

'Shit,' she cried.

'The fuck you're doing,' shouted Lois. She turned on me, and backed through the swinging door at the same time, then all three of us were through.

Another corridor took us to a glassed-in hall or foyer looking out from the ground level on to the airside tarmac. There were desks against the inner wall, Lyle Heart and Luther Davidson doing business at one of them. We sat on seats with our backs to the glass. The big planes thundered in and out behind us. Eventually a coloured girl, very smart in a uniform, glossy hair in a bee-hive, stamped documents and handed them to him. You didn't have to read her lips to guess: 'Have a nice trip, Mr Heart.' He put them in a slim document case and they came across to us.

'Got him? Well done. Just in time, eh Kit?' He turned back to the two women, lifted the document case. 'We might as well get on board. They've approved the flight plan and they'll give us clearance in twenty minutes.'

He pushed at the glass doors and by some freak of acoustics or whatever for a moment or two we could hear the PA system again.

'Mr Christopher Shovelin, this is your last call. Please proceed to gate 8 where flight VS20, Virgin Atlantic for Heathrow, London, is preparing for take-off, will Mr Christopher...' and then we were in a red painted Moke and zipping round the edge of the field to where the private planes were parked.

Chapter 25

It was a great flight. OK, I was agitated and the offer of a drink, Buck's Fizz with freshly squeezed, though unlike the girls the oranges can't have been Californian since it was July, was irresistible — agitated and bewildered, but I couldn't help enjoying it. A bit. I reckoned I stood little chance of getting out of it all alive so why not risk half a flute of champers? After three years off the booze it went straight to my head.

The first bonus was the take-off of VS20, Virgin Atlantic for Heathrow. Precisely because it was utterly normal. It didn't blow up. Nor did the United American jumbo which followed it.

As we taxied and then waited for final clearance at the end of a runway I had time to think. My larger bag had been swapped for another like it — probably in the Handlery luggage room, maybe by Luther Davidson while we were at the airport. Perhaps the Handlery luggage room had just been the place where its near twin had been identified. Or maybe the cases had not been swapped at all, but just their contents. Anyway, it would be possible to show that a case I had checked into the Handlery had been manipulated by me to travel on a plane I was not on, a plane that later crashed. The case against me would be compounded when a similar case was pulled off Virgin Atlantic VS20 at Heathrow and shown to be packed with stuff not mine, though it was tagged with a number corresponding to the one stapled to my ticket. None of which would be looked into until after the fat lady sang, that is after the plane, not VS20, had blown up. I'd got that far when we started moving again.

Just as we got airborne we had what looked like a near miss which put my heart in my mouth. The thing is the take-off and landing runways at San Francisco International form an X and cross each other. I sucked in breath but Lyle Heart, in front, said it was quite normal. But it was enough to break my train of thought and there were more distractions on the way.

Nicola sat opposite me, our knees almost touching, Lois Cooper made with the drinks and the canapés (this time I stuck to orange juice) Luther piloted the Lear with Heart next to him as co-pilot. We took a turn over the Bay, got a farewell glance of the skyscrapers and then the Golden Gate Bridge, gleam of sun on both now, the Pacific, then inland again over San José. He took us down the San Andreas

Valley at ten thousand feet, the Sierra Nevada's peaks level with us on the left, the coastal ranges and the ocean on the right. Almost as soon as we were clear of the Bay the sky cleared to a perfect blue. Nicola explained as if to a child:

'Hot air inland, cold over the ocean. The Golden Gate makes a funnel, the cold air is sucked through as the hot air rises, and its humidity condenses into fog. It's much better once the summer's over and the temperatures are not so different or work the other way once the snows hit the sierra...'

'That's not the only thing that needs explaining,' I muttered.

'No, I suppose not.' She nibbled the side of a finger nail for a moment and her eyes, the same shifting pale topaz to green as her mother's, held mine, serious, calculating. I wondered: did they both use the same lipstick or breath-freshener? The one with the blackcurrant tang? Then she tossed her hair back and looked over her shoulder.

'Dad? Is there any reason why I shouldn't tell Kit what's been going on?'

'I guess not. If he lives long enough he'll figure it out anyway.'

'OK.' She leant forward so we were almost cheek by jowel and I caught the fragrances that took me back to the Golden Gateway Inn. I reckon I was a bit mean about the way I told you about that before. Maybe I wasn't that good, and she was a touch self-centred about it, but what the hell. Experiences like that don't come to a fifty-year-old bloke like me that often. Anyway, put it like this. During what followed I wasn't that unaware of animal magnetism and even a sort of longing closer to nostalgia than desire. Especially when she put her hand on my knee.

'I guess you've realised we're broke. Properly broke. The oil dried up, the aquifer dropped. We got caught in a couple of scams, pension funds, Savings and Loan, Okie oil, that sort of thing. Grandad will keep buying arms and so forth from dodgy sources and selling them on to the vigs and the militias at a loss. Anyway, we're way beyond what our assets can raise. You get the picture.'

I nodded. I even composed my face into a seriousness I hoped she might take for sympathy.

'So. Together we dreamed up this scam to extort a hundred million.'

'By blowing up planes?'

She shrugged, almost petulantly, perceiving perhaps a hint of disapprobation in my tone.

'It seemed as good a way as any other.'

'And part of it was you needed a fall-guy. Or two.'

'That's right.' Quicker now, as if she had detected a note of understanding this time. 'It worked out like this. First thing was Grandad had a room full of Russian stuff, AKs, rocket grenade launchers, that sort of thing, from Nicaragua. He'd picked it all up from a colonel in the Pentagon who'd been in charge of collecting the ex-Sandanista weaponry that was handed in after the armistice between the Sandanistas and the Contras. And one day, about eight weeks ago, it all vanished. Well, Lois and Luther had a little sideshow importing medicines from Tijuana, through a guy called Guzman, and to cut a long story short we worked out that Jerry and your friend Jefferson, had stolen the AKs and exchanged them for a truck-load of the latest anti HIV and AIDS drugs. So it seemed only fair to make them the fall-guys. And we began to set it up that they'd be seen in or around LAX, then we'd put a guy on UA324 who looked a bit like Jefferson and was using documentation that identified him as such, and then he'd walk off the plane, just the way he did. That all worked out fine. And we had Jerry lined up to meet Jefferson in the Da Vinci that evening where they'd be collared by the LAPD... well, you get the picture.'

'But it went wrong. How?'

'Jefferson rumbled us. So he... had to go.'

'And then?'

'Well, we already knew a bit about you. We'd got into his files and so forth and it wasn't difficult to get the picture.'

'And you got me over to fill his place?'

'We reckoned another fall-guy could be useful. Yep. Once we knew you were on your way we could go ahead with offing him. Trouble was... somehow you got to La Jolla a whole six hours earlier than we thought possible.'

'Once I got the message it was urgent I traded in the BA ticket you sent and got a Virgin Atlantic instead. So. Jefferson's body was still there when I arrived.'

'Yeah. We were waiting for it to get dark before we got him out.'

'Waiting? Where?'

'In his bedroom closet. By the time you got through the door.'

'Christ. Who?'

'Me, Luther and Lois. Then Lois followed you down to the sea.

Why didn't you search the apartment?'

I thought back. I should have done. It's what private eyes do.

'I was spooked. In shock. Grieving.'

She paused, looked out of the window. I guess she sensed she was coming to the part where a sort of apology might be in order, and she felt a touch awkward about it.

'Yosemite National Park over there on the left. Not that you can see it properly from this distance and height.'

I looked past her shoulder. Range after range of mountains, the rock almost as white as snow, so only the presence of some real snow on the north-facing slopes, told you it was rock, rose out of rolling valleys of dense coniferous forest. Quite a sight.

'See that twisting valley, really deep, deeper than the others. And that huge rock like half a sugar loaf? That's it.'

It was almost gone, almost behind us.

Her Dad intervened.

'Did they catch the axeman?'

'Sure, they caught the axeman.'

She looked back at me, eyes now, through some trick of the shifting light, flecked with yellow shards.

'Then, after UA324,' I resumed, 'you sent me down to Santa Monica so Jake Carson could off me.'

'Yeah! And you handled that real well!' The admiration in her voice matched the shininess of those eyes. She meant it.

'But later you changed your mind. Why? I get it. You realised they weren't going to pay up. You needed a second plane to crash.'

'That's it. And we already had one lined up... as a sort of fail-safe. Once we knew they weren't going to pay we had two objectives. To get you to San Francisco, and with baggage too big to be cabin baggage.'

All that stuff about buy yourself some decent clothes. And the FBI scam. I thought about it, tried to be objective.

'You know, once the basic idea was there, you, someone, was very good at improvising, coping with new situations, and so on. Daring, quick, clever.'

'Mother mostly.'

'Oh come on!' Heart again, looking over his shoulder.

'Well you too Dad. And that was sometimes the trouble. You didn't always let the other know what you were up to, or had said.'

I looked out my window. The San Andreas Valley, from this height flat as the proverbial, chequered by all the different crops, netted with rivers, roads and irrigation canals, stretched to the coastal ranges and the deep lilac haze over the Ocean. California's, indeed much of the US's, salad bowl.

'And of course Jerry Lennox, the real Jerry, wasn't missing at all,' I said.

'Oh no. Of course not. He lived and worked in San Francisco. You could have looked him up in the telephone book there. His law firm's office anyway. Where he lived was another matter, and he moved around. Used the Handlery as a post office. Once he realised we were on to him for stealing the AKs he kept a very low profile.'

'Why did you kill him?'

'You met him an hour or so before we expected you to. You had a long talk with him. We didn't know how much you and he had pieced together what was going on, and Dad here reckoned he'd be seriously in the way while we got the bags on to the particular plane we wanted them on.'

'And Carson?'

'His first loyalty was always to Jerry. As soon as we realised you were going to meet him we guessed it was to ask him how you could find Jerry, and if he felt it was in Jerry's interest to tell you, he would.'

'Someone must have been following me. All morning. I didn't see anyone. I wasn't aware of that.'

'Yours truly some of the time. And Lois.'

'Lois?' How could I have missed her? Her, of all people.

'She's very good.'

And of course, that sort of obesity is a lot more common in America than England. I probably saw dozens of really fat women that morning without registering them.

'So there you are, that's it.' She pulled away into her back rest, that slight sad smile on her face again.

'Hardly!'

'You're safe until Dad decides you're more nuisance than you're worth.'

'That's not what I had in mind.'

She lifted an eyebrow.

'Another plane has my bag on it. Presumably now filled with explosive. It's on its way somewhere. It'll blow up somewhere on the way or as it lands. Where?'

'Well, we're not going to tell you that.'

'Why not? You might as well.'

She leant forward, touched my knee again.

'You're a slippery customer, Kit Shovelin. So don't ask. The moment we think you know, we'll kill you.'

She put her finger to her lips and then placed it on mine. Nuff said. But there was one more thing.

'Who actually killed Jefferson? Pulled the trigger?'

'Don't you know?'

'It was someone he knew. Someone he had allowed into his apartment. From his position when I found him he could have been sitting on the settee while the killer sat or knelt on the floor beside him. That implies some sort of closeness, doesn't it.'

Again the misty look in her eyes, the sad smile, the hand on my knee. But what she said was gently mocking.

'Gee, Mr Shovelin, that's the first time I've heard you talk the way a detective should...'

Between Fresno and Bakersfield we were buzzed by an F16.

'Is he really interested in us,' Heart asked, 'or is he just fooling around?'

'Shit knows,' Davidson answered. 'We're not far from Vandenburg, though.'

'Vandenburg?' I asked.

'Big airforce base on the coast. North of Santa Barbara.'

They were polite with me. Almost jolly. Wanted me to relax, keep from thinking too hard.

'First trip to the States nearly over then, Kit,' Heart asked. 'What do you think of us?'

'All he's seen is Californ-eye-ay. That's not America.'

'How true. Kit, the Californian Republic is a country on its own, geographically, economically, culturally....' and so on.

'I enjoyed the seals,' I said, thinking of La Jolla. It was all I could think of saying. 'And the sea otters at Carmel.'

'Come back in Spring. When the whales migrate along the coast. That is something. We always take the boat out from Santa Barbara, at least once each season. Cruise round the Channel Islands.'

The boat. Their own, of course. And probably as big as the Britannia. Like the plane, the pad on Russian Hill, Homage, trips from coast to coast to hear Domingo. Bastard. Cancelling Sydney so he could sing at the Met.

'LA on the right. We're just crossing the San Bernardino Freeway. Twenty minutes.' Davidson again.

'Have we a plan?' Nicola leaned towards her father. He'd taken off his jacket. Looked as neat as a tailor's dummy in razor-creased slacks, piqué short-sleeved shirt a sort of olivey rather than charcoal black. His eyes too were dead like a dummy's beneath his silver hair. Seeing him more and more as he really was I realised what a good performance he'd put on as Agent Fowler.

Had it been necessary? That charade? Probably not, but typical of the way these people worked: they improvised, they did not always tell each other what they were doing, they muddled through. Which was why being dropped or sucked into this muddle in the middle of it all had been so confusing. All of which was now borne out by Heart's urbane shrug.

'We'll see how bad things are. If we can't talk our way round it we'll pick up the General, and fly on to the Costa Rica spread.'

'Won't Bella mind? I mean you just blew her son away.'

'Bella's out to lunch on another planet. Forgotten she ever had a son. China's the one's going to be pissed off about that. If anyone's stupid enough to tell her. She always carried a flag for Jerry, even though he turned out a gay leftie nerd.'

Nicola chewed a knuckle, looked out of the window at the dried up, yellow sierra below, dotted with scrub like a rash.

'San Diego on the right. Lindbergh wants to know what the fuck?' Luther had earphones on now, and a stalk mike angled towards his mouth.

'Tell them what the fuck. Just get us over the border and then take us home on the Mex side. I don't want them to guess who we are if we can prevent it. Speak Spanish. Tell him we're heading for Tijuana. Sound drunk. Make 'em think we're Spic joyriders. More money than sense.'

Luther flipped a switch, rattled away, slurring his consonants, speaking a sort of hybrid Spanglish. Then with San Diego downtown glittering back at us we banked, began to lose height and headed east. But for a second or so the sun filled my window, warmed my knees. Then we banked the other way and the bay shone up at us like a silver shield neatly sliced by the white boomerang curve of the Coronado Bridge.

'*The fuck?*' Heart called. He sounded angry.

Luther pushed his earphones back.

'There's the Naval Air Station at Border Field on the coast, and shit like the Naval Space Surveillance Station ten miles east. They think we a Mex plane overflying them they'll put a missile up our ass. I'll cross the border when we're downwind of them.'

He flew on. There were dried up valleys below now, deep and narrow enough to be called canyons, then a lake, artificial, dammed, almost empty. He turned south again.

'We'll need two fuel stops to get to Ticoland,' he said.

'Make the first at the ranch.'

'Here's the border. Three minutes. Seatbelts.'

I leant towards Nicola.

'He knows what he's doing, does't he? I mean he's not just a cook. Talented guy.'

'Don't put me on, Kit.'

She looked nervous, nearly frightened. The landing? Or what would happen after?

'Tell me,' I asked, 'you said this whole jape has just been for the loot, yes?'

'The loot. Yes.'

'And where, how, do you get to spend it?'

'No problem if no one knows who did it all. If we're compromised, and it looks as if we might be, we split up adopt other, prepared identities... it's all arranged.'

'Must have cost.'

She looked at me like I was dumber than she'd thought.

'There'll be change out of a hundred million bucks, believe me.'

'Yes. I suppose there will.'

I looked out again. Suddenly it seemed we were much lower, the ground streaming away as our deep purple shadow streaked ahead of us and on the right. What had it cost to set up. A million? Even five? Peanuts. Fences, towers, the border again. A track winding lazily through low dried up pasture. I remembered. They used this plane or one very like it, to go on safari, hunting for Mexican illegals coming over the border. And if they found any they dropped napalm on them.

We crossed the black top east of Heavengate, made a wide circle, losing height all the time, crossed the road again, and there they were, less than five hundred feet below us. They were parked up against the wind-pump on the hill and the water-tank, a small convoy of trucks and vans with a portable aerial sticking up high enough to make you think for a moment we might hit it. The Flag — on its own freestanding flagstaff. Men in uniforms, displacement pattern but basically yellow, desert boots, round peaked caps, some with carbines. Some even waved.

'Oh fuck,' said Heart. And the wheels bumped, bounced and rumbled on levelled hardcore and for twenty seconds or so we towed a cloud of dust in our slipstream. !

Chapter 26

Heart covered the mouthpiece of the telephone handset he was holding.

'They say it's to do with firearms and weapons. In short, the General's collection. That's why they've got the AFT with them. I don't think they're connecting us with UA324.'

He looked round at us all. We were in the main reception room at the front of the house, the Southern-style mini-mansion. The cannon, the flagpoles, the lawns and cedars were framed by muslin curtains which swelled like sails on faery seas in front of partially open casements. Inside, the westering sun turned the ormulu and crystal chandelier into gold and diamonds, formed dark brown ice on the central round mahogany table. A Lennox in kilt and sporran, with a basket-hilted claymore at his side, posed against a Highland mountain landscape above an Adams fireplace that had probably never been used as such. Not, at any rate, since it was shipped out.

'Bullshit,' the General rasped from his motorised chair. 'The marshalls' office knows all about it. It's just a fucking collection. Like stamps.'

I was standing near Lois and Luther, close up to the door, in a corner the sun had gone from, leaving shadows behind like cast-off garments. I noticed now how, though growing anxiety was etching deeper lines on their faces, they exchanged half-grins.

'They want to check it out,' Heart replied, still holding the handset. 'Documentation against what's there, see what's missing.'

'The fuck they do. Why don't they just drive up to the gate and ask for admittance then? It's an excuse. It's your ass they want to fist, your pussy they're sniffing at. Once they're in they'll find something, anything, to warrant holding us, turn the place over.'

His face had gone crimson, like the sun was setting over the fissures and pinnacles of a rock-face, and spittle gathered in the corners of his sharkish mouth. But his eyes remained alert, sharp, like needles.

'Maybe,' his son-in-law still had a shot, as they say, in his locker, 'and maybe they'll find where you keep your tactical nuclear device.'

'What do you think we should do then, Grandpa?' Nicola asked. She was sitting on the edge of a deep chair covered in emerald satin. I guess it was meant to go with the green damask on the walls.

'Tell them to come back tomorrow. When we've got our lawyers in.'

'We owe Wedenfeld and Christoffersen three million dead presidents and they won't get out of bed for us until we've paid off some of it. You know that Granpa.'

'I know that, but they fucking don't.'

It was the first real indication I'd had that the family was genuinely short of a dollar or two.

'May be they do,' Heart said. Then he took his hand away from the mouthpiece and spoke into it.

'I'll call you back.'

He replaced the phone. He looked round.

'I wish we could speak to China.'

Nicola looked at her watch. 'Seven hours to go.'

What did she mean: seven hours? China was in New York where it was now what? Half-past ten at night? Watching the last act of *Madame Butterfly*. If it wasn't over already. Puccini's no Wagner for passing time that would have passed anyway.

*

'They've got a company out there at least,' the General croaked. 'For all we know they've got missile launchers, mortars in those trucks. They know there's more at stake than a foolish old man's toys. I tell you what. They're looking for another Waco. They enjoyed that. They loved that. They want to do it again.'

'Listen,' said Nicola. 'I'm trying to think the way Ma would if she were here. Let's suppose they know who we really are. That we've got more to hide than a collection of weapons, some of which we might not be able to explain. Let's suppose they know, or at any rate suspect we got that bomb on to UA324 and blew it. That we're the people threatening to do the same again. This is what Ma would say to them: OK, you're right. But what you don't know is that the second bomb is in place, it's in the air, a radio signal will set it off just before touchdown. Give us the money, and let us fly our plane out of here. When we're safe we'll cancel the explosion. You've got seven hours to make up your minds and do it. Shift ass. That's what Ma would say.'

*

It's in the air. It's primed to go off. We'll cancel it. Seven hours.

*

Either because of the situation or because the last direct rays of the sun had slipped up into the sky, Heart's face had gone from pasty to a sort of luminous, blueish chalk. He pulled a big pink paisley patterned handkerchief out of the top pocket of the jacket he was wearing again and wiped his palms. He sighed.

'It's one fuck of a risk,' he said. Then: 'It won't work, Nicola. They'll pull every plane out of the sky. Make them land anywhere but where they're supposed to land.'

She thought for a moment.

'Hey, that's assuming they know the bomb will be detonated at the plane's scheduled landing place. Maybe I was wrong just now. They don't have to know that, we don't tell them that. Come to think of it we don't say seven hours, we don't say when. Just that it blows on touchdown. Like that film with Brad Pitt, when the bus stops it blows. When the plane lands it blows. Meanwhile we can stop it, or we'll tell them how to stop it as soon as the Banco de Corpus Cristi Internacional has accepted their transfer of a hundred million.'

'Keanu Reeves,' I said.

'What?'

'Keanu Reeves in *Speed*. Not Brad Pitt.'

'Shut the fuck up, why don't you?'

The General wheezed, then croaked: 'It might work.'

'If we're going to convince them, we've got to work it out very, very carefully.' Lyle Heart again. 'They've got to believe we're telling the truth. They've got to believe the bomb will go off if we don't stop it, they've got to believe we can stop it, and we've got to do this in such a way we don't give away how it's done.'

'So let's sit down and think it through.'

Again Heart popped a couple of pills. Duraphet or ritalin — uppers anyway. I could have done with a lift myself. Especially in view of what came next.

'What about the Limey? What's his name? Over there?' The General meant me. 'He's no use now, is he? Take him outside and put

201

a bullet in his head, why not?'

Oh shit.

Nicola looked across the room at me. A sort of half smile glowed in her eyes for a moment, like sunshine on heather, then it was gone. I'd seen that wistful smile once before. When we were shagging in the Golden Gateway Inn. I shrugged. Sydney fucking Carton. I could hear the tumbril rumbling. Nicola turned towards Lois.

'Lois,' she called. 'Take Shovelin somewhere safe and well out of the way and cuff him to something he can't move. Kill him if he's a nuisance. Take Luther with you to be sure.'

But at that moment, as Lois put her fat paw on my shoulders, a dull roar that had been increasing in volume suddenly became unavoidable, unignorable, and a peal of headlight beams swung round the walls and ceiling of the big room.

'The fuck?' the General asked.

The three of them turned to the windows, from behind them we shifted to get a view round them. A fleet of RVs, recreation vehicles, at least ten of them, more if you counted the ones towed by SUVs as two, was trundling into the big semicircle of gravel outside. Flags fluttered from aerials and masts, Old Glory, the Confederate flag, the Texan lone star and the California bear amongst them; men stood on running boards and waved shotguns and rifles or just their huge hats, Stetsons but the ten gallon variety. Above the noise of their engines rose the high cries and cheers one associates, in the cinema, with rodeos and bronco-busting.

Lois could see the question on my face.

'They come every year at this time. And these are just the vanguard. Come Sunday there'll be another hundred vehicles.'

'Why?'

'They love the General and what he stands for is the official reason. In fact they buy up the excess stock from his collection, duplicates, ammunition, and so forth, he let's them go cheap if he reckons they'll be put to good use.'

'Which is?'

'Defending our rights to life, liberty and the pursuit of happiness. And to carry side-arms.'

'Will they fight for him? Will they take on the National Guard.'

'Who knows?'

The general hollered: 'Is that bastard Limey still here. Get the motherfucker out.'

Lois prodded my left kidney with the muzzle of her .38 special. 'Make a break for it,' she said, 'make my day.'

*

They marched me halfway round the estate trying to find something they could feel very certain I wouldn't shift. They seemed to credit me, like the village blacksmith, with the strength of ten. I ended up in the old *finca*, with one cuff on my wrist and the other fastened to the bar on a window facing out on to the desert. They had to take out the framed moveable mosquito netting to do it. The room was empty. Maybe the one Jefferson and Jerry Lennox had taken the AKs from.

'And if you want a piss, you've got a hand free, just piss on the floor.'

'Listen. Before you go. Which of you killed Wilbur Jefferson? Just so, if I do get a chance, I can pay off a debt.'

They looked at each other, shrugged.

'Miss Heart,' said Lois. 'She done it. Nicola.'

I nearly, very nearly vomited. Again.

*

The sun had gone. The same sun, it occurred to me, that would soon be rising in Australia — tomorrow. What if all that stuff about Domingo cancelling Sydney and going to the Met was guff. The true McGuffin. Right from the start, from before my visit to Homage, China Heart had been booked to fly to Sydney a week later. Yesterday? Suddenly I felt icy cold. What was going on? She'd gone. She wasn't going to blow up her own plane. Somehow leave a device on it after she'd got off? Unlikely.

But even while all this was forming in my mind the first explosion came. I happened to be looking out of the window at the time — in fact the cuff and bar were so arranged it was difficult not to — and I saw the orange fireball, spinning in on itself against the night sky like a great whirligig marble, a second before the crump came. A few moments later a gust of hot air and that smell of burnt kerosene I'll always associate with Nicola-Lola's Mona Lisa smile as she looked down at me. The mingled smell of kerosene and sex. Before the air in the Golden Gateway Inn began to smell like a dirty oven.

203

The Lear? Not just the jet, maybe not the jet at all, but if not, then the fuel dump. Refuelling for Ticoland, at Homage anyway, seemed no longer an option.

It was annoying. It interrupted a train of thought. I was almost there. Supposing China Heart had flown to Sydney after all, supposing UA128 was the flight to Sydney she'd taken yesterday as well as the plane we had seen take off today. San Fran to Sydney? How long? Christ, I had no idea. About the same as London to San Francisco or Los Angeles? That was ten or eleven hours. Leaving yesterday roundabout four thirty she'd never have made it in time to get to the opera house that night. Yes she would. Going with the sun. Actually crossing the International Date Line... my head was beginning to swim. I was just no good at this sort of thing. Was it already tomorrow today in Sydney? Did it make any difference? Anyway, if she was in Sydney, it wasn't to hear Domingo.

Shots. Distant and then close to. Small arms, carbines, nothing bigger. Yet. Then an amplified voice, booming across the grit and dried up thorn and the little sky-blue daisy-like flowers that still bloomed. Distorted by feedback but the words 'talk it through', and 'we'll give you ten minutes, no more' were there.

Then suddenly there was a hail of bullets, the crump and percussive bang of mortar fire, and the heavy clatter of a powerful machinegun. Outside, in the yard, a huge diesel engine coughed, roared, settled to a loud steady rumble. A gust of black fumes, strong enough to make me retch, swirled in through the unglazed window, then came the squeal of wheels tortured by the tracks that held them as, I supposed, the big tank slewed and trundled out of the yard.

They seemed to come from all sides. A couple of mortar bombs landed in the armouries to the side and opposite the room I was in, and they began to burn. The end of a burst of tracer smacked along the stucco wall outside my window but, as I struggled to get as low as the cuff would let me, gave out before it reached me. The bombardment lasted two or three minutes at least and was followed by smoke bombs which doubled me up, retching again and coughing, so I felt I'd have my lungs down my shirt front before anyone came.

Since the smoke clung to the floor I got up again to breath and saw a line of National Guardsmen, a squad twenty strong, deployed in scatter formation, trotting briskly over the visual ridge and down through the brush with carbines across their chests, the light from the flames flickering across them, across the masks they wore with staring round glass eyes. Padded with body armour they looked like Michelin men.

Ahead of them holes had been blasted in the security fence, possibly by rocket-propelled grenades. They were a touch clumsy coming through these: one guardsman got his padded jacket snagged on a loose wire and the men behind him piled up in a vulnerable line as he struggled to get free. They ended up under my wall, crouched, out of breath, and waiting for orders. Right there beneath my sill was a sergeant. He had out a map, a blown up aerial photograph of the whole of Homage.

'I think you've got it upside down,' I shouted, peering through the bars.

He leapt as if he'd been shot and thrust a big Bruniton-coated Beretta 92SB at my head. Bruniton? Sort of Teflon-type finish. I like to keep up with these things.

'*Stop*,' I screamed, 'I'm on your side, can't you see? They've fucking cuffed me to this bar...' Something like that anyway.

I don't know how well he could hear me through all the ambient noise and the gear he had on his head. He pulled some of it off and peered through the bars at me. He had a red face, plump like a plum, cropped white or sandy hair, looked about forty.

'Is there a garden and a pool up on the other side of all this?'

'Yes. Get me out of this before I fry and I'll show you.'

He stumbled along the wall towards the corner, waving at his men with his Beretta to follow him, which most seemed rather reluctant to do. However, he found his way through the arched gateway into the old *finca*, and down through the garden past the space left by the tank, and Heart's rooms which China Heart had told me were Jerry Lennox's. Coming over to me, and coughing with the smoke, which was swirling round us, not from the bombs now but the burning buildings, he placed the muzzle of his huge pistol up against the linking chain, just below the point where it joined the cuff Lois had closed on the bar.

'Jesus,' I said. 'I hope you know what you're doing.'

He shifted it all so the bullet would, hopefully, end in the wooden frame rather than ricochet about the room. I closed my eyes. This sort of thing always works in the movies, I thought, but does it in real life?

The bang, even with all the other noise, was enormous, and my wrist took a nasty jolt, but it came free all right, though of course with the other cuff still on and the chain hanging from it.

'Sergeant Jaruwelski,' he said. He stuffed the automatic in his belt, and held out a huge hand, took mine, crushed it.

'Kit Shovelin,' I said.

'Glad to meet you, Kit. Now,' he peered at the map again, 'Op Comms are that we come through a garden area, past a pond, a swimming pool perhaps, towards the back of the house.'

'I'll show you.'

'Much obliged, I promise you.'

The sky had taken on that soft velvety look, rich with colour, that goes with a sub-tropical nightfall. Big moths cruised the borders, fire-flies dithered, the glow from several flowers flickered over dark foliage and what wind there was kept the smoke back from the pool. Its ebony surface reflected flickering lights and flames. One of the nubile nudes had lost her head, the giddy young thing. Way out beyond the sunset, thousands of miles away, where the sun was still high and bright, UA128 had been airborne for nearly four hours. That is, if I hadn't got it all wrong and it was in pieces somewhere in the Ocean north-east of Christmas Island.

Beyond the pool the house, a greenish white in that light, was just beginning to burn behind the big semicircle of glass crowned with its glass dome, housing that tall, straight flowering palm. In front of the curved glass doors, flanked by their ornamental urns, a huge peacock strutted across the gravel, head bobbing for seeds, dragging its train behind it. Was it deaf, or what?

Jaruwelski waved those of his men who had actually had the nerve to follow him into cover below the outer rim of the pool, but he himself crouched behind the headless nymph with his carbine across the hollow her waist made between her hip and her chest. I sat with my knees up and my back against her plinth. I guess he thought she was made out of marble, but you could see from what was left of her head that she was only plaster.

Night and silence. For a moment. Distant shouts, a shot or two, someone screaming. I thought of the caravans and Winnebagos on the other side of the house. Were those amateurs really taking on the pros? Looking up I saw Jaruwelski caress the nymph's buttocks, his finger finding the cleavage and running up to her back. He looked down, saw me looking at him.

'Just testing,' he said.

Testing? For what?

'We've been told to cover the rear exits,' he went on. 'The main attack is coming from the front.'

Hardly had he said that when two fireballs, almost as big as that caused by the fuel dump blowing up, soared up on the other side of the house, casting an orange glow over everything.

'Hey,' Jaruwelski bellowed, 'I guess that's the tank taken out. Them's the fireballs from our new RL 35 missiles. They just burn their way in and fry what's inside.'

But there was still something or someone left to shoot at. The fireballs were followed by a cacophonous pandemonium of small arms fire punctuated with the crump of mortars and the whoosh of more missiles. Most of the windows lit up with white, blinding phosphorous and blew out. The dome shattered outwards as the cast iron frames twisted and glowed like fiery snakes, a splash of glass and burning palm fronds against the plum-coloured sky.

Yet a patch of blackness remained at the back of where the glass doors had been and in it chrome tubes flashed for a second before the General's wheelchair came gliding out of the darkness, through a shower of melting glass and on to the parterre. The General himself had relinquished the press-button controls: behind him, crouched, with her head down, Lois Cooper was now both the power pack and the control system. He had an M 60 heavy machine gun, Rambo's favourite weapon, across his knees, trailing a belt of heavy shells behind him, and as he came clear he fired, sending an arc of tracer high over to our right, then bringing it down in a graceful parabola towards us. It needed only two of its shells to complete the destruction of the nymph and mince Sergeant Jaruwelski into burger meat from the waist up.

Shaking his blood out of my eyes, I rolled down below the rim of the pool, scooping up the huge automatic he had dropped as he fell. Some of the National Guardsmen were already bolting back through the darkness, smashing madonna lilies as they found their way into a grove of arbutus, but three at least, out on the flanks, kept their heads, literally, and returned the general's fire with a hail of bullets from their semi-automatic rifles. The M 60 clattered to the ground, the wheel chair slewed to the side and he toppled out of it and into the pool like a ripped ragdoll. His body bounced up to the surface, still pumping blood, then slowly sank again. Meanwhile Lois attempted to scuttle away on the other side, on all fours, bum in the air, palms and stockinged knees scrabbling through the gravel, before she too was knocked sideways into a climbing plumbago which shed blue stars on her corpse.

It wasn't over yet. I'd been wrong about the Lear. Fuel-dumps maybe had gone, but the jet was still in action. It came howling over the roof, through the smoke and flames, bending and shredding them, its cannon blazing so shells smacked into the water, pluming steam like geezers. But they were hitting the ground now at ten yard intervals and again I escaped. I rolled on to my back to watch the plane hurtle on, and just above me it loosed its black turd. Forward thrust carried it beyond me, to the furthest edges of the gardens. Meanwhile the Lear soared upwards and just as it went beyond the glow of all the fires that raged beneath it, a missile like a dart swerved with its swerves, closed and struck like a snake. A beat, then it shattered in a starburst that would not have disgraced the biggest firework display in the world.

And down below the bomb exploded, the sudden tower of orange flame, the black smoke curtaining across the stars. The smell was the smell of loss and exhaustion, despair and defeat.

There was still Nicola-Lola.

She too came through the flaming arch where the doors had been, holding in each hand not one but two chrome-plated Colt .44. She blazed away at us across the pool. She stood for a moment, a Goddess, still in her billowing duster coat and denims, spitting lead and lightning from each hand. No one on my side of the pool seemed to have hung around to return her fire. Or they were all dead. I still had Jaruwelski's huge Beretta in my hand and I sighted on her, thinking of Jefferson, but I knew I'd miss. Over ten yards, I'd miss. The fingers of my other hand found the laser-torch I'd bought Richard in Tijuana. I turned it on, swung the red disk it threw on to the wall above her, down till it settled in her eye, spread at that distance to fill the whole eye-socket. She felt it, saw it, could presumably see the source. She lifted one shiny Colt and pointed it at me. Worked the mechanism, threw it away, she'd already emptied it, raised the second. Gripping Jarulwelski's gun now in both hands with my left hand clamped over the barrel, holding the torch so its tiny bulb was over the muzzle and keeping the circle of light in her eye, I squeezed the trigger.

The bullet went right through her head and came out the other side with a blast of hair, skin, bone and blood, but left her standing. Then, by some fluke of heat draughts and wind, a huge swathe of burning muslin drifted out of the flames and darkness behind, and, in a sinuous adagio, wrapped its lower lengths about her body. Dead already, she surrendered to its gentle rape.

Chapter 27

There was a general. Much younger than the General and with only one star on his helmet which was on the table in front of him. Fair hair razored to above his ears then flattened across his head from a parting on the left. Thin, white hands protruding from pressed buttoned cuffs. When I told him Mrs China Heart was in Sydney, possibly already in one of the lounges of the airport, or in a hotel room overlooking the arrivals runway, with a radio signalling device which would initiate an explosion in the freight hold of UA128 as it came into land, he refused to believe me.

'Frankly, Mr Shovelin, that's all horseshit. The lady you killed tried something like that on us, without actually naming names and places, before we attacked, and frankly I've never heard a greater pile of horseshit in all my life. Now, I can see what her motive might have been, and I can guess at yours. Your association with these people is proved, and no doubt you are laying the ground for some sort of plea-bargaining, but it won't wash. Not with me, no way.'

He bowed his head towards his laptop computer screen, head forward, the green light from it reflected in his steel-rimmed spectacles. Laboriously, inexpertly he continued to tap away, one-fingered, at the keyboard. We were in the huge Winnebago-type leisure vehicle that served as his CCC, command and control centre.

'General,' I tried again. 'If all this wasn't connected with the bombing of airliners, what was it for?'

'The feds working on information garnered by the Puzzle Palace located Homage as a centre for the warehousing and distribution of weaponry and other matériel to various vigilante and militia groups up and down the country.'

'And how do you think they were financing this operation?'

'Shit knows. Oil wells. Construction industry. Tourism.'

'They were broke, General.'

He looked up at me over the screen, eyes narrowed behind the spectacles. The tie-clip on his neat khaki tie caught the light now. Apart from the colouring of what he wore he could have been an IR inspector.

'Bastards like that don't get broke, Mr Shovelin.'

I sighed, turned away. Fuck it, I thought, I've done my best to save his ass. But then I thought of the English family on their round-the-world trip and turned to a female sergeant sitting in a corner with a stenography machine.

'Miss,' I said, 'please make sure what I have said about Mrs Heart, Sydney airport, and UA128, is on record.'

At that the general left off doing whatever he was doing to his keyboard, pushed back his chair, pushed his hands out to the sides and grasped the edge of the camping desk he was sitting at. His spectacles flashed.

'Clever dick, Mr Shovelin.' He turned to another sergeant who was sitting at a large comms desk that looked like a synthesier in a recording studio. 'Sergeant,' he said, 'I don't know who the fuck is in charge of this sort of thing, you may have to go right up to the NSC, but find whoever it is.'

She was a nice looking woman, part spic, part oriental, lots of black hair, skin the colour of those very pale yellowish olives. The khaki didn't do a lot for it.

She did her best to be polite.

'What sort of thing, General?'

'Getting airlines to turn their planes round.'

I looked at my watch, the Casio.

'General,' I said. 'You've got three hours.' I thought about it. 'Maybe only two.' I thought about it some more. 'Maybe four.'

The general appeared to ignore me, but to himself he muttered: 'What the fuck's he on about now?'

'Just do it,' I said. 'Meanwhile, I need a toilet. There must be one in here somewhere.'

'A rest-room? The flush isn't working. They forgot to fill the tank. You'd better go outside.'

'I've got the Pentagon Control on the line,' the sergeant said. 'Will that do?'

'It's a start.'

*

Outside it was cold, pitch dark apart from starlight and the glow that filled an eighth of the sky on the other side of the hill. I had a pee in a bush, emptied my bladder. I was dead tired. I found a Jeep. No one challenged me when I peeled back the tarpaulin and got in the back and curled up on the rear bench, pulling the tarpaulin over me.

I awoke stiff and cold at very first light. There was some movement around me, but not a lot. An engine somewhere revved, feet tramped by, skittering through the gravelly soil. Someone swore, someone else pissed into a bush. Maybe the same bush. I smelled coffee.

I raised my head. There was a mobile canteen with a short queue, fuck, line of National Guardsmen. No one queried me when I joined them. The coffee was good and a doughnut came with it, the first I'd had in America. No. Tell a lie. The second. The one I bought at the takeout in La Jolla before taking the taxi to San Ysidro. My first Californian Girl. Still haven't tried a peanut butter with jello sandwich but when I have I guess I'll have run the gamut.

Then I walked over the hill and down the scrub towards the ruined house and wrecked gardens. The sun threw my shadow twenty feet in front of me, purple on the pale grit.

Footsteps behind me, broke into a trot.

'Mr Shovelin? Mr Kit Shovelin?'

I turned. It was Felix, the sassy Afro who'd opened doors for me on my first visit. Usual broad white grin in his dark face. Only difference was, he was wearing a neat pale khaki uniform, pressed, tie, a captain's bars.

'Going down to the house? I'll walk with you.'

He fell in beside me. 'The gear surprise you? Don't ask!'

He went on: 'Thought you'd like to know. The Sydney plane was diverted to Auckland, I already had that checked out but maybe if something had happened to me your intervention could have been vital. China Heart was picked up on the observation deck at Sydney International with a Discman in her purse whose innards no way matched manufacturer's specs.'

We walked on down, I at any rate occasionally slipping a little when the slope got steeper. A pair of small birds, one blue all over, the other grey with blue wings flew across the dried pasture. Our feet rattled through dried stalks with tiny cottony seed-cases. They shed a little fluff round our knees.

'You were some sort of undercover agent?'

'That is correct.'

'Yet you couldn't stop the bombing of UA324?'

'Not without blowing my cover.'

'Oh, come on.'

Silence as we slipped and scurried. Then it clicked. Rubber pads in his cheeks to push them out, complete change of clothes, shades.

212

'But it was you. You who got my case out of the luggage store at the Golden Gateway Inn after the boy had put it there, you who checked in on UA328 as Jefferson and got it into the hold.'

I was looking at him, waiting for a reaction and I almost tripped. He caught my elbow, steadied me.

'Take your hands off me you fucking black bastard.'

But I was too tired to hang one on him.

'Why Jefferson?' I asked, a moment or two later, when I'd got my breath back.

'Friend of Jerry's. Close, close friend. The General hates queers. Long leftie past. Ideally placed. You available to take his place. And no way was he going to check in that bag for us.'

'But it was... Nicola Heart,' I choked on her name, 'who actually shot him. I mean... she was around that evening.'

His face took on that serious look Americans use when they want to show sincerity.

'Oh yes. She did it.'

*

'How did the Lennoxes know all this? All the things they needed to know to set it all up?'

He said nothing, walked on, looking at the ground, but with a secret sort of grin on his lips.

'Oh I get it. You fed it to them. Entrapment.'

'Something like that.'

By now I was thinking like I was Einstein. Holmes, anyway.

'Oh, I get it,' I said again. 'Someone somewhere wanted that plane downed. The Japanese nuclear scientists who were against expanding the domestic industry? Were they the target?'

He wouldn't say anything, but I detected a sort of shrug. Then...

'You know how it is, Kit. These things are always done on a need to know basis.'

*

A short avenue of acacias brought us on to the gravel forecourt, the cedars. The façade of the house was patchily blackened, all the windows broken. There was a litter of burnt out RVs, three of them. The rest must have survived and been driven or towed away. And of

213

course the burnt out shell of the tank. A detail of National Guardsmen were coaching lumps of barbecued meat into black bags and zipping them up. Out of all the questions I could have asked, I chose the daftest.

'Why's it called Homage?'

'Homage to the American way of life, is what the General used to say. He wanted it to be a centre of excellence, a shield against all that threatens what is truly American.'

For a moment I felt sick to the marrowbone. Cold and sick.

We paused on the step.

'Why have you come down here?' Felix asked.

'Get my hat, coat and bag.'

'They're in a cloakroom, to the right. I put them there.' Back in the days when he was the house flunkey.

He paused on the top step, held out a horizontal pale palm. What do they say? Lay on five? Fuck off, Felix.

Apart from a broken window the small room was undamaged but filled with the sick smell that soaks into all burnt buildings. There was an old porcelain wash basin, brass fittings, soap, mahogany surrounds, a toilet, and a mahogany table beneath a plain mirror. My things were on the table. I turned on the taps. There was still cold water although the hot was dead. I had a wash, got off most of the black smudges, found a razor in my bag and gave myself a bit of a scrape.

Then I picked up the hat, turned it over. Inside, gold lettering on the leather band. The Sovereign Stetson. John R (or was it a B?) Stetson Company, and in the crown, on the white silk lining, a coat of arms with supporters — a beaver and an eagle.

A brown fedora. The real thing. Beware of imitations. They do some things well, I thought. I put it on, pulled down the rim, gave it a tilt, it made me look good, feel better. I picked up the coat and my bag. The gravelly voice murmured in my ear: 'You did well, old pal. Couldn't have done better myself. At least you didn't get shot.'

Once outside I felt good, spirits lifted as I walked down the avenue, yes I walked down the avenue... or rather up it, getting a lift from a sergeant in a jeep who took me back to the main road where, from Heavengate, I got a bus back into town. You know how it is at a good wake. After a drink or two people get as jolly as they ever do: poor sod I'll miss him, but hey, I'm fireproof. Bang, bang you're dead! Yah-boo, missed me! That's how I felt.

*

But as a cab took me round the San Diego beltway, past all those brave and beautiful flags stretched by the Pacific breeze in the Californian sunshine it was the G and S that was in my head:

In spite of all temptations
To belong to other nations
I remain an Englishman
I remain an Eng...lishman!

And then, damn it, I remembered. All that GAP stuff I bought for Rosa. Still in a bag, at Sydney airport with fifteen pounds of Semtex? Object of a controlled explosion? Or being pulled apart by the forensic department of the Aussie police? Something like that. Bugger.